Tha

Continued Support.

KILLING ME SOFTLY WITH HIS WORD

DENISE COOK-GODFREY

Denise Cook-Godfrey

CONTENTS

ISBN 979-8-9899654-1-0

FICTION

Disclaimer: Certain scenes in this novel may depict themes that could be sensitive to some readers. However, these scenes were carefully crafted by the author with the intention of raising awareness, promoting wholeness, and fostering healing overall.

"The Sin-N-Me" Series

"The Sin-N-Me" is a captivating stand-alone series searching intently into the complex journey of Christianity through the lens of Romans 7:17.

Now then it is no more I that do it, but sin that dwelleth in me.
Romans 7:17

PREFACE

In a community built on tradition and religion, Chloe Rhodes struggles to reconcile her identity with the expectations of her church and family. The fortifying walls guarding her most intimate life story are about to be torn down by a single message that will shake her world to its core.

Chloe, a spirited and fiercely independent young woman, has always known she was different. Yet, the mere thought of revealing her truth to her conservative community fills her with fear and trepidation. Determined to live an authentic life, she embarks on a journey to convince her loved ones to accept her lesbian lifestyle.

However, Chloe's quest for acceptance is not without its internal conflicts. Her past is riddled with traumatic experiences that have left scars on her soul, making it difficult for her to fully embrace her own identity. As she navigates the complexities of her emotions, she finds herself drawn to the captivating words of a young minister named Aaron.

Aaron, a passionate preacher and believer in the transformative power of scripture, becomes a beacon of hope for Chloe. Yet, their budding connection only intensifies her inner turmoil.

"Killing Me Softly with HIS Word" is a gripping novel that delves into the depths of human experiences. It takes readers on a journey of self-discovery, redemption, and the pursuit of personal truth, regardless of the price. This story is part of the stand-alone series, "The Sin-N-Me," which explores the tension between human desires and the transformative power of scripture, capturing the essence of Romans 7:17.

ACKNOWLEDGMENTS

Acknowledgement is made to my Heavenly Father for granting the grace to delve deep into the "Sin-N-Me" series. I am grateful for the courage to explore the dynamics of the themes within this work. The Christian journey, as complex as it is, is filled with twists and turns, worthy of being woven into a narrative. I am blessed to have received a breath of inspiration to create this ongoing stand-alone series.

I acknowledge my family, my wonderful children and grandchildren. I would like to especially thank my beautiful sisters and nieces for the heartfelt feedback on the cover choice.

I would also like to give acknowledgment to my husband, Pastor DeForest L. Godfrey for all the years of mentorship and spiritual covering.

May God bless each reader as the plot of this story unfolds... page by page.

CHAPTER 1

CHLOE (AGE ELEVEN)

Chloe could feel her heartbeat in her throat as she walked down the long hallway toward the living room. The sound of her shoes tapping against the hardwood floor echoed around her, making her feel small and insignificant. She felt like an intruder in her own home, like she was not supposed to be there. Still, she pressed forward, her long, and perfectly formed legs strutting while her silky pressed hair bounced freely with each step.

When she finally reached the living room, her expressive, deep brown eyes covered the room, while her nostrils absorbed the rich scent of vanilla and cinnamon coming from the freshly baked desserts on the polished mahogany table. The room, adorned with vibrant artwork and the soft glow of ambient lighting, held an atmosphere of both elegance and warmth. Then she saw her mother, Starla, surrounded by guests. Chloe's stomach tightened with an unwelcome heaviness. She didn't want to interrupt such an important gathering, but she had no choice. She needed to talk to her mother, who always made certain her gatherings were full of gala and stimulating fellowship. Starla was slender but tall and curvy. She easily stood out in a crowd, with her hair framing her beauty in perfect, natural arches. Chloe resembled her mom but took her personality from her father.

Taking a deep breath, Chloe approached her mother and whispered in her ear. "Mom, can I talk to you?"

Starla looked at Chloe, surprised by the interruption. She then regained her composure and smiled at the guests. "Excuse me, everyone."

The guests murmured, some of them nodded, and Starla led Chloe to a quieter room in the house. Once they were alone, Starla turned to Chloe and asked, "What's wrong, honey?"

Despite her normal independent, brave momentum, Chloe's eyes welled up with tears. She struggled to find the words to explain what was happening to her. Finally, she blurted out, "Mom, I think I got my period."

Starla's eyes widened in genuine surprise, momentarily breaking through her composed exterior. She always figured Chloe would not start until about thirteen, like she did. A quick flashback of her own experience with the curse of women, or at least that's what her grandma called it, rolled across her mind. "Oh, sweetie," she said, her tone softening as she pulled Chloe into a hug and subtly assessed whether her daughter had grown or changed. "Are you sure? I was thirteen when I got mine."

"Positive. It happened just like Auntie Macy said it would."

A sense of guilt and fury whisked through Starla's soul as she thought about the reality of how her mother never had *the talk* with her, now she seemed to fall into those same footsteps. In that fleeting moment, Starla's mind replayed memories of her own adolescence, the absence of crucial conversations with her mother, and the awkward silence that surrounded such pivotal moments. The weight of unspoken words lingered in the air, a silent echo of missed opportunities. "Okay. Sweetheart," Starla said frantically as she grabbed Chloe by the hand and led her into one of the downstairs bathrooms. Despite her poised exterior, a storm of conflicting emotions raged within. Success as an investment banker at one of Charlotte's largest banks didn't shield her from the realization that, as a mother, there were conversations she had overlooked. "Look, there are not any sanitary napkins…pads here. I'll bet if you run over to Kennedy's you'll find exactly what you need. I'll talk to you later about hygiene stuff, cramps, you know. I've got to help your dad with the guests. Love you. Awe, my little muffin is growing fast. Go ahead, honey. We'll talk later," Starla assured as she took note of Chloe's confused expression.

As Chloe walked down the hallway, she started feeling uneasy again. She picked up some fresh clothes and other essentials and left through the back exit to visit Kennedy across the street. Despite being cousins, they had an incredible bond, like sisters. Both Kennedy and her mother Macy were always there for Chloe whenever she needed them. However, Chloe longed for her mother to spend more time with her, as well as her dad.

Walking slowly to Kennedy and Macy's home, the climate was mild, as it normally is in Charlotte during late spring, but seemed as if it was the middle of a scorching summer night to Chloe, as sweat covered her forehead. She felt torn between wanting to stay at her own house or take refuge with her aunt. Even though she knew their house was her home away from home, it bothered Chloe to always seem to fall back on her Aunt Macy when her mother was not available. Ringing the doorbell, Honey, the family poodle could be heard scratching at the door right before Macy opened the door.

"Well, hey, babe, did you leave something when you were here earlier?" Macy asked as she widened the door for Chloe. She was already in her pajamas with her hair bonnet in place. Although she hardly ever dressed up like Starla did most of the time, Chloe's Aunt Macy was a beautiful woman whose natural features sparked with little make-up.

"Nope. I'm here because mama is busy and…and…well, it's here."

"What's hear Sweetie?"

"My period. I just got my period," Chloe said in a lowered tone. Despite feeling embarrassed and uncomfortable about having to ask for help, she also felt a sense of relief knowing that her aunt could help her out.

"Oh! Oh my, that was quick, but hey, this is normal. Are you okay? You look so conflicted."

"Mom said you would have sanitary pads. There were none at our house."

"Of course! Kennedy has plenty of those. Oh, Chloe, don't worry - you're entering a great time in a woman's life! Try to remember our conversation?"

"I do."

Grabbing her by the hand, Macy knew exactly how to handle the situation and the three of them engaged in girl talk, popcorn and a movie for a couple of hours.

"Mom, you're so funny. I can't believe you've never wore tampons," Kennedy remarked as she gulped down the last of her diet coke. "What did you do when you went swimming?"

"Shoot. Nothing. I wase not allowed to go anywhere but to school and church during that time of the month," Macy answered.

"At least you were ready, I mean your mother talked to you and all," Chloe chimed in as she gathered the empty popcorn bags and disposed of them. "Anyway, I guess I'll live."

The three chuckled. By the end of the night, Chloe felt better about the situation; relieved that she had somewhere else to turn even if it meant relying on someone else rather than her mom.

After Macy left them alone, Chloe and Kennedy continued reclining on the sofa. Kennedy leaned forward, her caramel skin glistening with sweat as she shoveled the last handful of popcorn into her mouth. The crunchy kernels tumbled out onto the pale blue carpet in the family room, an area that Kennedy rarely ever saw occupied.

"Spending the night?" Kennedy asked quickly, not wanting to miss a beat in their conversation.

Chloe glanced up at the window, noticing how Kennedy's thick braid had fallen in front of her eyes from peering outside. Kennedy loved braided hair, especially during the spring and summer months, while Chloe's mom always insisted that she straighten her hair, regardless of the season.

"Naw I think I'll head back across the street," Chloe replied, thinking about how quiet Kennedy's house must be compared to her own; tonight was yet another evening of adults who slid between conversations filled with laughter and loud music blaring from the kitchen speakers.

"Yea, I see only a car or two in your drive. Don't know how you put up with a whole bunch of adults sipping liquor, laughing at corny jokes, and acting all important. My mom and dad hardly ever have company over."

Chloe shifted on the couch cushions as Kennedy continued to speak and peer out the window, remembering what it felt like to retreat away to her bedroom whenever these visitors came by.

"You're the lucky one, cousin. Anyway, I mostly stay in my room, reading, writing, whatever," Chloe said as she made her way to the door, Kennedy dragging behind her.

~

As she woke up the next morning, Chloe could hear distant voices and footsteps. Starla was on her phone while her father, Reginald, was rushing around the house getting ready for work. Despite it being a Saturday, he usually worked from the office. When Chloe asked him why he didn't work from home, he explained he preferred working in his office, in front of the window, with no distractions. Reginald, an imposing figure standing at a commanding six feet tall, boasted an athletic build that showed forth strength and discipline. His clearly defined masculine facial features framed a serious-minded countenance, and he was known for his attention to detail in both his work and personal life. The financial security of his family stood at the pinnacle of his priority list, reflecting the unwavering dedication that defined Reginald.

"I just wished you'd told me you'd already talked to her about her period," Starla said, a hint of concern in her voice. Chloe walked into the room just as she slung the phone on the bed.

"Mom, is everything okay between you and Auntie?"

"Sweetheart, I didn't know you were standing there. Why do you ask?"

"I overheard you mention Auntie not telling you about our conversation about how things would be when I got my period."

"Oh, we were doing girl talk, is all. Everything's perfectly fine. Want breakfast?" Starla asked, attempting to change the subject. She always tried to conceal conflicts between her and Macy, but little did she know… Chloe was well aware of it.

"If you're cooking," Chloe answered. Playing right along with her mom.

"Cooking? Girlie…let's go out. It's Saturday morning."

"Okay. Shopping afterward?"

"Okay," Starla replied before quickly grabbing her phone. After scanning through her messages, she said, "Oh my goodness, I completely forgot about my meeting with the 'Young Bankers Association' at the library at eleven. I apologize."

"It's only nine. Do you want to grab breakfast at the Waffle House before your meeting?" asked Chloe.

"Sure thing. Alexa, can you please call the Waffle House?"

Chloe felt disappointed their time together would once again be cut short for a quick drive-through meal before the meeting.

"When you're old enough to drive, there'll be a lot of things you can do by yourself. You've always been so independent and understanding when your Dad and I have to work or travel. It's all for your benefit. We want to make sure you know how proud we are of your grades and attitude," Starla said as she kissed Chloe's forehead before running off to shower.

"The best thing would be if you spent more time with me and took me on a real vacation once in a while," Chloe murmured. She'd gotten into the habit of muttering about her feelings privately for some time. Just then her phone buzzed – it was Kennedy.

"Hey!" "What are you up to?"

"About to grab breakfast from the Waffle House drive-through…What's going on?"

"You won't believe what I just found out. Okay, so I was scrolling through social media and this post popped up….and then my phone went crazy…."

"Kennedy, slow down! Have you taken your medication yet? Jeez! You must be sitting on some hot gossip!" The two girls broke out laughing.

"Alright, alright… Daphne and Tavares did it…. Yes girl, they did it! We're seriously the only virgins left in Ms. Freeman's Sunday School class. Like, no one else except us!"

"Looks like Daphne and Tavares didn't follow the abstinence instructions from the sexuality classes from summer camp last year," Chloe said, scanning her eyes toward her mother's bathroom.

"Speaking of…are you packed for camp yet?"

"Somewhat. Not so exciting since you'll be leaving early this time. You know I can hardly function without you by my side," Chloe said.

"Same here, but you'll be fine," Kennedy answered. "You'll only have to endure three nights after I leave for my basketball camp. Not sure why they changed the date. Anyway, I hear Mom walking this way. Come over soon. I want us to call Daphne and get some details, cause...I think I'm next."

"What? Girl, you're something serious. I'll be over after breakfast," Chloe said as she sat on the edge of her mother's bed contemplating her conversation about sex with Kennedy. She'd often wondered about sex and how it would feel. She knew what it was, of course, but had never experienced it herself. Her mother had changed the conversation quickly when she'd asked about the sounds coming from their bedroom when she was six, and Chloe had never asked again. The thought of a boy's private parts inside of her sparked all kinds of emotions. She often wondered when it would happen to her. She had seen it happen in movies and on the internet. Dismissing the thoughts, she exited the bedroom to prepare and go for breakfast.

CHAPTER 2

MACY, MIND YO BUSINESS

"Kennedy! Someone's at the door...Kennedy!" Macy called out from the kitchen as she quickly filled a basket with snacks for summer camp. The church's youth group had been taking part in this annual event for some time now, but Kennedy and Chloe had lost interest.

"Mom, it's Aunt Starla...and Chloe!" Kennedy shouted as she rushed back into her room. Her mother was always reminding her of how much of a procrastinator she was compared to Chloe, and why punctuality and focus were so important. Kennedy was still packing.

As Macy turned the corner from the kitchen and into the living room, she stopped in her tracks when she saw Starla standing by the door, checking her clothing. Starla wore a dark, form-fitting business suit with a red blouse. Her hair was pulled back into a bun, her makeup was applied with a light hand. "Morning...I'm just finishing up and about to start loading the car."

"Hi, Auntie Macy. I'm gonna go help Kennedy," Chloe said before leaving the two women alone.

"Thanks for driving again this year," Starla said without

looking toward Macy, as her nose twitched at the scent of the fresh strawberries Macy had just sliced and then rinsed in the sink mixed with the scent of the cleaning products, she had used to clean the countertops. "I couldn't get out of my Board meeting."

"No problem," Macy replied. "I look forward to the drive; it'll give me a chance to sightsee on the way back and reflect on things."

"Just to clear the air about our conversation the other day..."

"No need for a rehash. You had every right to be angry. You should be in charge of talking with Chloe about her period, not me," Macy said as she began grabbing snacks. Giving their history, Macy often walked on eggshells to keep peace between her and Starla.

"We seem to have different opinions on a lot of topics, and I wish we could respect each other's thoughts, even if we disagree sometimes," Starla said while inspecting herself in the hallway.

"Nice suit, by the way."

"Thanks. Just because I'm not as good a homemaker as you are doesn't mean I'm not a good mom," Starla continued. "And frankly, last month when I overheard you telling Reginald you felt like Chloe was having trouble due to all the business trips I take, I didn't appreciate it."

Macy's heart was pounding in her chest, and her head felt foggy. "I understand you're upset," she said, trying to calm the tension. "Maybe my words were misinterpreted. All I wanted to do was express concern for the changes I've noticed in Chloe lately. She's here almost as much as she is at home, after all, and it's hard to miss."

"Yes, but she is my daughter," Starla replied, "and since you and I are both adults here...I'd prefer if you bring your concerns to me first instead of to Reginald." An uncomfortable silence filled the room, broken only by the steady hum of Macy's refrigerator and the dull sound of a half-dripping faucet.

"Ready," Chloe declared as she and Kennedy lugged assorted items from Kennedy's bedroom. Chloe wore a slight grin, while Kennedy still wore her night bonnet. She seemed half-asleep.

"Fantastic. I'll take the food to the car now," Macy said as she thrust herself past Starla. Despite only seeing Macy for a few seconds, Chloe sensed something was amiss between the two of them without asking what was wrong. She embraced her mom more firmly than usual before departure. Macy noticed this yet wanted to stay silent. As Starla high stepped back onto the other side of the street, they loaded up Macy's vehicle while making small talk. Finally, they drove away toward camp.

The two-hour drive to camp went by without a hitch as the girls did their normal routine, half of the drive was filled with music, and the rest spent sleeping. Ahead, the road was flat and wide enough for three lanes of traffic, but only two shoulder lanes on each side. Macy blasted her favorite gospel songs and inspirational sermons from her phone, trying not to think about Chloe's emotions as she held onto her mother while leaving for the trip. She reminded herself to be extra careful with her words after Starla had given her a stern warning back at the house. It was going to be hard, but she prayed God would help her stay silent in this situation. She had a deep affection for her family and desired peace between them all. Chloe, who was a year younger than Kennedy, represented the second daughter she'd never had. Unlike her own child, Chloe reminded her a lot of herself, leading them to grow close to one another. It made her sad to observe the changes taking place in Chloe. Changes like drifting into space during conversations, a lack of confidence, and other mood swings.

"Come on up, girls! We're here at last!" Macy declared cheerfully, as both girls yawned and stirred in response. After enduring seven years of this annual camp routine, she was convinced this would be the last one. For the past two years, she could detect that the girls were not as enthused about the camp experience. Exchanging camp stories was one of those things that kept the bond growing between the three of them.

"Yeah, right," Kennedy said sarcastically as Chloe gave her a nudge. "Seem like we just left home."

"Everybody else is already here by the looks of things," Chloe noted as she and Macy began lugging their bags from the car. The air was thick with the scent of pine, as towering trees surrounded the campsite, their needles forming a fragrant carpet beneath. The distant hum of a river flowed nearby, offering a soothing melody to the lively chirping of birds above.

"You know you can call me if you need anything while you're here...okay?" Macy queried. She stole a glance at Chloe, the worry lines on her forehead deepening.

"Sure thing, Auntie. Is everything alright with you? You seem kind of off," her perceptive superpowers kicking in and detecting Macy's emotional state.

"Yes, honey. Just thinking about some stuff. But I mean it. Call me if you need me."

"Of course, but you know how I roll. I'm sure I'll be just fine."

"Come here," Macy said as she wrapped Chloe in her arms. "Remember, you don't have to be all grown and independent all the time. It's okay to ask for help. It really is okay to need somebody. Kennedy, out of the car!" She added after they let go of their hug, sharing a smile. Although in her heart, she continued to be anxious about Chloe's emotional well-being, despite her holding to her brave and independent persona. Macy could discern desperate cries from within Chloe's soul.

CHAPTER 3

CHLOE'S UNIQUE GIFTS

As the sun embraced the summer campgrounds, Chloe's anticipation flickered a bit of excitement within her at the sight of Ms. Monet. Ms. Monet gracefully gliding across the pathway to the gathering cabin, added a ray of electric energy to the air. Ms. Monet, affectionately known as Ms. M, was a recent addition to the camp's roster of facilitators. Chloe and Kennedy had met her the previous summer and instantly connected with her vibrant personality. Unlike the other instructors, she was approachable and down-to-earth, and exuded an understanding of youth culture that made her the favorite of campers. Everyone adored her, except for Mrs. Kramer, whose reasons for harboring a mysterious dislike for Ms. M remained a mystery to Chloe and her fellow campers.

With a final tight hug, Chloe and Kennedy bid farewell to Macy. The sound of rolling luggage wheels filled the air as she and Kennedy made their way into the spacious cabin, joining the lively voices and laughter. The atmosphere buzzed with the joyful anticipation of reunions and new adventures.

Approaching the registration table, Chloe and Kennedy were greeted by a cheerful attendant. "Hello, young ladies, and welcome back!" the attendant exclaimed, handing them their name tags and housing information. The girls smiled and eagerly headed toward their assigned cabins to unload their belongings.

Just as Chloe and Kennedy were about to step away, a familiar voice called out to them. "Hello! You two have grown a bit since last summer. Good to have you back," Ms. M said with a warm smile, her eyes gleaming with genuine delight. Her hair differed from last year as she rocked a short, classy, natural afro. Chloe felt a surge of comfort and familiarity wash over her in Ms. M's presence.

"Yea...most kids always come back, especially those who aren't planning college or have other commitments," Chloe replied, her tone mature and composed. She cast a glance at Kennedy, silently urging her to rein in her playful antics.

Ms. M nodded in agreement, her gaze sweeping over the bustling crowd of campers. "Indeed, it's wonderful to see so many familiar faces returning. It adds to the sense of community."

As if summoned by fate, Mrs. Kramer, the camp's stern and rigid director, appeared from around the corner, her eyes narrowing in disapproval as she noticed Ms. M engaged in conversation with Chloe and Kennedy. The tension between the two women was undeniable, a dark undercurrent beneath the surface of the camp's usual cheery atmosphere.

Before any more could be said, Ms. M abruptly excused herself, her quick steps leading her in the opposite direction. Chloe couldn't help but wonder about the mysterious dynamic between Ms. M and Mrs. Kramer. There was an unspoken animosity that tinged their interactions, leaving an eerie sense of intrigue hanging in the air.

Lost in her thoughts, Kennedy's naughty remark brought Chloe back to the present. "Look at her butt...she knows she should've gotten a size larger. My mom would have a fit if I wore pants that tight," Kennedy whispered with a mischievous grin, resuming her gum-popping habit.

"Kennedy! You're crazy, but I can't deny the truth…those pants are snug," Chloe agreed as she and Kennedy slapped a high five with laughter and more small talk. "It's a bit crazy how Mrs. Kramer and Ms. M still seem to be at odds and yet no one seems to know what the deal is."

"Usually when females have beef there's a man involved, but I wouldn't think that's the case here, since Ms. M is younger and all," Kennedy added.

"Right. Anyway, let's not keep the cabin waiting. We have plenty of settling in to do," Chloe continued, a mix of amusement and annoyance lacing her voice. Getting organized was one of her least favorite tasks when arriving at camp.

With that, they both made their way toward their cabins, carrying with them the weight of the mysterious tension and the unspoken questions that hung in the air. The summer camp, once a place of carefree joy near the Carowinds, now held something different, but neither could come up with an explanation.

~

After supper, the group gathered around a well-lit area with a stage. It was the perfect setting for the evening's agenda. Laughter and chatter filled the air as campers introduced themselves, highlighting their talents through song, dance, and interpretive signing. The camp emphasized the use of creativity and the arts for both church services and preparing the youth for Bible study and public speaking.

Amidst the lively atmosphere, Mrs. Kramer, the stern camp director, addressed the group, her eyes scanning the eager faces.

"Chloe, are you still interested in perfecting your ASL skills?" she inquired, her voice cutting through the buzz of conversation.

"Yes, Ma'am. I think it would be wonderful to learn, especially since we have members in our congregation who are deaf," Chloe replied, her eyes shining with enthusiasm.

"Very well. Ms. Monet will take over the class. Those interested in ASL can follow her to the right, while the others will stay here for a brief lesson on preparing to teach a Bible study topic," Mrs. Kramer explained, the words hanging in the air.

The youth dispersed, forming separate groups. Kennedy, visibly bored, idled around, toying with her nails before engaging in conversation with one girl from their cabin. Most of the older campers seemed equally uninterested in the lesson at hand.

Amid the commotion, a whispered voice reached Chloe's ears, and she turned to find Danny "Dan Dan" Pots, a figure from her Sunday school days, beckoning her. Chloe had always harbored a secret crush on him, even though he had often teased her mercilessly. To her surprise, Dan Dan was no longer the scrawny looking rascal that always brought on an annoyance but seemed to have sprouted up overnight. His eyes, a striking shade of green, stood out against his creamy caramel-colored skin. Most of the kids found it fascinating for him to have such a rare green eye color, but none of them teased him for it. Chloe overheard some of the older women at the church once gossiping about his mother and the milkman, although it confused her greatly.

"What is it, Dan Dan?" Chloe responded, a trace of frustration filling her voice. She was eager to join the ASL class, fearing she might miss something.

"We're heading to the pool area. Jabari swiped the keys. And guess what? Kennedy is in too. She wanted me to find you," Dan Dan revealed with a mischievous grin, tempting Chloe with a taste of rebellion.

"You're all crazy! You'll get caught and end up in trouble," Chloe protested, her responsible nature firmly rooted.

"You're such a goody-two-shoes. Come on, Chloe. It'll be fun," Dan Dan urged, his eyes gleaming with the thrill of adventure.

"No thanks and tell Kennedy she better get back here before she gets into trouble," Chloe replied, her voice unwavering.

"We'll only be gone for about fifteen minutes. By the time we get back, change our clothes, and sneak back into our cabins, we'll make it in time for the closing prayer. Don't you ever wonder what it's like to take chances?" Dan Dan asked, a hint of curiosity in his voice.

"I said no," Chloe firmly stated, dismissing the enticing offer.

Joining the ASL class, Chloe settled into her seat, her mind still wandering to Dan Dan's proposition. She had always played it safe, never venturing beyond the boundaries of what was expected of her. But a nagging thought lingered in her mind—was she missing out on the thrill of life's uncertainties?

As the class ended, Chloe nervously scanned the room, searching for Kennedy. Ms. M, noticing her restlessness, approached her with a warm smile. "Good job, Chloe. How about you lead the closing prayer using ASL?" she suggested, her eyes full of encouragement.

"Me?" Chloe stammered, surprise and uncertainty mingling in her voice.

"Absolutely. You have a gift indeed. Your passion will undoubtedly bring value to your congregation," Ms. M praised; her words enveloping Chloe like a gentle breeze.

"Thank you, Ms. M," Chloe responded, a mix of gratitude and bewilderment in her voice. Being the perfectionist that she was, she always thought that she needed more training and development in the craft.

Before she could further contemplate the exchange, it was time for the closing prayer. Chloe gracefully blended her ASL skills with heartfelt words, capturing the attention of the engaged campers and those who had previously appeared disinterested. A sense of unity and captivation settled over the group as her prayer unfolded.

As the prayer concluded and campers dispersed, Ms. M approached Chloe, her eyes filled with admiration. "Outstanding, Chloe. I'm truly blown away by the way you bring your movements to life. Your gift is remarkable," she remarked, her voice brimming with genuine appreciation.

"Thank you, Ms. M," Chloe replied, her heart fluttering with a mixture of pride and uncertainty. She was taken aback when Ms. M changed the topic, her voice laced with a mischievous grin. "By the way, I couldn't help but notice how you were looking at the young man earlier. First crush, perhaps?"

Startled, Chloe blushed, her cheeks turning a shade of pink. "Dan Dan? Oh, no. We've known each other since grade school. He's just a friend," she clarified, her words betraying a hint of defensiveness.

Chuckling softly, Ms. M continued, "Certainly, just a friend. But don't be shy, Chloe. You're at an age of discovery, and if you ever have any questions or want to talk about your journey of self-discovery, I'm here for you. That's what camp is all about."

Before Chloe could respond, Mrs. Kramer intervened, interrupting their conversation. "Is everything okay here?" she inquired, her gaze shifting between Chloe and Ms. M, a note of suspicion creeping into her voice.

"Everything is great, Mrs. Kramer. I was simply discussing Chloe's signing abilities," Ms. M quickly clarified, her tone friendly but guarded.

"Well then, Chloe, why don't you join the others? Catch up with everyone. I'd like to have a word with Ms. Monet," Mrs. Kramer suggested, her voice carrying an undertone of authority.

"Yes, ma'am. Goodnight to both of you," Chloe replied, feeling a twinge of unease as she hurried away in search of Kennedy and the rest of the group. Glancing back, she couldn't help but notice the intense conversation unfolding between Mrs. Kramer and Ms. M, their hand gestures and expressions conveying a sense of confrontation. A shiver ran down Chloe's spine, leaving her with a lingering sense of foreboding.

CHAPTER 4

CHLOE'S SCIENCE PROJECT

It was the second week of camp, and Kennedy was preparing to leave. She would need to join the students on her basketball team for camp for the next week. Chloe was feeling sort of lost. This would be her first camp in seven years where she and Kennedy were not together.

"Are you sure you can't skip this week and join basketball camp next week, or at least at the end of the week? You know I don't have a lot of folks I hang out with," Chloe said as she pulled clothing out of her bag.

"Already checked. I'd lose demerits if I'm even late arriving. Our new coach is tough. She doesn't play," Kennedy answered all the while lying flat on her back with cucumbers covering her eyes, which were stolen from the kitchen the night before.

"Yo Kennedy, your folks are here," Dan Dan said as he stuck his head in the cabin.

"Boy, you are not supposed to be on this side. I swear you are so crazy," Chloe said frantically.

"Hahaha, I'm gonna miss all this but I'll see you kids later," Kennedy said jokingly as she grabbed her bags and rolled them out to her parent's vehicle. They were already in the main camp area, signing her out. Chloe felt a lump in her throat as she hugged her best friend and watched her leave the camp in her pajamas.

~

The camp buzzed with laughter and chatter as fellow campers gathered around bonfires. Despite the lively atmosphere, Chloe remained distant, her heart heavy with the absence of Kennedy. She sat on a weathered bench, huddled over her phone, scrolling through a collection of photos from last year's camp, each image emphasizing the void even more.

Suddenly, Dan Dan approached Chloe with a mischievous grin. He tugged at one of her braids, catching her attention.

"What are you sitting here looking all lost for, Chloe?" Dan Dan asked, his tone laced with curiosity. "And what do you keep staring at on your phone?"

Chloe sighed, her gaze shifting from the photographs to Dan Dan. She couldn't help but feel a twinge of annoyance at his interruption.

"I miss Kennedy," Chloe replied, her voice tinged with longing. "And honestly, I'm just ready to go home."

Dan Dan leaned closer, his playful demeanor attempting to offer a distraction from her dreary mood.

"Yeah, we all miss Kennedy," he said, his voice filled with a hint of empathy. "But you don't have to be alone. You can hang out with us. We've got some fun planned for this last week."

Chloe's brows furrowed, skepticism etching her features.

"I've already told you, Dan Dan," she replied, her tone firm. "I don't want to get in trouble with you guys."

Dan Dan's grin widened, his eyes sparkling with mischief as he tried to persuade Chloe.

"And I've already told you," he said, jumping up from the camp bench and joining his buddies in a huddle nearby. "You should stop being so serious all the time. It'll be fun, I promise, and we don't plan on getting caught."

Chloe hesitated, her longing for connection warring with her cautious nature. She watched as Dan Dan laughed and playfully nudged his friends, their bond contagious. Perhaps, just this once, she could let go and embrace the spontaneity of the moment. Taking a deep breath, Chloe mustered a tentative smile and stood up from the bench. She walked towards the huddle, ready to let the last week of camp unfold in unexpected ways, hoping it would help fill the void left by Kennedy's absence.

The night raced by, but every step Chloe took felt like slow motion. She regretted hanging out with Dan Dan and his friends. They were all drinking alcohol from their water bottles. Was this what life was about? The smell of toxic waste flooding the ground under their feet made it harder to breathe. Ms. M's soft voice pulled her back to reality and brought her back up the path toward the campground.

"Chloe? Are you okay? You seemed distant, and I missed you at ASL tonight?" Ms. M said as she stepped off the path toward her cabin.

Ms. M reached down and grabbed Chloe's hand, a move which surprised her, but also acted as an anchor pulling her away from the plastic horror show into which she had wandered.

"Oh, hi there. I'm sorry. I have to admit I chose to spend time with Dan Dan and the others instead of going to class. Big mistake on my part."

"I understand. There's about an hour before lights out; why don't you come over to my cabin so we can chat? I want to make sure you're okay," Ms. M said as she stepped away toward her cabin.

The dimly lit cabin exuded a soothing ambiance, flickering candles casting dancing shadows upon the walls. Chloe nestled into the snug chair, her senses enveloped by the tantalizing aroma of the candles. As a soft, secular melody drifted from the blue tooth speaker, memories of distant years echoed in her mind.

Ms. M, a woman of wisdom and creativity, possessed an uncanny ability to paint vivid pictures with her words. Her voice, as gentle as a bird's song, wrapped around Chloe like a comforting embrace, evoking memories of her beloved Aunt Macy.

"I saw you with him again," Ms. M's voice was barely above a whisper, laden with knowing. Chloe's heart skipped a beat, her curiosity piqued. This unexpected conversation held an air of mystery and intrigue.

"Him? What do you mean, Ma'am?" Chloe responded, her voice tinged with uncertainty.

A knowing smile graced Ms. M's lips as she approached Chloe, gracefully settling on the edge of the bed, her eyes locking with Chloe's. The atmosphere grew electric with anticipation.

"Oh, come now, my dear," Ms. M urged, her voice like a gentle caress. "I understand the complexities we face as we journey into adulthood. Mrs. Kramer and the others may never truly guide you through the changes your body undergoes. But fear not, for I shall offer you something invaluable."

Perplexed, Chloe shifted uncomfortably. The line of questioning felt invasive, treading into unchartered territory, which made her squirm with unease.

"Dear child, fret not," reassured Ms. M, her eyes fixated on Chloe's. Drawing closer, Ms. M reached out, her fingertips hovering above Chloe's chest, between her blossoming breasts. "Allow me to enlighten you. When ardor and infatuation grip one's heart, the female nipple area might stiffen and become taut. It's a perfectly normal response, Chloe."

The unexpected touch jolted through Chloe's body, nerves ablaze with apprehension. This conversation had spiraled into uncharted territory, morphing into something far more unsettling.

"Ms. M, I... I..." Chloe stammered, her voice trembling with fear.

Her interruption did nothing to deter the determined Ms. M. With a blink of her eyes, Chloe felt a flood of emotions wash over her, her vulnerability laid bare.

"Chloe, has your mother ever spoken to you about these matters?" Ms. M inquired, her tone laced with a mix of concern and astonishment.

"No, well, my Aunt Macy talked to me about menstruation a couple of years ago. She always said I could come to her with questions..." Chloe trailed off, her voice heavy with uncertainty.

Ms. M's eyes sparkled with determination as a thought took hold. "Listen carefully, my dear. Sex education shall grace the curriculum of this camp. I have already drafted a comprehensive syllabus and shall present it to the advisors during our next meeting. Fear not, for you will be the first to benefit from this enlightening addition."

Curiosity tugged at Chloe's mind, inching her closer to a forbidden desire for knowledge. Ms. M's words hung in the air, promising her the answers she had been denied.

"Can you explain..." Chloe hesitated, mustering the courage to voice her curiosity. "Can you explain what happens within the female body when longing and affection take hold? With anyone, regardless of gender?"

A sly smile graced Ms. M's lips as she sensed Chloe's burgeoning inquisitiveness. The atmosphere crackled with anticipation, and in a moment of daring, Ms. M extended her hand, ready to guide Chloe into uncharted territories of understanding.

Chloe's uncertainty grew, a knot tightening in her stomach. This encounter had become too strange, too intrusive. In the depths of her being, a storm of emotions raged within, threatening to drown her fragile sense of innocence. As her mind struggled to make sense of the incomprehensible, fragments of peculiar melodies echoed in the recesses of her consciousness, entwined with memories of a peculiar tenderness she experienced for a classmate. The discordance of it all left her bewildered, questioning her own desires and the boundaries that defined them.

Yet, amidst this disorienting inner chaos, a buried memory shimmered, offering a temporary sanctuary within her tormented mind. Transported back in time to a fleeting encounter with a classmate during her fourth-grade days, she sought comfort in the fragmentary remnants of that delicate connection. It became her refuge, a secret hiding place she retreated to as the agonizing touch of Ms. M invaded her personal space.

Paralyzed in the moment, she wrestled with the same question... *Why did it feel as if she had craved the touch of another girl to caress her in that forbidden way?* The tenderness that lingered in the memory of Britney, her fourth-grade classmate, now danced alongside Ms. M's invasive touch, leaving her bewildered and trapped within her own thoughts.

In that tormented silence, Chloe clung to the lingering memory of that fourth-grade encounter, using it as an explanation, or a lifeline. It became a flickering glimmer of hope in the darkest corners of her mind. As the touching continued, her young soul hung in the balance, teetering on the aspect of self-discovery and understanding.

The campsite, once a place of wide-eyed innocence and joyful anticipation, now transformed into a twisted wasteland of sinister secrets. The scars of this illicit encounter would forever mar her tender heart, leaving behind an imprint that would shape her future journey.

Her instincts screamed for her to leave, to escape this discomfort, but she convinced herself that it must have been the norm.

Firmly repressing Chloe's moments of hesitation, Ms. M pressed on, her touch persisting night after night, their connection shrouded in secrecy until the fateful day Chloe was checked out of the camp, her mind burdened with unsettling memories which would forever remain a haunting mystery.

And so, the wrongful intentions of a trusted mentor tarnished a part of Chloe's innocence, igniting a flame of inquiry that would forever burn within her.

~

Finally, it was check-out day for camp. Like they often say, 'Another one on the books', but this one was no ordinary last day of camp. Feeling numb all over, Chloe sat like a manikin in the rear seat of her parents' vehicle. Everything seemed blurry. Even the sound in the atmosphere was like a song dragging from one of those old CD players.

"Honey, you okay back there? You've barely spoken two words since we picked you up," Starla said as she peered at Chloe through the rearview mirror.

"Yea, you're not babbling about all the excitement like you normally do," Reginald chimed in, his eyes still glued to his work tablet.

"I'm okay, just exhausted," Chloe answered, resting her head against the top of the seat. She had not slept soundly in the last four nights. Mainly because of the three nights she spent in Ms. M's cabin. Chloe was confused, frightened, and filled with all the different emotions from the traumatic event. *Should I tell? But what would I say exactly? Was there anything wrong with spending time in Ms. M's cabin? She was only showing me what my body parts would experience as I grow into a mature woman, right?* These are the questions that danced in her head. But then there was the thought of the non-binary lifestyle that she had heard some speak of. Whether she was a part of that group haunted her like a horror movie. So much so, until she broke out in a cold sweat. Something deep inside felt like excitement, almost like home, but on the other end, she felt as if she would let her parents, her Aunt Macy and cousin Kennedy, and her church family down. The weight she carried was much too heavy.

CHAPTER 5

FRAGMENTS OF A BROKEN INNOCENCE

Months passed by each day dragging Chloe deeper into the clutches of her secret. The weight of her encounter at summer camp with Ms. M consumed her every waking thought. It was a gnawing darkness that permeated her soul, leaving her isolated, disconnected from the world around her. After returning to school, strangely enough, same-sex relationships appeared to be normal for most. Chloe had not noticed this before, although she'd heard Kennedy speak of it a few times. All she could do was to ignore the inner turmoil that now existed because of the strange incidents years ago in the fourth grade. Ever since her encounters with Ms. M, other buried memories from fourth grade had now resurfaced. For instance, Britney, one of her classmates, would offer her gum, but rather than giving a fresh piece of gum, she'd remove the piece from her mouth and extend it to Chloe. Britney introduced her to a game where they would chew their gum and kiss, while attempting to retrieve the piece of gum from each other's mouths. Then there was the touching, but nowhere near as detailed as the touching that Ms. M introduced to her.

"Hey! What are you daydreaming about, girl?" Kennedy asked, breaking through the thick maze of thoughts that had engulfed Chloe. They were hanging out in Kennedy's room, selecting clothes for the upcoming school day. Chloe had just finished a club meeting after school, while Kennedy had completed cheerleading practice.

"You've been acting strangely lately, and why do you keep hiding when you change your clothes?" Kennedy raised an eyebrow with each question. "It's like you're ashamed or something. I've seen your naked butt plenty of times. What's going on?"

"Nothing's going on. Why do you assume there's something wrong just because I want a little privacy?"

"I'm not assuming anything. Even my mom has noticed how distant and unusual you've been acting lately, especially since you returned from camp."

"Is that what she said? Did Auntie call me weird?"

"No, she actually used the word 'peculiar.' It's me who thinks you've been acting weird," Kennedy replied, clearly frustrated. "Mom! Hey, mom...come in here, please."

Rushing into the room with wide eyes and curiosity, Macy, standing in the center, asked what was wrong. "I'm here. What's the emergency?"

"Mom, tell her. Go ahead and tell her how strange she's been acting. It's getting even weirder," Kennedy said as she walked out of the room, huffing with frustration.

"It's like she's gone crazy or something. I don't know what's going on," Chloe said in disbelief, while fidgeting and tapping the tips of her nails on her shoulders while crossing her arms.

Seeing the sadness etched onto Chloe's face, the haunted look in her eyes, the lack of eye contact, and the signs of profound pain she held inside, Macy knew she had to uncover the truth and break down the walls Chloe had built around herself. Summoning her courage, Aunt Macy spoke.

"Sweetheart, something isn't right," she gently voiced with empathy. "I see the weight upon your shoulders, and so does Kennedy. Please, you can tell me anything."

Chloe's heart pounded within her chest, torn between the trust she held for her aunt and the fear that clung to her like a venomous vine. She wrestled with the memories of her fourth-grade encounter with Britney, a tangle of emotions and confusion she had buried deep within. The thought of revealing her recent traumatizing experience with Ms. M now seemed unimaginable, Chloe's eyes darted around the room, continuing to avoid eye contact with her aunt, she thought, *How can I ever explain the knots tightening in my stomach over what has happened*? The weight of unspoken words pressed on her, threatening to spill forth the tangled mess of emotions she had kept buried since fourth grade.. Then there was the guilt she felt about not trusting Kennedy with the camp issue. They had always been inseparable and shared things with each other. Chloe's independent nature had persuaded her to protect Kennedy from feeling guilty for leaving her alone at camp, so she concealed it.

"I'm okay, really. It's just... well, you know, lots going on. School, friends, stuff." She forced a half-smile, hoping Aunt Macy wouldn't press further, "I'm going home now. Mama will be there any minute, and I'm supposed to be making the infamous hamburger helper," Chloe continued as she hurriedly placed her sneakers on.

Aunt Macy tilted her head, studying Chloe's hurried movements. "You seem a bit off today, sweetie. Are you sure you don't want to talk?" Concern etched her face"Because I've got a box of hamburger helper with your name on it. We can go downstairs right now and whip some up, and by the time Starla gets home, you'll have it ready. Plus, you and I would have had a heart-to-heart while cooking a delicious meal, like we used to do with the cupcakes...What do you say?"

"It sounds tempting. You know I like to cook with you, Auntie, but I'll pass this time," Chloe said as she managed to discontinue the fidgeting and pecked her aunt on the jaw, quickly exiting the room, down the stairs, and out the front door. As Chloe hurriedly left, Aunt Macy sighed, a mix of worry and helplessness clouding her expression. The door closed behind Chloe, leaving Macy alone, with this prayer: "Lord, please help Chloe to roll all her worries and trouble on You, because I know you see the weight she is carrying, in Jesus' Name...Amen.

It was hard to believe that October was already in full swing. Fall was typically Chloe's favorite time of year, but she couldn't embrace the usual festivities - the ball games, social outings, and preparations for the holiday season. Even her grades seemed to suffer because of a lack of concentration. As she sat in a daze in her classroom, a rolled-up piece of paper hitting her snapped Chloe back to reality. She quickly turned to see Dan Dan back to his old tricks. *This was not the day,* she thought, as she picked up the paper and tossed it back in his direction. He would have thrown it back, but the bell rang, and the assistant principal entered the classroom. All the students straightened within their seats to give Ms. Walker their full attention.

"Good morning, students. As you all know, Mrs. Strode has been ill for the last week. We received word this morning that she will not be returning for the rest of the semester."

The students expressed their disappointment with sighs and

exclamations of "Oh man" and "What?" Mrs. Strode was a beloved teacher among the students.

"I know. We were disappointed to hear this news as well. But instead of the substitute teachers who filled in last week, we're fortunate to have someone experienced in teaching English and other subjects. Please join me in welcoming Miss Kramer, whose a retired teacher but have volunteered to serve Mrs. Strode's position until she is able to return."

"Miss Kramer, you may come in now," Ms. Walker called out, and the serious minded, round-faced Miss Kramer from Chloe's camp entered the classroom. "Everyone, this is your new English teacher for the time being. Miss Kramer, they're all yours."

"Thank you, Mrs. Walker, and good morning, students," Miss Kramer greeted them cheerfully. All the students returned the greeting in unison, except for Chloe, who sat wide-eyed and in her seat. Panic enveloped her as she struggled to breathe. She wheezed, coughed, and sweat uncontrollably, and Miss Kramer hurried to her side, guiding her through calming breaths. After a moment, Mrs. Walker returned with a bottle of water. Chloe's breathing gradually returned to normal, and she had given everyone quite a scare. After that, Chloe found it increasingly difficult to concentrate on the lesson plan Miss Kramer distributed. All she could do was speak affirmations to her thoughts as she had learned during one of her Sunday School classes, I can do all things through Christ, who gives me strength, I am more than a conqueror because Jesus Christ loves me. These affirmations from the scriptures she'd learned provided some comfort as she proceeded throughout the class. Thoughts of embarrassment of what the others would think about her attack continued to push through her mind, but she would continue with her affirmations.

. . .

As the bell rang and the students prepared to leave for their next class, Chloe hastily gathered her belongings, her heart racing with intimidation. She desperately wished to avoid encountering Miss Kramer. Every glimpse of the counselor triggered the haunting memories of a few months ago, replaying like a relentless recorder. Her anxiety surged as she heard Miss Kramer's voice calling out to her, drawing Chloe's troubled history into sharp focus.

"Chloe, can I talk to you for a moment?" Ms. Kramer asked as she finished erasing the blackboard.

"Yes, ma'am," Chloe answered sheepishly, her voice barely above a whisper.

"Are you okay? Have you ever had a panic attack before today?"

"A what? I mean, no, ma'am. Never."

"Hmm, that's odd. You might want to discuss this with your parents. We want to make sure you don't need any special medication or treatment."

"I will. I... was just surprised to see you again."

"Surprised? Oh, you mean the camp, right?"

"Yes."

"Small world. I had no idea that you attended school here. It's great to see you again. Speaking of camp…dear I can't say much now, but I need to speak with one or both of your parents and yourself. It's confidential, so I will be contacting your parents over the next couple of days as a matter of fact."

"Yes, ma'am. I've got to get to my next class," Chloe mumbled and hurried out of the classroom, her anxiety growing.

As Chloe left Miss Kramer's classroom, her thoughts raced, and her heart hammered in her chest. Just when she thought things might get better, they only got worse.

In the hallway, Chloe unintentionally overheard a conversation between two teachers, their voices hushed in secrecy.

"Did you hear about that other woman that works with her at that camp?" one of them asked.

"Yeah, I heard about some sort of investigation, or at least one of my reliable sources said she heard about an investigation," the other teacher replied.

Chloe froze in her tracks, her mind racing with thoughts of the camp, memories she had tried so hard to suppress. Pressing on to her next class, she once again relied on her past Sunday School encounters. This time, she clutched at a prayer seeking serenity in her faith as the shadows of the past crept closer. It went like this: "Lord, God, you are my helper. I can do all things through You, because You give my strength, In Jesus' Name, Amen.

CHAPTER 6

BUT I DON'T WANT TO REMEMBER

Chloe trudged home from school, tossing her backpack onto the sofa. The lingering effects of not only her recent panic attack but also the onset of insomnia rendered her movements zombie-like. To her surprise, her mother was home, which was rare during this time of day. Her mother's presence piqued her curiosity.

"Unusual. She's never here during this time," Chloe mumbled to herself as she prepped herself for her usual routine of concealing the inner turmoil she had been carrying. Slowly she navigated her way to the kitchen, her steps heavy with uncertainty. "Mama…is everything okay? Are you sick?" Chloe's voice carried the weight of her confusion as she approached her mother.

"No, baby. I'm fine," Starla replied, her voice filled with apprehension. She had received a call from Miss Kramer. "Miss Kramer called this morning, said she has an urgent matter to discuss with your father and me. But, as usual, your father is running late."

"You mean …she's coming here?" Chloe's heart raced, and she offered her assistance, grabbing a dish towel to help her flustered mother, who was no master in the kitchen. Fighting the tightening feeling in her stomach, Chloe took a deep breath in and then released it. "Do you want me to help you with dinner?"

"Yes, she's coming here," Starla confirmed, a sense of disarray clouding her composure. She too had been a bit raveled in her thoughts as to why this woman was requesting an urgent meeting. *Perhaps it had to do with the contributions that they typically paid into the camp,* was her immediate thought. "I invited her for dinner, although I didn't have anything prepared. I've been rushing to the market, tearing around like a madwoman. Oh, and isn't she also working at the school as your teacher now?"

Chloe nodded slowly, her apprehension deepening. She couldn't fathom what Miss Kramer could want to discuss with her family, and it filled her with dread. All she wanted was to forget about camp, to erase every memory from those days.

"Mom, I'm not feeling well," Chloe said as she wiped her hand over her eyes and then over her head while releasing a deep sigh. "Do you mind if I skip the whole dinner thing?" Chloe's voice trembled with a mix of dejection, fear, and nervousness.

Starla hesitated for a moment, then responded, "Well, she mentioned she wanted you to be a part of this urgent matter. Is something wrong? Are you sick? Is it a virus or your cycle or something?"

Chloe shook her head, readjusting her demeanor, not wanting to delve into the real reason for her unease. " I'm okay, Mom, just not in the mood for dinner."

"Alright, I'm glad you're not sick sweetheart and I'm sure the visit from Miss Kramer won't last long. Why don't you go wash up, or even change your clothes?" Starla shifted her attention to Chloe's attire. "What did I tell you about those jeans? They're so dingy. Where are all those clothes we bought at the mall right before school started?"

Chloe nodded and replied, "Changing now, Mom." Yet, deep inside, she couldn't shake the feeling that the impending visit from Miss Kramer held the key to a past she desperately wanted to leave behind. She simply did not want to remember anymore.

About a half hour later, as the sun dipped below the horizon, casting long shadows throughout the room, the doorbell rang. Reginald, who had arrived a mere five minutes earlier, greeted Miss Kramer with politeness, inviting her to make herself comfortable in the gorgeously arranged guest room. Starla, always one to make an entrance, had changed her clothing and applied makeup for the occasion. Her countenance exhibited an air of prestige.

Chloe, however, felt a deep unease that had been gnawing at her since the moment she'd learned of Miss Kramer's impending visit. Her stomach churned with nervous fear as she took her place in a chair opposite Miss Kramer. Starla was there too, hastily finger-combing Chloe's ponytail to make it look less messy.

"Mr. and Mrs. Rhodes, thank you both for allowing me this time today. Thanks for the invitation to dinner. What a lovely gesture," Miss Kramer began, her voice measured and tense. "I'll get straight to the point, as this issue is rather unpleasant. We have a young woman who is new to our counseling team over at the camp. There was an allegation from a young lady about this new counselor. I'll not mention her name, since no investigation has begun yet," she said, pausing between sentences. "Anyway, the young female has accused the counselor of making inappropriate advances toward her. The counselor has denied these allegations, but we have two other young ladies that we wanted to question, since there were rumors that someone saw these two additional ladies spending time inside of this counselor's cabin after the normal camp activity times."

Starla, playing her normal difficult act, asked, "And...?"

"Miss Kramer, are you saying that our daughter is one of those rumored additional young ladies?" Reginald inquired, his gaze unwavering as he signaled to Starla, indicating that he would handle the situation. Taking charge, he could fill the sweat forming on his brows.

"Unfortunately, Sir, yes," Miss Kramer replied with a heavy heart. "Someone said that they saw Chloe on at least two or three occasions entering into the counselor in question's cabin at an unusual time during the night. I agreed with the head of our camp to talk with Chloe in your presence. We only want to get as much factual information as we can, so that we will know how to proceed," Miss Kramer responded, her head hanging low with embarrassment. "Excuse me. This is the first time I've had an incident of this nature. I'm a bit beside myself."

"Well...Chloe?" Starla interjected without responding to Miss Kramer, her voice betraying her nervousness all while sitting with her shoulders squared, abdominals tucked, and her chin held high

"Ma'am," Chloe responded, her countenance conveying numbness. She had developed a defense mechanism to escape from situations she was too afraid to confront directly. All she could think of was the plan she played out in her mind. The plan that promised to shield Kennedy from the burden of guilt, because she left her alone, the extra chaos that the situation would bring to her already dysfunctional family, and the chance that her parents may never find the time to give her the attention that she desperately craved. *I'm okay. I'm a big girl. I'm independent and smart. Someday this will all go away,* were the thoughts that she clung to in the heat of that moment.

"Baby doll, we need to know exactly what happened between you and one of your camp counselors," Reginald insisted, his tone loving but firm. "Did you visit a counselor's cabin after hours or not?" Reginald continued with the same tone…but inwardly, he was terrified at the thought of his little girl being violated.

"No, sir. I don't remember anything about that. I don't remember a cabin other than the one Kennedy and I stayed in," Chloe replied, maintaining her deception. The truth was so overwhelmingly difficult for her to say. She would stick to her story and continue to speak her positive affirmations from day to day.

"Let's just call Kennedy and ask her," snapped Starla, her nervousness seeping into her voice, her poised demeaner losing its shape. She grabbed the phone and dialed Kennedy's number. Kennedy, when reached, confirmed that during their time at camp, Chloe was always fast asleep in their cabin before anyone else. Starla and Reginald accepted Kennedy's reply, and since Miss Kramer had no recollection that Kennedy had left the camp a week earlier than everyone else, the conversation was dropped. This brought Chloe temporary relief. Now everyone is safe, she thought as she felt the painful tension in her shoulders ease off a bit.

The tension slowly dissipated as Miss Kramer entertained several questions from Reginald and Starla regarding the camp's by-laws. Playing with her hair and escaping to her world of daydreaming, Chloe imagined herself positioned in a small boat, sipping her favorite strawberry lemonade. Everything seemed pleasant until a boisterous storm seemed to appear out of nowhere. With that, she jerked and felt lightheaded.

"Dear, are you alright," Starla asked as she and the others were about to enter the dining area for dinner. You look like you've seen a ghost?"

Embarrassed, Chloe held her hand to her head. "I think it's because I didn't eat all of my lunch today," Chloe answered as she gently stood to her feet, with her dad coming to her side. "I'm okay, really."

The four of them enjoyed a lovely dinner, as the aroma of the rotisserie chicken filled the atmosphere. The polished silverware clicked against the elegant dishes as the conversation revolved around mundane topics like school, community activities, and other subjects Chloe found extremely boring. For a fleeting moment, Chloe felt she could relax. The aroma of the food and the conversation gave her a sense of normalcy, but she had no inkling that suppressed memories always had a way of being resurrected by the slightest trigger lurking beneath the surface, waiting to resurface and haunt her once more.

After Miss Kramer's departure, Chloe retreated to her room to finish homework. As Starla rose to tidy up, Reginald approached her with concern.

"Do you believe her?" he asked.

Frozen in the moment, Starla could not help but unload the heavy burden that Miss Kramer's visit brought on, despite Kennedy's confirmation that Chloe had been safely in the cabin with her the entire time. "I guess the question is more like…do we know what's going on with our daughter?' Starla's voice was laced with both regret and fear. " I mean what if…Reginald…"

"Alright…stop. Let's not get carried away. Kennedy confirmed what we needed to know."

Starla nodded but still held a look of uncertainty.

"We did our homework years ago before enrolling her in the summer camp and each year, we check that the camp is still accredited, fully regulated, and even that the facilitators have the background checks performed," Reginald said, consoling Starla with a gentle hug.

"You're right. Miss Kramer, who is the director, is a pillar in the community and a long-time educator. Most of the instructors are retired nurses, schoolteachers, and some are even youth ministers from various churches."

"True. I won't lie though; I almost lost it when I thought that Chloe could have been violated. Let's be thankful that she's safe and pray for the other families."

After convincing themselves that they didn't have anything to worry about, the two retired for the night.

CHAPTER 7

A MYSTERIOUS DISCOVERY

Chloe had grown into a young woman since the incident with Ms. Kramer, blossoming in ways she hadn't before. The visions had lessened; however, she began to have nightmares more often. If any event triggered memories from the camp experience, she stubbornly clung to the positive affirmation approach that she swore by. In moments of distress, she repeated her favorite motto from the Bible, "A joyful heart is good medicine," reminding herself of the strength within her faith.

Despite the nightmares and tightening muscles, Chloe remained determined to erase the memories that haunted her. The fear of being alone with adult females who held authority positions lingered, but she pushed through, relying on her affirmations and faith-based values. Continuing to apply these disciplines appeared to stabilize her until the next trigger, guiding her through the challenges she faced.

She kept up her studies and extracurriculars, earning her place at the top of her class while Aunt Macy helped to fill those motherly roles that Chloe was missing from her own home.

As they made plans to go shopping for accessories for Chloe's prom, Kennedy offered her the keys to the Altima. "No, I'm good," Chloe replied, though Kennedy gave her a judgmental look. She knew what her cousin was thinking - Chloe needed to get more experience behind the wheel if she had any hope of getting her license soon. Pulling on the door handle and sliding into the car, Chloe could feel anticipation bubbling inside her as their adventure began.

"I can't drive you everywhere you know. I'll be going off to college before you and you know Uncle Reginald won't buy you a car until you have lots of experience and your license," Kennedy said with a hint of frustration.

"Calm down. I drove all the way to church on Sunday. I know how to drive. I took the driver's education course, and I'm okay. I'm in no hurry. I'll get the license this summer," Chloe responded. She knew that Kennedy meant well, but over the past couple of years, she had trained her mind to watch every decision. Only decisions that affected her education were prioritized. Driver license was not at the top of her list.

"You better. Besides, all the cool females drive their own vehicles. It's what's up," Kennedy mouthed as her thoughts focused on how weird her cousin was to not be in a hurry to get her license. "You are so different girly."

"Yea, yea. I know. I'll drive on the way back and for your information, dad and I have already decided that I'll take my road test at the end of the summer. Speaking of cool females, wonder how Daphne is doing? I feel bad that she won't be able to make prom. She and Tavares were hoping that their baby wouldn't come until after the prom," Chloe said as she soaked up the satisfaction of knowing she was a shrewd teen who made healthy decisions, but thoughts of Daphne and Tavares having sex and now has a baby on the way sent chills down her spine.

"I know right. But maybe it's for the best," Kennedy answered as she was now taking the exit to the mall. "By the way...I can tell you've been dieting to fit in that fancy looking dress your mom bought last year! Who does that?" Kennedy went on. But little did she know Chloe's weight had been up and down for a while because of a lack of appetite at times, but then there were times she would binge eat.

"I really hope I can keep down the pounds. This morning I swear I smelled doughnuts in my room upon wakening."

The girls continued chatting and laughing as they wandered through the outlet mall, enjoying the cloudy but dry late afternoon. Their laughter echoing against the walls of discounted shops. The air was infused with the scent of freshly baked pretzels, enticing their taste buds. Despite the outward appearance of enjoyment, Chloe's gaze occasionally drifted away, her emotions hidden beneath a facade of casual conversation. Suddenly Chloe's attention was drawn to a luxurious restaurant, where she saw her father with another woman - someone who was not her mother. Her stare became intense as she tried to make sense of what she was seeing. Kennedy noticed Chloe's distraction and asked what was wrong. "It's daddy. I mean, who is that lady he's with? He's normally still at work," said Chloe, confused and alarmed. Suddenly, Reginald took the stranger's hand and kissed it gently. The couple stared into each other's eyes, laughing and enjoying each other's company. "Girl did you see that?" Kennedy gasped in shock as Chloe made her way toward the door of the restaurant, determined to confront Reginald about his inappropriate behavior. But Kennedy grabbed her arm and urged her to stay out of it. "Alright! I can't believe this. The nerve of daddy being with some woman while my mom is slaving her tail off," Chloe complained bitterly.

"I know, but you can't get involved," warned Kennedy wisely.

"Why not? Did you see how he was looking at that woman? I mean, I never see him looking at mom that way," replied Chloe, confusion and anger lacing her words. Slamming a shopping bag to the floor. For the first time in a long time, Chloe was not choosing to act out her mature role.

"Girl, I understand why you're upset, but sometimes these things just happen. It's life," Kennedy said. "Wow, I've never seen you this angry, or at least not slinging stuff. Wow."

"But they can't go around preaching about morals and values when they don't even practice them! This is so unfair to my mom." Chloe felt rage bubbling up inside of her, but it was Friday night—their movie night—and she didn't want her parents' issues to ruin that. So, she took a deep breath and said, "Let's go get something to eat...but I don't know if I can just forget this. I mean, maybe, but... taking a deep breath in and then out, and repeating her breathing exercise, Chloe closed her eyes and looked deep within for an affirmation. Nothing came to mind.

Kennedy's gum-smacking intensifies as she watches Chloe. Almost lost for words, Kennedy offered advice to Chloe. "Listen, I'm telling you it's not a big deal. Your mom may already know or maybe she's stepping out on Uncle Reginald too. Hey, remember that night a couple of years back when we were snooping in the spare bedroom at your place?" Kennedy asks with unshakeable confidence. Perhaps if Chloe thought her mom was doing the same thing it would help with the aggravation.

"Yeah, how can I forget?" Chloe responds nervously, wary of her friend's intentions.

"Exactly. Your mom had all sorts of sex toys and stuff hidden away. So, we don't know what secrets either of them is keeping from each other." Dark images run through Chloe's mind - thoughts of her father and that strange woman, and the memory of her mother using sex toys. Then suddenly, there it was. A haunting thought. It had been several weeks since the camp scene came for a visit in her thoughts. Biting her bottom lip and rubbing her head, Chloe repeated her favorite affirmation and chose to exhibit self-control. Counting backward from ten, she decided to let the matter go for now.

"Okay, you're probably right." She concedes reluctantly. "But wait…how do you know so much about these things?"

"Girl, please. Do you even have to ask? ." Kennedy cackled cruelly without answering the question. "You need to lighten up. I've noticed lately that you have some weird mood swings," Kennedy fired off while simultaneously winking at a cute dude passing by. "Speaking of sex…my last prom and your first one is only a couple of weeks away. A few couples are planning to meet up at one of the hotels downtown at around ten o'clock. Dan Dan is down if you are."

Chloe shuddered as the suggestion enveloped her like a thick fog and chilled her bones. All the talk about sex made her both uncomfortable and inquisitive at the same time. Despite knowing that her parents would never approve of such an idea, some part of her yearns for adventure - something dangerous that will set her free from their confining expectations. Especially after witnessing what she did at the restaurant. How dare they lay down the law to her.

"No," she answered firmly before quickly adding: "And thousand times no! Besides, none of you are of legal age to book rooms."

"You are such a nerd cousin. We have connections," Kennedy replies sinisterly with a raised eyebrow, letting her words linger in the air like smoke from a fire. "It's already done. So... are you in or not?"

Chloe considered her options carefully and took a deep breath before responding: "I don't want any trouble."

"It won't be any trouble," Kennedy said with a sly smile spread across her face. "It'll just be some of us having a good time. Your folks won't find out. I promise and if they do, I'll cover for you,"

"I guess so, oh, I don't know. Let me think about it," Chloe responded as she placed her thoughts on speed dial, trying to work out every detail.

Kennedy ran her fingers through her braids in thought before responding. "Fair enough, "she answered, not once considering the amount of pressure she placed upon her cousin. It was her who was ready to venture out and experience the wild side of life, not Chloe. Kennedy had always been the most adventurous one and Chloe knew it but held no judgmental thoughts about her cousin. The only secret thoughts Chloe held was wishing her mom had the same traits as her aunt Macy, and if this was so, she'd never do anything that would bring disappointment.

In the midst of the sudden change of subject matter, Chloe tried hard to shake the thoughts of her father and this strange woman from her mind, and also the curiosity that the memory of her mother using sex toys stirred up. She fought against the distractions as she and Kennedy proceeded to find a place to eat dinner and afterward catch a movie. But despite her best efforts, she couldn't help but feel overwhelmed by the inner turmoil that threatened to consume her first ever prom night. Was she ready for the adventure that Kennedy introduced? Would she be able to enjoy the night without the memories of her past? Who was the strange woman with her father and why did her family seem to never get past all their dysfunctions? Her thoughts swirled like a roller coaster. It did not take Chloe long to see that her coping mechanism was becoming fragile. There would need to be something else in addition to her affirmations and her faith. Perhaps she was in the wrong line of living. Maybe she should take Kennedy up on the proposal, but of course, be extremely wise.

CHAPTER 8

A NIGHT TO REMEMBER: PROM, SECRETS, AND SHADOWS

Ever since Chloe had witnessed her father and the mysterious woman at the restaurant, her world felt like it was spinning out of control. She continued to have nightmares and her mood swings became more evident during her classes. One of her teachers even recommended a counselor visit, but Chloe managed to talk her way out of it. The looming pressure from Dan Dan, urging her to join the others at the hotel after the prom, coupled with the meticulous attention she paid to her diet to ensure her dress fit perfectly, left her in a constant state of disarray.

"Are you okay, Chloe? You seem lost in thought," Starla observed, concern etching her face as she joined Chloe at the breakfast table. "Prom should be an exciting time, but you appear distressed. What's been bothering you?"

Chloe's gaze was distant, and she hesitated before responding, not wanting to reveal the turmoil she'd been wrestling with ever since that fateful night at the mall. Deciding to keep the ugly truth to herself until further notice was her decision, but each day became more difficult. Especially when she would see her father parading around the house as if nothing was wrong. Straightening her posture in her chair, she answered. "I'm fine, Mom. It's just that I've taken on a lot lately. Volunteering for the prom committee, juggling my schoolwork, and managing all the decorations are starting to wear on me," her voice holding a subtle strain as she felt a stain of guilt from hiding the truth.

Starla raised her brow, not entirely convinced by Chloe's explanation but deciding to let it go for now. Long winded conversations with her daughter were not the norm. "Well, remember, it's not every day you get to experience your first prom. Try to enjoy it. Oh, and don't forget about your appointment tonight at six. The salon is top-notch, and if you're more than fifteen minutes late, you may risk losing your slot. So, be on time."

"Sure thing, Mom. See you tonight," Chloe replied, her eyes holding a mix of tension and uncertainty as she heard her father enter the kitchen.

Reginald grabbed a cup of coffee, inquiring about his wife's departure. "Did Starla leave already?"

Chloe responded bluntly, avoiding eye contact, "Yes, she did," as she rushed to exit the room. Fury filling her belly, threatening to spill over. *I ought to confront him right this moment…*she thought as she high stepped toward the door. But just as she reached the door, her father halted her in her tracks. "Slow down there, young lady. Where's the fire?"

Chloe paused briefly, her mood still hanging heavily over her. "I'm running late for school, Dad."

Reginald persisted, reaching out for a moment of connection. "No hug? You're off to your prom, but you'll always be my little girl, you know?"

Chloe looked down, her jaw clenching, a mixture of resentment and frustration bubbling within her. She forced a tight smile, masking her inner turmoil. "I know," she replied with strained cheerfulness, her emotions getting the best of her. She muttered a hasty goodbye and swiftly grabbed her purse and bag, making a beeline for the door. In her rush, she couldn't bear to meet her father's gaze. *You make me sick,* was her final thought as the door shut behind her.

Outside, she crossed the street to Kennedy's house, her mind a whirlwind of conflicting emotions. The images of her family playing the perfect role were disrupted by the reality she felt caught in—the family dynamics shattered, a façade of togetherness that masked the true disconnection. She replayed flashbacks of the family life dynamics from her home economics class, where the happy family scene seemed like a distant dream. Chloe also revisited all the times she stood at her church's altar with other congregants and petitioned for her family to be closer. She wondered if her requests were still lingering in the atmosphere...unanswered because of her father's folly.

Chloe's bedroom was bathed in the soft glow of lights, creating a magical ambiance that mirrored the enchantment promised by the upcoming prom. The air was filled with a sweet fragrance from both perfumed lotions and scented candles. Her reflection in the mirror revealed a mixture of excitement and fear in her expressive hazel eyes. As she applied a hint of makeup, she couldn't help but recall the events leading up to this night – the discovery of her father with another woman, the subsequent emotional turmoil, and the persistent nightmares that haunted her.. The weight of her emotions was momentarily lifted as she admired herself, a fleeting moment of joy in the midst of the chaos. With a final glance at her reflection, she took a deep breath, steeling herself for the night ahead.

The excitement continued to be evident as Chloe arrived at the high school gym for her first prom. As Chloe entered the ballroom, the subtle fragrance of flowers from the decorations intertwined with the warmth of the lights, creating an enchanting aroma. The venue had been transformed into a fairy-tale setting. Dazzling lights cast a warm, soft glow on the beautiful decorations, setting the scene for a night to remember. The soft, mellow tunes of a live band filled the air, as couples swayed elegantly on the dance floor.

Chloe had chosen a stunning royal blue gown that flowed gracefully with her every step, and her updo was elegant and adorned with sparkling accessories. Also, the other students were taken aback since Chloe was always known for her plain attire and low-key disposition.

Kennedy appeared in a deep crimson dress, dancing with her date. The two couples, with their youthful energy and bright smiles, blended seamlessly with the more experienced dancers gliding across the floor. As she immersed herself in the enchanting atmosphere, the soft rustle of her gown and the subtle clinking of her accessories blended seamlessly with the rhythmic beats of the music.

Laughing and feeling free, Chloe's attention was drawn to a prom couple that stood out. It was two females, one dressed in an elegant silver gown while the other one wore slim-fit pants and a white button-up blouse with a necktie. Even though there had been much debate concerning these types of relationships in the community, most people looked upon same gender couples at the prom as normal.

Chloe was immediately haunted by memories of those nights in Ms. M's cabin during summer camp. Her chest felt tight, her breathing suddenly became ragged, and she wheezed uncontrollably. One particular memory resisted affirmation – the scent that lingered in the cabin. The aroma of candles and flowers, forgotten until this moment, flooded her senses. Why is this memory resurfacing now? she questioned herself as the panic attack persisted, the familiar scent lingering in the air. Could someone be wearing that same fragrance? Chloe found herself hunched over, overwhelmed by the vivid recollection.

"Hey, you good?" Dan Dan asked, his voice filled with worry and concern. He placed his large hand on her back and motioned for Kennedy to join them. As Kennedy quickly came to her cousin's side, Chloe, slowly returning to a standing position, glanced around the room; some students were staring at the strange scene before them. Others were pointing, laughing, and recording the scene on their phones. Still, a few were concerned and quickly stepped into her space to offer assistance.

Kennedy let go of Chloe's hand and rested it on her shoulder instead. "Okay, girl, that's it…breathe in, hold, and out…come on, come on, breathe," Kennedy said as she took charge of the situation; she was familiar with coaching Chloe into settling down from sudden panic attacks after the incident happened a few years ago during class. Although these only happened occasionally, Starla and Reginald had taken Chloe to see a doctor once about a year ago who prescribed medication but also gave instructions for controlling her breaths on the onset of an attack. Chloe had taken the medication for several months but discontinued it when she felt like she no longer needed it anymore.

"Okay, okay enough," Chloe muttered under her breath as she noticed some of the students still staring in her direction. The last thing she wanted was to cause a scene on prom night.

"I'll get something for us to drink," Dan Dan offered as he left Kennedy and her date standing with Chloe.

"Excuse us Cameron," Kennedy told her date as she yanked Chloe by the hand and walked to the nearest corner of the room.

"So, what's up?" and I do not want to hear some lame, cool and confident answer with a Bible affirmation. "What is going on with you?"

"I don't know...I, well I just felt an attack coming on out of nowhere." Kennedy was visibly frustrated, and her annoyance grew with every second. She wondered why Chloe had constantly kept secrets.

"Girl, I was with you on those doctor visits. Your attacks come on when you are anxious. When you are overly stressed and out of control you have those attacks. You've not had one in a while, so what's up? Why are you keeping secrets from me? Answer me.

Chloe tried to remain calm but her emotions were getting the best of her. She wanted to scream and cry as she felt a mix of fear and anger bubbling up inside of her. She especially felt guilty for not being open with Kennedy about the camp experience. "I said I am okay! I don't want to talk about it, Kennedy. Let's go back and dance. Please!"

But Kennedy wouldn't budge. "No. I don't want you messing the night up for all of us, now we need to get to the bottom of what's bothering you and do it now."

The situation got heated quickly as Chloe began to yell in frustration "You're not my mother, Kennedy, now let go! See, you're causing a scene." The gathered crowd grew restless as rumors swirled around them. Chloe felt exposed, her secret threatening to unravel in front of everyone. She glanced around, catching glimpses of pity, curiosity, and judgment. The incident would undoubtedly leave a mark on her reputation, due to all the cell phone video clips streaming into social media sites. Dan Dan and Cameron reached out to their dates in an attempt to diffuse the situation before intervening themselves.

"Ladies, everything alright?" Cameron asked softly, his expression of concern was clear on his baby-face.

Kennedy, feeling betrayed as if the bond between her and

Chloe had been fractured, curled her lips into an even more serious expression and replied curtly "We're fine. Just had a moment. My cousin seems to think it's always about her. Never willing to see things from anyone else's perspective," sending another wave of anger through Chloe's body. "I'll let this go for now, but it's not over girly."

Before either could speak again, their fight was interrupted by an elegant woman approaching them--one of the chaperones who had been nearby since the start of the conflict.

"Ladies is there a problem?" she asked with a warm yet concerned expression on her face, though Chloe's eyes widened as recognition struck her like lightning; she knew this woman from somewhere else--from somewhere private.

With her mouth opened wide in total awe, Chloe spoke..."It's you!" Chloe shouted angrily, pointing at the woman accusingly "Who are you? Why were you with my father?!"

"I beg your pardon?" the woman asked, her facial expression exuded confusion and concern. Her hand placed on her chest as she looked around the room carefully. She was indeed the woman that Chloe and Kennedy saw a couple of weeks ago in the restaurant with Chloe's father.

Kennedy's eyes widened in disbelief as she stared at the chaperone. "Wait...it is you," Kennedy intervened. She turned to Chloe, who was now nervously biting her lip and tugging on her earring. Kennedy gently grasped Chloe's arm and led her away, shooting apologetic glances at the chaperone as they passed. The group of students had stopped dancing and were now murmuring excitedly, their eyes darting from Kennedy and Chloe to the mysterious woman with a stern expression on her face. Kennedy cleared her throat and flashed a winning smile, speaking in a calm and collected manner. "Ahh ma'am, thanks for coming over, but we're fine. Just a misunderstanding," she said as she ushered Chloe and their dates out of the building. "Don't mind us, everything is cool,

Y'all go on back to your groove thing now." As soon as they stepped outside, Kennedy quickly closed the door behind them to silence the noise inside. The students resumed their dancing and things returned to normal - or so it seemed. However, the mysterious chaperone lingered in the back of their minds, leaving a sense of unresolved mystery. Who was she, and what connection did she have with Chloe's father? The night held more secrets than anyone could fathom.

CHAPTER 9

LET ME IN

As the night progressed, Chloe found herself retreating into a corner chair, overshadowed by the carefree laughter and dance of Kennedy, Cameron, and Dan Dan. Her thoughts echoed with the haunting traces of Kennedy's ominous words, "this is not over," and the enigma surrounding the mysterious chaperone seemed to have taken root in her mind, claiming a permanent residence. "Ready to get back out there?" Dan Dan asked as he sat down next to her, still catching his breath from dancing.

"For what reason? The night is almost gone. I had a miserable time, and I still don't know who the supposed chaperone is, and Kennedy thinks she's supposed to control my life. Listen to me, obviously, I've ruined your prom."

"Listen, you haven't ruined anything. Don't you know?

"Don't I Know what?"

"How much I am into you. Just being here with you tonight is enough." Dan Dan reached out and gently touched Chloe's cheek as he spoke, causing her heart to flutter.

Blushing, Chloe looked deep into his eyes before taking his

hand and leading him onto the dance floor. One of her all-time favorite love ballads was playing, and they swayed together slowly at first before gradually pulling closer until they were embraced in a tight hold that made Chloe feel unique sensations of both tension and excitement coursing through her body. As the song reached its sweet conclusion Chloe and Dan Dan took their ten-year friendship to another level by sharing an intimate kiss. In each other's presence, their figures resembled a captivating silhouette on the dance floor, making it seem as if they were alone at that moment. The music shifted, and Dan Dan's soft words stirred the air, a whisper meant only for Chloe's ears. "Let me in. Just let me love you." Dan Dan felt a mixture of excitability and nervousness as he succumbed to the romantic feelings that had blossomed for his long-time friend. That night marked the beginning of a journey, a pivotal moment to cultivate the chemistry he knew they both shared

"Love me? Dan Dan, we've been friends since pre-school. This feels unusual," Chloe responded, her heartbeat beginning to quicken, matching the tempo of the music. Her thoughts swirled back to the traumatic memories and the unanswered questions that had plagued her concerning her past experiences with same-sex attractions. First Britney, and then Ms. M. It was a part of her history buried beneath layers of pain and solitude; a secret she dared not share with anyone. Now, with the kiss she had shared with Dan Dan, her confusion intensified. In that moment, all she knew was that her body seemed to respond with sensations akin to those from her past encounters with Ms. M at the camp, memories that felt as vivid as if the camp incident had occurred just yesterday.

Interrupting her thoughts, Dan Dan, grabbing Chloe's hand and caressing it gently, spoke his heart. "Well, we've secured a room at the Hilton. Perhaps we can discuss it further there. In fact,

I'm starting to lose interest in this prom. Let's get out of here," Dan Dan suggested, his voice resolute and commanding.

Chloe's heart pounded in her chest as she stared at Dan Dan, her mind racing with conflicting emotions. She wanted to trust him, but the tangled web of her past experiences made it difficult for her to fully embrace this new connection. Still, there was an undeniable pull between them, a magnetic force that drew her closer. Looking for an affirmation from her faith, she found none. Her walls were completely torn down.

As they made their way through the crowd, Chloe's thoughts swirled like a hurricane. She couldn't help but wonder what awaited them in the hotel. Would it bring clarity or only fuel her confusion further? She hesitated, torn between the desire for answers and the fear of what she might uncover. Still, she proceeded on. As she and Dan Dan reached the parking lot of the hotel, he turned off the car and turned to Chloe to ensure she agreed with hanging out at the hotel for the remainder of the night. "I won't force you. It's your choice," he said, leaning closer and gently kissing her on the cheek. Her heart fluttered, thoughts racing. Closing her eyes briefly, visions of reading her devotional or crying herself to sleep played out in her mind. Her first notion after opening her eyes was to ask Dan Dan to drive her home. But something in Dan Dan's gaze reassured her. There was a genuine concern in his eyes, a warmth that melted away her doubts. With a nod, Chloe decided to come out of her normal shell of safety. Besides, Kennedy always got on to her about living a little, so here was her chance.

Walking into the night air felt enchanting as Chloe and Dan Dan held hands. The gentle breeze caressed their faces, carrying with it the soft notes of distant laughter and the sweet aroma of cuisine and fresh pastries from the adjacent restaurants. Their steps seemed to glide with every stride, creating a rhythmic dance on the pavement.

Chloe, gently lifting the train of her elegant gown, felt the luxurious fabric brush against her fingertips, adding a huge dimension to the enchantment. As they ascended the steps and entered the hotel, the warm lighting inside embraced them, casting a cozy glow that contrasted with the cool outdoor air. Once inside the Hilton, and even though Kennedy and Cameron were in the adjacent room, the atmosphere changed. The dimly lit room seemed to transport them into their own world, separate from the chaos of the prom. The soft hum of distant music and muffled laughter filtered through the walls, serving as a distant melody to their own private world. Dan Dan stepped closer, his voice barely above a whisper. "Chloe, I want you to know that I care about you. I've known you for so long, and this... this connection we have is something I've never felt before. You know me, we've been friends a long time, and yes, I could've spent this night with any of the others. It's you that I want to be with."

Chloe's heart skipped a beat. She mustered the strength to speak, her voice trembling. "Dan Dan, I trust you. But... there's something I need to tell you. Something..."

Dan Dan's expression softened, but he didn't want any further conversation. He stepped closer, gently reaching for her hand. The plush carpet beneath their feet added a softness to their connection, as the scent of vanilla-scented candles in the room whisked through the air, creating an atmosphere of warmth and comfort. "It doesn't matter...whatever it is. I just want us to lose ourselves in this moment. Shoot, you got me talking like some old romantic man in a movie or something girl," Dan Dan continued as they both exploded with laughter.

Chloe's laughter faded as a loud, persistent knocking echoed through the room, shattering the intimacy they had created. Confusion etched itself into their expressions, both frozen in the sudden tension now filling the atmosphere.

Dan Dan's jovial expression vanished, replaced by a frown. "Who could that be?" he muttered, shooting a questioning glance at Chloe. Without waiting for a response, he cautiously moved towards the door. "Who's there?" Dan Dan asked, with a loud but firm voice. Twisting the handle of the doorknob, two uniformed policemen stormed into the room, identifying themselves and flashing their badges.

Chloe's heart leaped into her throat. She felt the moisture in her palms, the sudden tension suffocating the air. Breathing in and out, she stepped closer to the gentlemen.

"What's going on?" she managed to ask, her voice barely above a whisper.

"Are you Chloe Rhodes?" one of the policemen asked.

"Yes, Sir," Chloe answered, her voice fluttering and raspy as she cleared her throat and swallowed hard. Her heart beating fast in her chest, she looked intently at the policemen.

"What time did you leave the prom?" the other asked. "There's been an incident following the prom tonight involving Henrietta Lawson. She was assaulted and was found lying in the parking lot beside her vehicle."

"I…I guess, I'm not sure," was Chloe's nervous explanation.

"Officer, we left at around 9:30," Dan Dan intervened as he grabbed Chloe's hand, trying to console her. Although shocked and nervous, Dan Dan managed to keep his composure.

"Several of the students witnessed some sort of misunderstanding or argument between the two of you tonight?"

"If you're referring to the chaperone, then, well, I snapped at her. We didn't really have an argument; I mean she was nice. I was the one doing the loud talking."

"Officer, Chloe and her cousin were in an intense discussion… family stuff, and so the chaperone, Henrietta, I believe you called her, intervened to see if all was okay. Chloe must have thought she… Henrietta was someone else, but it turned out it was a misunderstanding. Nothing came of it," Dan Dan explained, holding up well under the pressure

The policeman asked a few more questions, documented notes, and left the scene.

"Why did you lie?" Chloe asked, as she paced the room.

"What do you mean? I told the truth as I saw it. You yelled at that lady and she didn't know you, so I assumed, as Kennedy said, that it was all a misunderstanding. Anyway, it worked. It got those cops off your back."

I know, but...well, you're right. I don't know her, but I did see her with my father in that restaurant! Now, someone has assaulted her. This is too much," Chloe said falling onto the bed as if she'd fainted.

'Hey, don't sweat it. Everything is going to be fine. You were with me the whole night. You're innocent."

"I know I am, but...can you imagine what the social media sites are gonna do with this issue? What if word gets to my parents or what if they arrest me?"

"Baby, they are not going to arrest you. Chill...okay," Dan Dan assured, caressing her gently.

As the two continued to discuss the matter, they were interrupted again by a knock at the door. This time it was Kennedy.

"Hey! I just got questioned by the cops!" she said as if it was an adventure.

"So did I," Chloe responded in dejection. "That lady, by the way her name is Henrietta something or another was attacked tonight. Someone told the cops that this lady and me were arguing at the prom."

"I know. Girl, this has been one crazy night."

"Tell me about it. Now can we go back to our room now?" Cameron asked as he stood behind Kennedy. I don't know. Chloe looks out of it. I think its best that we go on home now."

"Are you serious?" Cameron asked, his voice full of disappointment.

"No, we can stay a bit longer. Just need to process it all," Chloe said as she hugged Kennedy. "I'm okay. Really."

The couples continued to enjoy their time at the hotel, but eventually, they decided it was time to call it a night. As Chloe and Dan Dan approached her house, the evening took an unexpected turn. They were taken aback by the sound of shouting echoing from inside.

"What is that all about?" Dan Dan asked, his face reflecting shock.

Chloe shook her head, puzzled. "Beats me. I didn't even think they'd still be up." She fumbled for her key and inserted it into the lock. Turning to Dan Dan, she added, "I'll call you tomorrow." She placed her hand on his chest, preventing him from stepping inside. The night had already been a rollercoaster, and she wanted to avoid her parents getting involved, especially since it was already one in the morning.

As Chloe entered her house, the tension in the air was thick as fog. She could still hear her parents arguing, their voices rising and falling in a heated exchange. Closing the door behind her, she took a deep breath and braced herself for whatever awaited her on the other side. Momentarily, the thoughts surrounding the events of the night would be laid to rest, but they would spring forth like rivers of water in their own timing.

CHAPTER 10

ADULTS!

"What is up with the two of you? We could hear you outside of the door," Chloe said, anxiety pouring forth like water as she stared at her mom's wine glass and her dad's countenance. It had been a long time since she'd witnessed an argument between her parents. When she was a young girl, it always made her nervous to hear them disagree or get loud with each other. Now that she was older and especially with the knowledge of her father and Henrietta's mysterious relationship, her desire for healthy family dynamics was slowly starting to feel out of reach.

"We? Who is we?" Reginald snapped, as he eyed his daughter from head to toe.

"Are you mad, or just plumb crazy. Tonight was prom night and her date walked her to the door. I'm sure you've embarrassed the stew out of her," Starla responded, tossing the remaining drops of wine into the sink. She was in a provocative night gown, and her hair was in curls. Typically, she would be in leggings with her hair bonnet on.

"Mom, dad...what's going on?" Chloe asked again. This time

her voice seemed to transform into that of a sheepish child. Her anger toward her father and her resentment toward her mother always placing work as a priority did not prevent the painful emotions from erupting.

"It's nothing. You should go to your room, or something, wash that makeup off your face. You look too grown," Reginald snapped. This was shocking to Chloe since her dad was usually so mild mannered. She'd seen him get rowdy a few times over the years, but it was not with her or her mom. "Look, I didn't mean to snap. Your mom and I…we've got some adult issues we're plowing through."

"Does those adult issues involve Henrietta?" Chloe asked, her heart pounding. She had become quite bold ever since seeing her dad and Henrietta in the restaurant. Her newfound boldness surprised even herself, but she had resolved to speak her truth.

Placing her hand over her mouth, Starla was taken aback while Reginald, who had started walking out of the kitchen, froze in his tracks. Turning around slowly, he spoke, but with a lighter tone.

"How do you know Henri?" he asked, as his light complexion rendered his face a reddish color that Chloe had seen only a couple of times.

"I saw the two of you a few weeks ago when Kennedy and I were at the mall. Dad, mom, you two are not getting a divorce, are you?"

"Baby…no, we are not getting a divorce. Look, you're sixteen, so you're not a child. Adults sometimes have issues that can be too complicated to explain. Ms. Henrietta, or Henri, is what we've always called her, is an old friend of ours. She moved away when you were much younger, but even before you were born, your father and I cut ties with her, "Starla said reaching for her wine glass, pulling it to her mouth, and frowning upon discovering the empty glass.

"Yes, sweetheart. Henri came back into town a year ago, and I ran into her, and...well we were catching up. I'm sorry you saw us together, but your mother and I are fine."

"It just looked like you were on a date, from what Kennedy and I witnessed."

"It was nothing more than two old friends catching up...dear you look tired, why don't you call it a night, or morning...I didn't realize the time," Starla said as she stared at the time on her cell phone. Chloe glancing intently at the two of them could discern a cover up.

"Your mother is right. Get some rest."

"There's something else I may as well tell you, since we're being open," Chloe said as she took a huge swallow. "Your friend Henrietta...Henri, was assaulted tonight. The police...well, actually Ms. Henri was a chaperone at the prom. I jumped all over her for being with dad, and lots of folks heard me yelling at her," Chloe breathed deeply while staring at the floor. On one hand she was relieved to get the ugly incident out in the open but on the other, she was embarrassed by her behavior and wondered what the consequences would be.

"Go on," Starla urged, walking up to Chloe and grabbing her hand, and obviously anxious for what would come next.

"Someone attacked her tonight after the prom. I don't know if she is okay or in the hospital or what. The reason I know is because the police questioned me and Kennedy, since folks heard me getting loud with her. They assumed that Ms. Henri and I had an argument."

"What!? You did what? How could you be so disrespectful?" Reginald asked. His face was red as fire, and he began to scratch his head.

"I'm sorry. I was angry. I thought she was trying to come between you and mom. Dad you've got to understand."

"It's okay," Starla said, embracing Chloe, all the while giving Reginald a sharp, dark stare.

"Dan Dan and I both told them that it wasn't an argument. Ms. Henrietta was nice about the situation. Kennedy also talked with the police. They believed us and they left."

"Okay, but…did they say how bad the attack was?" Reginald asked, the intensity in his voice was evident, while the look on Starla's face evidenced an undercurrent of darkness. The atmosphere was even colder than when Chloe interrupted their argument.

"Alright, at least our daughter is home safe. She was questioned but nothing came of it. Actually, one of us should contact the police department tomorrow or Monday at least to find out why they would question a minor without our presence," Starla said.

"Good thought," Reginald said as he cleared his throat and exited the room. Relieved, Chloe embraced Starla once more and headed to bed. As she laid down, her mind raced. *Was that it? Was it settled between her mom and her father? Were they being truthful about their relationships with Henrietta?* The weight of uncertainty hung in the air, and Chloe could not shake the feeling that there was more to the story.

In the quiet of her room, Chloe reflected on the events of the night. The investigation into Henrietta's assault, her parents' argument, and her own bold confrontation with them all swirled in her thoughts. It was a night she would not easily forget. With each stroke of her pen on the pages of her journal, she delved into her parents' actions like never before, seeking clarity amid the shadows that seemed to envelop their lives. The journey to unravel the mysteries had just begun.

Weeks had swiftly passed since the prom, and Chloe could not shake her suspicions about her parents' true relationship with Henrietta. While they appeared closer, there was an underlying tension that she could not ignore. She discovered that Henrietta was discharged from the hospital the day after the prom, having suffered no life-threatening injuries. Rumors swirled that she had identified her attacker in a police lineup a couple of days after the incident.

Chloe and Dan Dan chatted over a video call one evening as she lounged in her bedroom. Wearing comfy loungewear, she reclined on her bed, surrounded by an array of plush cushions. With her laptop closed and sitting on the nearby desk after a lengthy time of study, she and Dan Dan began to conversate. The topic naturally drifted to her parents and Henrietta. "Did you ever find out what's really going on between your folks and this Henrietta person?" Dan Dan asked, his face illuminated by the soft glow of his phone. "Their story seems reasonable, but there's something odd about the whole situation."

Chloe nodded in agreement, reclining on her bed. "I've thought about it too, especially since she showed up as a chaperone at our school."

"Remember, she's related to Angelica, or so Cameron said. With Angelica's mom passing away last year, someone mentioned that Henrietta has been primarily looking out for her."

"That does make sense. I recall how gentle she was with me when I was yelling at her. Seems like a nice lady underneath it all," Chloe conceded, her brow furrowing. "But it still doesn't explain the way they were looking at each other, or why my dad was holding her hand and kissing it."

"Nope," Dan Dan admitted. "But let's put that aside for now. We need to talk about us."

Chloe's interest piqued. "What do you mean?"

"I mean that everyone else has taken their relationships to the next level, and I think it's time we seriously consider it, I mean, not that I'm forcing anything on you," Dan Dan said, treading lightly on the subject."

Chloe bit her lip, uncertainty dancing in her eyes. "I've thought about it too, but I want to be sure, you know?" Chloe contemplated all her emotions and what had unfolded over the course of the year. She had set so many goals for herself. Mainly, to be a whole person who someday has a family with less dysfunctions than what she experienced with her parents.

Dan Dan's gaze held hers. "You know I love you. I have not been with anyone since that night we kissed" he said, his heart connecting deeper with hers.

Chloe's heart quickened at the thought of the intimate step they were contemplating, yet she felt insecure by Dan Dan's experiences with other females. "How many girls have you been with, Dan Dan?"

Dan Dan hesitated; his gaze unwavering. "Why does that matter? I don't even remember anyone else. I just want you, baby. Sex is a natural part of a committed relationship. To answer your question, I've only been serious about one other person."

Chloe could not help but experience tinge of jealousy as she questioned, "Big booty Tabitha, is that who you're talking about? "Chloe let out, as a hint of insecurity once again enveloped her mind. She oftentimes felt overwhelmed with the thought of human sexuality, especially with the aspect of touch, as she fought to keep the traumatic memories of the camp issue at bay. One of her affirmations had been to "forget those things that are behind and reach toward the mark of her life-calling.

"Let's not discuss Tabitha," Dan Dan replied, changing the subject. He used to like his reputation of not being a virgin. Now, he was not so sure. He did not want Chloe feeling some type of way about his past. "Listen, my mom won't be home tomorrow night; she has a work thing out of town. My uncle is coming over, but he doesn't finish his shift until 10."

Chloe considered his proposition. "And?"

"And... We can study for the chemistry test. Remember, you

promised to help me with it. After that, I think we can, well, you know, I mean...we can go as slow as you want, but I'm really into you."

"Let me think about it," Chloe replied. "Mom said I can go to your place after school tomorrow to help you study, given the upcoming exams," Chloe answered, her voice was that of the usual independent and intelligent Chloe, however, her heart held no confidence in her ability to navigate the complexity of the conversation.

"Sounds like a plan," Dan Dan agreed, with a voice of expectation and excitability and they concluded their conversation for the night, both pondering the path their relationship was about to take.

As Chloe continued to contemplate further, she fought the unwelcoming thoughts of how she and Brittany from her fourth-grade class touched and kissed. "That was so long ago. We were just kids playing around. It was nothing," she murmured to herself. *Brittany is a female. I'm a female. I'm sixteen and Dan Dan and I have an authentic relationship...this is the expectation of my parents, my church family and the community...right?* Her thoughts swirled as she reached for her laptop to surf the web. Next, she would shower and read in her devotional for solace and relaxation.

CHAPTER 11

UNDER PRESSURE

Dan Dan's home provided a comfortable and focused atmosphere for the intense study session. The room, designated as a study space, was well-lit with ample natural light streaming through the open blinds. The room was free from distractions, allowing Chloe and Dan Dan to immerse themselves fully in their study materials. Wading through several chemistry formulas and other data elements, Chloe and Dan Dan reluctantly decided to stop studying. The session had been intense, and they both knew how important it was for Dan Dan to pass the upcoming exam.

"Whew! This stuff is harder than I thought, but I'm getting there," Dan Dan said as he scratched his forehead. He moved closer to Chloe as she took a sip of her water bottle. "So, while we're taking a break...what did you decide?"

"I know you're not jumping to that again. Let's get you closer to the finishing line with these chemistry problems, Mister!"

"Cameron and Kennedy have done it," Dan Dan said with a sly smile. "It's just a matter of time for us."

"How do you know that? I swear you guys are all about kissing and then telling. It's disrespectful," Chloe insisted as she envisioned her and Dan Dan becoming like her parents. She recalled the story of how her mother became pregnant near the end of her senior year and how she struggled to manage her education and career with a baby.

"Naw…we're nothing like you females. I've heard how Y'all talk about us behind our backs," Dan Dan said as he devoured a handful of chips.

"Look, I don't want to end up like my mother. She got pregnant and her and my dad got married after that. They've done well for themselves, but it came at a high price," Chloe ranted as she stared into the atmosphere. "My identity is my own, and I need to protect myself."

Wait, nobody is trying to go there. I'm not ready to be a father," At that moment, both received a text message. "What tha?" Dan Dan blurted out.

Chloe grabbed her phone from her pocket and read the cryptic message from an unknown sender: *Go ahead, make your move*. She looked up at Dan Dan who had also received the same message on his phone.

"Did you tell someone about us?" Chloe asked frantically as fear flooded her heart.

"No! Why would I do that?"

Dan Dan slid his chair closer to hers and their faces were now only inches apart. They nervously exchanged phones to confirm they had both received the same message.

"Technically, there is nothing to tell," Dan Dan's attempt at humor fell flat in the face of Chloe's escalating anxiety.

"Not funny," she said aloud, her voice rising in frustration. "I wonder if it's Cameron and Kennedy playing a joke on us or something." The atmosphere in the room grew tense as Chloe and Dan Dan exchanged worried glances.

Dan Dan shrugged. "Could be. Anyway, let's finish the studying and then we can discuss the other matter at hand."

He had no sooner finished his sentence when another message arrived with the same strange words. Chloe's heart skipped a beat as the fear of being watched suddenly crept upon her.

"Okay, this is getting too weird," she said, biting down on her lip. Perspiration was also forming on her forehead.

Rising to check the window and ensure the doors were locked, Dan Dan consoled her. "No one is here but us. It's a prank. I mentioned to Cameron that we would be here alone studying."

"You're probably right and Kennedy knows as well," Chloe replied, still not fully convinced. "But why would they go through the trouble of sending these cryptic messages?"

Dan Dan grabbed his phone from the table and began dialing while nodding towards Chloe's

phone. "Why don't you call Kennedy and I'll call my boy Cameron. Time for these games to stop." Giving Dan Dan the thumbs up, she grabbed her phone and began dialing.

"Hey girl," Kennedy answered before Chloe could even finish her greeting. "What's up?"

Chloe's tone held a hint of anguish. "I could ask you that same question," she said. "Look, did you send two messages to my phone...one just now and another one about fifteen minutes ago?"

Kennedy quickly replied in the negative; her voice carried through the phone over the steady hum of grocery store chatter. "No. I'm with mom. We're at the grocery store and before that I was at the library. What's up?"

Through muffled sobs, Chloe related the unsettling incident to her cousin – both her and

Dan Dan had received cryptic text messages from an unknown sender which urged them to be intimate and indicated that the person knew they were alone together. "That is weird," Kennedy said after a moment of silence. Her words were heavy with concern; Chloe could tell that she was sincerely worried for their safety.

"I suggest you get out of there. Tell Dan Dan to take you home."

In response, Chloe dismissed her cousin's advice, saying that it was one of Dan Dan's friends playing a prank. She said goodbye and hung up, returning to her seat where Dan Dan waited anxiously. His expression told Chloe all she needed to know — Cameron wasn't behind this. Taking his hand in hers, she leaned into his embrace as he asked what she'd found out.

As Dan Dan tightened his embrace, Chloe felt the warmth of their shared connection. She was reminded of the first time they had kissed back at prom, but this moment was different. She could feel her heart racing and a flood of sensations all over her body as they held each other in an intimate embrace. Then memories of Ms. M's anatomy class came flooding back to her. She recalled how Ms. M had used touch to explore various emotions and sensations in various parts of Chloe's body. She grew overwhelmed with emotion and confusion, and reluctantly pulled away from Dan Dan.

"What's the matter?" he asked softly, concern etched across his face.

Chloe took a deep breath, fighting back the tears that threatened to spill down her cheeks, "I'm not like other girls, Dan Dan," she said in a quiet voice. "I'm scared by these messages, and I don't want to go too fast."

Dan Dan tried to reassure her, "I told you it's probably just some prank, but I understand if you're not ready yet and I get it about how you don't wanna become your parents." He stepped away from her and grabbed his backpack off the floor. "Let's finish up so I can get you home," he said sadly.

"It means a lot that you're so understanding," Chloe answered as the two shared a quick embrace, yet both felt the unease of the pressure to have sex and now the anxiety stemming from the messages they both received. *Who could be behind the mysterious messages and why? They both thought as they finished the studying.*

"After emerging from the warmth of the shower that night, droplets clung to Chloe's skin like transient jewels. The air in her room, thick with the comforting scent of lavender from her bath products, soothed her senses. A peculiar urge, a whisper from the depths of her soul, prompted her to reach for the youth group devotional resting on her nightstand, its worn pages holding the echoes of countless contemplative moments.

The sacred words, etched on the pages, seemed to resonate with a frequency only she could hear. With each scripture, she felt the weight of confusion lift momentarily, replaced by a gentle current of peace. Yet, the lingering uncertainty clung to her heart, refusing to be dispelled.

The room echoed with the solitary sound of her voice, the spoken question hanging in the air. "Am I a lesbian?" The words, once confined within, now danced into the air waves as Chloe sat in silence, awaiting an answer that never came.

Yet, as the night wore on, Chloe found solace in the reality of her faith to press forward in maintaining her identity and to find success in her future. And as Chloe drifted into the realm of dreams, the fragrance of lavender lingered, a subtle reminder of the peace she had found amid the storm of her soul. Her final verse was one of her favorites, *"And the peace of God that transcends all understanding will guard your heart and mind in Christ Jesus."*

The next day, Dan Dan asked each one of his basketball buddies if it was one of them who had perpetrated the prank. None of them owned up to it.

"I'll bet it was you," Dan Dan said to one of his oldest friends, Wally, who wore a smirk as they conversed about the situation. Yet Wally continued to deny sending the message, even after Dan Dan threatened to punch his light out.

Nevertheless, both Chloe and Dan Dan decided that it was indeed a prank from Wally, since he always held a secret jealousy of Dan Dan's success in sports and with the girls. It was the only solution that they could come up with, although it was a long shot.

Weeks turned into months and as Chloe continued to work on her goals of developing her self-esteem and dealing with the haunting memories from the past, she found herself with even more conflicting emotions about sex. Being the sponge she was, she absorbed lots of information from YouTube tutorials, internet articles, and certain movies.

As she and Dan Dan continued to spend time together, the pressure to experiment with sexual intercourse became more tempting, causing more confusion. For instance, the moments of arousal she would experience when they were close. The natural moisture in her vaginal area when they kissed, yet it all felt uncoordinated in comparison with a movie she recently watched about two females who were in love. The graphics of their natural relationship sent the same warmth through her body. This was concerning to her intellect and the student within her wanted answers. So, she decided to continue to discover and journal.

With Chloe's continued exploration of the question of her sexuality, coupled with the resurrected memories of her past traumas, she and Dan Dan never had the opportunity to take their relationship to that next level, which they both secretly ached for.

"I'm starting to wonder if you're as into me as you claim," Dan

Dan said, his tone laced with frustration and disappointment as he and Chloe sat on the sofa at his home. They had at least two hours before his mom would arrive and all Dan Dan wanted was to be intimate with her.

"You know I care for you, why would you say that?" Chloe's face showed her pain as she rubbed Dan Dan's hand, attempting to calm him. Over the past few weeks, the temptation had gotten to the point of frustration. The other night, the two of them had gotten extremely close to going all the way, but Chloe managed to extinguish the fire.

"I can't tell. Listen, why don't we cool it. I mean, take a break and maybe you can write out a plan in that journal of yours to grow up and take responsibility in this relationship."

"I beg your pardon. What do you mean by me taking responsibility? I mean, that's not fair. I explained to you about my emotional state and what my plans are. Why can't you wait?"

"I can wait, but not like this. I have needs, Chloe. Real men type of needs and hanging out with you is only frustrating me."

"But...you don't love me anymore?" Chloe felt her walls collapsing. Over the past few months, she and Dan Dan had grown closer. She had contemplated telling him the camp story, something she was not able to tell anyone else. "I...I'm sorry," she said sheepishly as she threw herself in his arms, kissing his neck desperately.

"Stop...Chloe, I said stop. I'm not trying to force you to do something you're not ready for. Look, you'll always have my heart, but I think we need to cool it for a bit. Think more on our college plans."

"That's your excuse for breaking up with me?" Chloe asked as she stood at her feet. Breathing in and out, she was determined not to cry, but to speak to her mind every affirmation she could think of and to square her shoulders and be the big girl that she knew she was. "Goodbye Dan Dan."

"Bye, Chloe," Dan Dan's expression spoke sadness; however, his mind was made up. It was not a quick decision. He had pondered it for a few weeks. "I'll check on you in day or so," he said as Chloe walked away, closing the door behind her.

Walking through the neighborhood, the sound of children playing and other public noises reminded her of her goals. Through the pain, she journeyed on. Her two-block walk seemed like miles as her mind contemplated her future.

~

As days stretched into weeks, Chloe persisted in wrestling with unresolved pain, never receiving the necessary help to cope with the traumatic memories. These included not only her fourth-grade encounter with Britney and the sleepovers at Ms. M's cabin but also the perplexing behavior of her parents. She continued to make peace with the reality that her dad was cheating on her mom and neither parent seemed interested in discussing it with her. She never accepted their story that everything was okay and that her father was only catching up on old times with Henrietta.

One of the most disturbing realities residing in Chloe's soul was her quest to discover herself. She had never even considered being with another girl, but many students freely embraced bisexuality and non-binary lifestyles. It would take much prayer, contemplation, and the grind to discover who Chloe Rhodes was underneath the independent, intelligent, and conservative characteristics for which she was well known. She battled with conflicting emotions when it came to male and female relationships. At times she felt proud of her independent spirit, but at other times she loathed the fact that she could not walk alongside someone else. Which way would she go?

CHAPTER 12

A NEW JOURNEY BEGINS (2 YEARS LATER)

The sun brightened the quiet suburban neighborhood as Chloe and Kennedy stood `outside Chloe's house. Chloe's suitcases packed and neatly arranged, rested by her feet, eager to embark on this new chapter of her life. Anticipation tingled in the air, intermingled with a hint of melancholy, as they prepared to bid farewell to the comfort of familiarity. Kennedy would not leave until two days later but wanted to be certain she spoke with Chloe before Chloe's mom and dad drove her to her new college. She had become extra nourishing toward Chloe after a difficult break up between her and Dan Dan. Dan Dan and Tabitha had been secretly seeing each other, which was a crushing blow to Chloe, especially with what she had witnessed between her father and another woman. This newfound information about Dan Dan and Tabitha came about only five days after the breakup.

Kennedy placed a reassuring hand on Chloe's shoulder. "You've got this, Chloe," she said, her voice carrying the weight of unwavering support.

Chloe's nervous gaze met Kennedy's, and a flicker of determination sparked within her. "Thank you," she replied, her voice infused with a mix of gratitude and resolve. "I'm ready for college, even if it's a little scary," she affirmed as she relaxed in the thought of a fresh start.

"Of course, you're ready. I'll only be a text message and a video chat away. Well, here comes the coach. I'm sure she's got a mouthful for you," Kennedy said as she motioned her head in the direction of her mother who was walking toward them. Chloe smirked as she noticed her aunt walking with a look of authority on her face. One Chloe had grown to love.

Macy, with her warm smile and nurturing presence, stood beside Chloe, the late afternoon sunlight casting a gentle glow around them.

Macy gently took Chloe's hand in hers, her eyes filled with a mixture of pride and bittersweetness. "Chloe, my dear, can we talk for a moment? I want to make sure you're feeling alright about heading off to college. I don't know…for some reason I can't help but feel like there is something unresolved."

Chloe, her excitement tempered by a touch of apprehension, nodded and gave full attention to Macy. "Of course, Aunt Macy. I'm a little nervous, to be honest, but I'm also eager for this new chapter in my life. Don't worry. I'm fine. All the things I've gone through over the past years…well, let's just say I've learned to keep it all in the past and move forward."

Macy gave her hand a reassuring squeeze. "It's completely normal to feel a mix of emotions, my dear. College is a big step, but you have always shown such strength and independence. I do not doubt you'll navigate this journey with grace. I just don't want any past issues presenting themselves as distractions."

Chloe smiled, gratitude shining in her eyes. "Thank you, Aunt Macy. Your support means the world to me. I don't know what I would do without you and Kennedy."

Macy's voice softened as she spoke, her gaze filled with affection. "Chloe, my sweet girl, you have always been like a daughter to me. Your parents, as successful as they are, may not always show it, but they love you in their way. Sometimes, their focus on their careers can make them miss out on the little things. But this doesn't diminish your worth or the love they have for you. Now..." Macy stopped suddenly while looking back toward Chloe's house. She didn't want Starla and Reginald to overhear her conversation. "Now, I cannot help but wonder about the last summer camp you and Kennedy experienced. I know it's been five years, but...seems like you changed, and I never had a peaceful feeling about it, is all. Even after that, all the other chaos...prom night and so many other things I know you went through..."

"No worries, Auntie Macy," Chloe abruptly interrupted. "Everything was and is still fine. I had some issues come up during camp all those years ago, after that, I experienced some issues with my parents, the breakup between me and Dan Dan, but all is well. I promise."

"But you never talked about summer camp like you normally would. Why, you spent the remainder of the summer in such a dry place. Your soul was not the same. I'll never forget it. Oh, I know it was so long ago, but for some reason, it comes back to mind over and over again."

"Like I told everyone...I had a bad experience after Kennedy left but it really wasn't a big deal."

"Okay, and you're at peace with your parents?" Macy asked while continuing to look over her shoulders.

Chloe nodded with a hint of sadness flickering in her eyes. "Yes, it's just sometimes I wish they could understand me better and be there for me when I need them most," Chloe explained with sadness. "But...my perspective of family dynamics has definitely been enhanced by the support you all have always given me. I'm good."

Macy's expression softened; her voice filled with empathy. "I understand, Chloe. It's natural to yearn for parental support, especially during important milestones. Remember, there is a strength within you, and it has carried you through so much. Lean on this strength, and know I am always here for you, ready to listen and offer guidance whenever you need it. Give your parents a bit of grace. I'm sure they will come around in time."

Chloe's eyes shimmered with unshed tears, touched by Macy's words. "Thank you, Aunt Macy. I am so grateful to have you in my life. You and Kennedy have been my rock."

Macy pulled Chloe into a warm embrace, holding her tight. "You're like a daughter to me, Chloe—-"

"If you'll excuse me, Macy, I wanna get MY daughter to her school so she can meet her roommates and get settled in," Starla said, interrupting a warmth between Macy and Chloe she had long grown to be envious of.

"Of course," Macy's voice trembled at the sound of Starla's command. "Goodbye, sweetheart."

Chloe clung to Macy, feeling the warmth of her love and support enveloping her before letting go and grabbing and loading her bags into her mother's vehicle.

As Chloe settled into the car, the engine roared to life, filling the silence with a low rumble. The car began to glide forward, carrying Chloe away from the familiarity of her childhood home and towards an uncertain future. Starla's stern expression reflected in the rearview mirror, intensifying Chloe's sense of unease.

The car journey was filled with an uncomfortable silence, broken only by the occasional soft sigh or the hum of the radio in the background. Chloe glanced out of the window, watching as the sprawling suburban landscape transformed into a blur of city lights and towering buildings. It was as if the world itself was preparing her for the chaotic whirlwind which awaited her in college.

After what felt like an eternity, they arrived at the dormitory building, its brick exterior bathed in the warm glow of streetlights. "Chloe could hear the distant sounds of laughter and chatter, a bittersweet reminder of the life she was leaving behind. Her decision to enroll at the University of North Carolina at Charlotte was driven by her passion for finance. As she arrived on campus, the university's size and beauty began to unfold before her eyes.

The campus was a blend of urban sophistication with a touch of Southern charm. Towering buildings, adorned with modern architectural grace, reached for the heavens, while at their feet, the immaculate landscaping unfolded like a lush tapestry.

The university bore the promise of a large institution, but as Chloe stepped onto its grounds, she could sense the essence of a close-knit community. Others who had attended recently had spoken of this unique blend, and now Chloe was experiencing it firsthand.

Amidst the landscape, dogwoods and magnolias were in full bloom, filling the air with their sweet fragrance, and the weather was typical for Charlotte—simply beautiful. A gentle, warm breeze played with her hair as she opened the vehicle door and stretched her limbs before gathering her belongings. Even with the picture-perfect surroundings, Chloe couldn't help but feel the weight of her own nervousness, the unknown future beckoning her forward.

Her parents helped her carry her suitcases up the flight of stairs, the weight of their neglect weighing heavily on Chloe's shoulders. As they entered the dorm room, Chloe's heart sank at the sight before her. Clothes were strewn across the floor, the sound of raucous laughter coming from the room next door. Two carefree girls occupied the space, oblivious to Chloe's presence.

Starla's face twisted in disapproval, her voice dripping with disdain. "Is this the kind of environment they expect you to live in? Absolutely unacceptable," she muttered under her breath.

Chloe, her face a mask of disappointment, tried to maintain her composure as her parents exchanged icy glares. "Mom, Dad, I know this isn't ideal, but maybe if I had my own apartment, I could focus better on my studies." Her voice quivered, portraying her vulnerability.

Reginald's voice was laced with authority as he replied, "Chloe, you need to learn responsibility and independence. This is an opportunity for growth. Moving into an apartment right away would be a disservice to you," Reginald said as his thoughts paraded around his own college experiences and the trouble some of his friends experienced when living off campus on their own.

Desperation surged through Chloe's veins as she pleaded, "But I can't concentrate with all the noise and distractions. I want to succeed in college, and having my own space is crucial."

Starla's face softened slightly; her voice filled with a hint of understanding. "Chloe, we want what's best for you. Maybe we can compromise. Give the dorm a chance for a couple of semesters, and if it doesn't work out, we'll reconsider the apartment."

Chloe's heart swelled with a glimmer of hope. It wasn't the solution she had hoped for, but at least her parents were willing to consider her needs. *The nerve of him saying I need to learn independence...I've been independent all my life,* she thought. With a nod, she agreed, a sense of determination replacing her disappointment.

~

The next few weeks were a whirlwind of adjusting to dorm life. The loud music, the late-night parties, and the constant stream of visitors became a hindrance and a nightmare that seemed impossible to escape. Chloe found herself struggling to focus on her studies, her dreams of academic achievement slowly slipping away.

One evening, as the noise reached its peak, Chloe's concentration shattered. Frustration mingled with exhaustion as she buried her face in her hands, feeling defeated. At the moment, all she longed for was a quiet space of her own, free from distractions.

Chloe was on the verge of tears when her phone rang, and it was Kennedy on the other end. She was relieved to hear from her cousin and raised her voice to be heard over the noise. "Kennedy, it's great to hear from you!" she said.

"Well, looks like somebody didn't waste any time adjusting to college life. I hear you cousin."

"What do you mean?"

"Girl, I hear it. Sounds like a party to me, and it ain't no Holy Ghost party either," Kennedy said as both burst into laughter.

"Believe me, it's not my music and I hate it here," Chloe whined, her voice shaky with a mixture of frustration and sadness. Just hearing Kennedy's familiar voice on the other end of the line made her tears flow more freely. "Mom and Dad won't get me an apartment. They say I have to tough it out for two semesters!"

Kennedy listened attentively, her heart aching for her friend. She remembered the struggles she faced when she first arrived at college, except she was fortunate enough to have great roommates and enjoyed the party scene. She tried her best to comfort Chloe, knowing words alone wouldn't magically solve her problems.

"Yep! Same thing happened to me, except, I had great roommates, and I actually loved the party scene," Kennedy replied, her voice infused with empathy. "Look, you're gonna be fine. You just need to adjust, is all."

Chloe sniffled, wiping her tears with the back of her hand. "I don't think so. I feel trapped, and I've only been here a short time."

Attempting to change the atmosphere of the call, Kennedy decided to engage in normal conversation. "Anyway, girl, how are your classes so far? Do you like your professors? Talked to fine Dan Dan?"

"Dan Dan? Please. The last time I saw him he was still following behind that big booty girl from Northwest."

"Right. But you know she's only your rebound, right? Think

about it. She is artistic and even looks like you, well, except for the booty and all," Kennedy said.

"I'm not even thinking about Dan Dan. All males are alike so don't even cut him no slack," Chloe said, as she found a way to change the subject. Dan Dan had broken her heart into a million pieces, but she didn't want anyone to know. "From what I can tell, the classes are fine, and the professors are cool. Just hope I can maintain my GPA."

"Are you kidding me? When have you ever had a GPA issue? Me on the other hand, well, that's a different story."

"You do okay," Chloe teased as the two prepared to disconnect the call. Preparing to grab books and other items to head to the library, Chloe noticed movement out of the corner of her eye. She turned her head to see her roommate, Chelsea, passionately engaged in a make-out session with her boyfriend, Sticks, on Chloe's own bed. Anger surged through her veins, her voice filled with a mix of betrayal and disgust.

"Chelsea! Up! I said get up and get away from my space!" Chloe's voice resonated with frustration and anger, desperately wanting her personal boundaries to be respected.

"Chill Mommy," Sticks muttered, his lanky frame towering over Chloe as he zipped up his pants carelessly. The audacity of their actions fueled her sense of isolation, intensifying her feelings of being trapped in a place where she didn't belong. The nerve of Chelsea, a striking contrast to Chloe with her vibrant presence. Chelsea's perfectly styled eyelashes were painstakingly glued in place, accentuating her captivating eyes, and her build resembled that of a runway model, with a graceful and striking appearance. Chloe's thoughts of her not belonging in the atmosphere, incited her to fight to win the battle of the mind. She would be resilient and stand her ground. "I will not be moved," she whispered as she paced back and forward. Soon after, both Chelsea and Sticks dismissed themselves.

Feeling a desperate need to escape after an hour, Chloe decided to head to the library, hoping the walls of knowledge would provide her with some relief. The weight of the world rested on her shoulders, dragging her down as she attempted to gather her books and belongings.

As Chloe walked toward the library, a song holding a special meaning to her drifted into her mind — "Something Has to Break". It was the last song she had passionately interpreted in American Sign Language for the church congregation. Now, its message resonated deeper within her than ever before, reflecting the tremendous pressure and frustration she felt.

Just like the theme of the song, at that moment, Chloe knew something had to change. She could not continue to feel trapped and suffocated in her current situation. The fire burning within her fueled her determination to overcome the challenges and find her place in this unfamiliar, overwhelming world. And maybe, just maybe, the song held the key to breaking free from her confined existence. A portion of the lyrics indicated the Lord having His way and causing things to change. Chloe resolved she would wait on her Lord to work in His timing for her, she only hoped He would come through sooner than later.

As Chloe entered the library, she could not shake the feeling that the coming days held a destiny she couldn't predict. Little did she know, her encounter with Chelsea was just the beginning of a journey that would test her resilience in ways she had never imagined."

CHAPTER 13

UNEXPECTED ENCOUNTERS

As she proceeded to leave the library on campus, a flyer announcing a networking event for finance students caught Chloe's eye. A woman named Nicole Weatherspoon, a real estate agent, would be giving a speech and discussing her mentorship services. The event grabbed Chloe's attention and she planned to attend. She also did research on Nicole Weatherspoon. Her resume was indeed impressionable. Chloe was excited and could not wait to check out the event.

The air buzzed with excitement as Chloe attended the networking event for finance students at her college. Nervously adjusting her blazer, she scanned the room, searching for someone who could guide her in her academic and professional journey. Suddenly, her gaze fell upon a charismatic woman with a warm smile and an air of confidence, her graceful poise commanding attention amidst the bustling crowd. Dressed in a tailored, charcoal gray pantsuit that accentuated her confident stature, Nicole exuded professionalism. Her blazer, perfectly fitted, bore a hint of pinstripes that added a touch of sophistication to her attire. Beneath the jacket, she wore a crisp, white blouse with a delicate silver necklace that caught the light as she moved. The ensemble was completed with black high-heeled pumps that clicked with each graceful step.

"That must be Nicole Weatherspoon," Chloe murmured to herself, recognizing the poised figure across the room. As she observed Nicole's commanding presence, Chloe couldn't help but notice the striking confidence etched into the lines of her face, which spoke to her years of navigating the complex worlds of real estate and finance. This woman also reminded her of her mother's poise and confidence when surrounded by a crowd.

Eager to gain insights from someone who had effortlessly maneuvered both fields, Chloe found herself drawn to Nicole's magnetic presence, unable to resist the allure of her poised confidence and intellect. "That level of success will be me someday," she whispered as she envisioned her future self.

Summoning her courage, Chloe approached Nicole, extending her hand. "Hi, I'm Chloe. I've read great things about your work in real estate and finance," Chloe's hand shook a little as she fought to overcome her nervousness in Nicole's presence.

Nicole's warm smile widened as she shook Chloe's hand, her eyes sparkling with a mix of warmth and calculation. She was moved by Chloe's tenacity. "Nice to meet you, Chloe. Call me Nikki. I'm impressed by your interest in excelling in finance."

Chloe blushed, grateful for Nikki's kind words. She didn't expect her to be approachable at all. "Thank you, Nikki. I've always been passionate about finance, and I hope to make a difference in the industry. Maybe we could discuss more over coffee sometime?" Chloe asked with boldness, deciding to take her confidence to a higher level. Feeling it was a pivotal season in her life, Chloe was determined to embrace every opportunity, adjusting and rolling with the punches.

Nikki's smile widened, and she nodded. "Absolutely. I love mentoring finance students like yourself. Let's meet tomorrow and chat about your career aspirations."

Excitement surged through Chloe as she agreed to the meeting. She couldn't believe her luck. Nikki Weatherspoon, an esteemed real estate agent, had agreed to mentor her. As Chloe left the event that evening, her mind buzzed with possibilities and a newfound sense of hope, regardless of the dorm issues she was still experiencing with her roommates.

~

The next day, Chloe nervously entered the small, but attractive café where she and Nikki had agreed to meet. The tantalizing aroma of freshly brewed coffee was enveloping the cozy space. Spotting Nikki in a warm and inviting corner, she approached with a mix of eagerness and timidity. She hoped she would not blow the opportunity, as she spoke to her inner self words of bravery from scripture.

Nikki smiled warmly as Chloe sat down. At the same time, carrying an enticing tray of steaming coffee, the waitress placed two cups on the table, its aroma filled the air, causing a hint of relaxing to be released into the atmosphere. "I'm glad you could make it, Chloe. So, tell me, what are your plans after graduation?"

Chloe took a sip of her coffee, gathering her thoughts. "Well, I've always been interested in real estate, too. I am considering pursuing a career in investment finance, specifically in the housing sector. I want to help people find their dream homes and make smart financial decisions."

Nikki's eyes glinted with excitement. "That's fantastic, Chloe. I may have a unique proposition for you. I have some investment properties I need assistance with, and I can offer you one of them to live in, completely rent-free. This way, you can focus on your studies and gain hands-on experience in the industry."

Chloe's eyes widened, her heart racing at the thought of such an incredible opportunity. "Nikki, this sounds amazing! Oh my God...He's heard my prayers."

"Prayers?" Nikki said as her eyebrows furrowed, tilting her head.

"Oh, I meant...I've been having dorm issues, and my parents wouldn't allow me to get an apartment, so I've been praying God would show me a way to resolve the issue," Chloe said with excitement. "I've been affirming that something would change sooner or later, without involving my parents. This will help me gain even more independence."

"Wow. I've never been the answer to anyone's prayers before. So, I take it you are accepting my offer?"

"I'd be honored to accept your offer... thank you."

Nikki smiled, her gaze lingering on Chloe. "There is one condition, though. You must maintain a high GPA and assist me with my real estate ventures. Consider it a partnership. You gain valuable experience, and I get a dependable partner."

Chloe nodded, determination flaring in her eyes. "I promise, Nikki. I'll give my all to excel academically and support you in any way I can."

"Great. Here is my card and I'm writing the address of the property on the back. Give me a call later this evening and we can arrange to have you move in."

"Yes, ma'am. Will do."

"Call me Nikki. Remember, we're partners now. Oh, and why don't you keep this between us for now? At least until I can arrange to meet with the school's board. I want to introduce this idea so a couple of other students can get in on the opportunity. Sounds good?"

"Sounds fantastic. God bless you, Nikki," Chloe announced as she prepared to leave the diner.

"Right back at you," Nikki responded, her lack of Christian culture quite evident. "Talk soon.'

Heading back to her dormitory, Chloe's footsteps faltered as she caught sight of her mom's vehicle parked in the visitor parking lot. A jolt of surprise shot through her veins, propelling her forward with a mixture of anticipation and curiosity. Hastening her pace, she rounded the corner and came face to face with Starla.

"Mom, hi! What are you doing here?" Chloe's voice carried a blend of excitement and bewilderment, her eyes searching for answers. She didn't know how her parents would respond to her moving out of the dorm so soon. She knew she needed to keep it secret.

With a gentle smile playing on her lips, Starla responded, "Surprisingly, our bank is considering opening a new branch in a nearby town, so I thought I'd surprise you and take you to lunch." Her gaze fell upon the coffee shop cup Chloe still tightly clutched, a hint of amusement dancing in her eyes. "But... looks like you've already had lunch."

"Nope, I just had a few sips of coffee with Miss Nikki," Chloe replied, her words flowed with a touch of pride and excitement.

"Miss. Nikki?" Starla's brows lifted, curiosity flickering across her face.

Chloe's enthusiasm bubbled forth as she explained, "She's a well-known investment banker who runs this amazing mentoring service. She's going to be my mentor for this semester." A sense of empowerment underscored her voice as if the path ahead were now brightly illuminated.

"Wonderful!" Starla said, her tone filled with genuine admiration. "There's nothing like the mentor-mentee relationship. I hope you take full advantage of it. Wow... have I told you lately how proud I am of you?"

A warm smile spread across Chloe's face as she wrapped her arms around her mother, savoring the moment. "No, but I know you and Dad are proud of me," she whispered, her voice brimming with gratitude.

"And Chloe, dear," Starla continued, her words carrying a touch of determination, "it was your father's idea to hold out on getting you an apartment, but I'll work on him. He has the crazy notion that you'll party your life away without dorm rules. Hopefully, we can get you out of that crazy dorm by the end of this semester."

Chloe's response was gentle and understanding. "Okay, no problem, Mom."

A chuckle escaped Starla's lips as she met Chloe's gaze, her eyes full of maternal understanding. "No problem? I saw your face when we told you to learn responsibility and stay in the noisy dormitory for two semesters!" Starla said. "You don't have to be so calm and independent all the time. Shoot. Yell, kick, scream…it's okay. I hope you're able to cope with your surroundings until I can get you out of there."

A mix of resignation and determination flickered in Chloe's eyes as she spoke, her voice laced with self-assurance. "I know, but Mom, you and Dad are right. I need to learn how to be responsible and work situations out on my own, and that is exactly what I'm doing."

Starla and Chloe set off to find a nearby restaurant where they could savor a delicious meal together. An hour passed, and Starla, with a tinge of reluctance, bid farewell, her presence required at a gala in one of the convention centers in Charlotte. Chloe couldn't help but feel a sense of relief, grateful she didn't have to delve into the details of her impending move to Nikki's property. She had planned meticulously, taking most of her belongings out of the dorm while leaving a few items behind, ensuring her transition remained discreet, just as Nikki had requested. And though her dorm mates scarcely noticed her whereabouts, Chloe knew she'd return from time to time, keeping up appearances, even if it meant simply showing her face. Her journey to independence beckoned, and she was determined to answer its call.

~

Days turned into weeks, and Chloe settled into Nikki's investment property. The proximity allowed their professional relationship to blossom into a deep friendship. They spent countless hours discussing finance, real estate, and their shared dreams for the future. Chloe felt at ease with Nikki, just like she did with Kennedy, whom she hadn't spoken to in a while. Both of their schedules had become increasingly busy. Nikki was now filling the void places that Kennedy filled. This caused Chloe to unknowingly begin to share about some of her most personal issues, and Nikki reciprocated the same. Their bond began to take root rather quickly.

~

The morning was crazy, rushed, after Chloe and Nikki had worked into the late hours of the night on real estate ventures. Feeling a hint of dread, Chloe sat in front of the mirror of the master bedroom, staring into the mirror and wishing for just one more hour of sleep.

"Knock knock…" Nikki called out as she peeped into the room. "A bit late, aren't you?"

"Good morning. I didn't hear you come in. Yep, I'm dragging."

"Aww, did the mentor keep the mentee up too late?" Nikki asked as she entered the room. She was dressed in her usual Prada. Chloe admiring her countenance from the mirror. Taking a brush from the dresser, Nikki began to brush through Chloe's silky straight hair as she unwrapped it. The strokes of the brush felt soothing, causing Chloe to sink into a relaxed position. Bending, to work the brush into a certain angle, Chloe felt Nikki's breath gently upon her neck.

"Thanks, I can take it from here. You must be in a hurry. It's almost eight," Chloe said, as her heart filled with discomfort from Nikki's gesture. Past memories making their way through her mind. It had been a while since she dealt with them.

"You're right. I'm just gonna grab my laptop. Left it here last night. Have a good day."

"You as well," Chloe answered, her gaze following Nikki until she was out of sight. "What was that all about," Chloe whispered as she quickly got up and dressed for the day. She reassured herself that it was nothing, emphasizing the need to take extra measures to guard her heart from wandering thoughts and to continue learning all she could from Nikki.

However, as their connection deepened, Chloe couldn't ignore the subtle gestures and lingering gazes from Nikki. These surpassed the boundaries of mere friendship. A wave of regret and confusion washed over Chloe, her past experiences clouding her ability to recognize and interpret Nikki's true intentions. While her journaling practices and prayers offered some solace, an inner turmoil began to take hold, gripping her like a tight squeeze. Something constantly nagged at her regarding Nikki, but she couldn't quite figure it out.

It wasn't until a moonlit evening, as they sat on the terrace of the investment property sharing their hopes and fears, that Nikki bared her heart to Chloe.

"Chloe, there's something I haven't told you," Nikki began, her voice trembling with vulnerability.

Curiosity mingled with apprehension, Chloe urged Nikki to continue, her heart pounding in her chest.

"I'm gay, Chloe," Nikki confessed, raw emotion coloring her words. "And I've developed romantic feelings for you." Nikki swallowed, as she struggled to go on. "I know this is abrupt, but I wanted to be open with you."

Stunned silence followed Nikki's revelation. Chloe's mind raced as she tried to make sense of her own emotions, her past traumas intermingling with her present reality. The difficult break up with Dan Dan coupled with trauma from summer camp, she had submerged her feelings for men, but this unexpected twist forced her to question her own identity. She wondered how Nikki could develop feelings for her after a few short weeks. Besides, *how would she reconcile this revelation with her upbringing and the faith she held on to?* The question resounded in the depths of her soul.

As their eyes locked, Chloe realized Nikki's feelings evoked a safe familiarity she longed for, a connection that transcended gender stereotypes and heartache. But what would she do about the teachings she grew up with and all the biased ideologies she was so familiar with? One thing is for sure, she did not see this coming. The impact of Nikki's admission forced Chloe to question her beliefs, leading her down a path of growth and self-acceptance.

In the midst of her internal struggle and external confusion, Chloe received an anonymous message from someone unfamiliar on her social media page. Hesitantly opening the message, it read: "The threads of fate are interwoven with secrets. Beware of what lies beneath the surface." Intrigued and slightly unnerved, Chloe wondered if this random post was a mistake or was it fate. Was the message divine? She was unable to shake off the feeling that her journey toward self-discovery was intertwined with a web of mysteries waiting to be unraveled.

CHAPTER 14

EMBRACING TRUTH

Bringing her attention away from the social media post and back to the matter at hand, Chloe's heart raced as Nikki's words lingered in the air, their weight sinking deep into her consciousness. The revelation of Nikki's feelings, extending beyond friendship, had thrown Chloe's world into disarray.

"With that, I'll leave you alone to pray, journal, or do whatever it is you do to get centered. I can see my words are crashing down upon you like a tower," Nikki said as she stood, grabbing her wine glass and shoes. "I'll check on you in the morning."

"Certainly…that's fine," Chloe responded, her voice shaky and uncertain.

Uncertainty and a wave of emotions surged through her, compelling her to seek a haven in the one person she trusted most —her cousin and best friend, Kennedy. Grabbing her phone and with

trembling hands, Chloe dialed Kennedy's number, her thoughts swirling like a tempest. As the line connected, she took a deep breath, hoping to find the words to convey the turmoil that now consumed her.

"Hey, Kennedy, it's Chloe," she greeted, her voice quivering with a mixture of apprehension and anticipation.

Kennedy's warm and familiar voice resonated through the phone like a lifeline amidst the chaos. "Hey, I know your voice girly! It's been too long. How's college life treating you?"

A moment of hesitation gripped Chloe's soul. She knew confiding in Kennedy meant bearing her vulnerability, exposing the tangled emotions consuming her. Kennedy would have it no other way. "Kennedy, something happened... with Nikki," she finally revealed, her voice barely above a whisper.

Silence hung in the air, heavy and pregnant with anticipation. Chloe's heartbeat quickened as she anxiously awaited Kennedy's response, her mind swirling with an abundance of thoughts and fears.

Finally, Kennedy's voice broke the silence, gentle and reassuring. "Chloe, whatever it is, I'm here for you. You can tell me anything," Kennedy, who knew Chloe better than anyone else, sensed something was off. She could always tell when something was bothering her but had learned since the prom night incident when to press for answers and when to keep quiet. *Listen and choose your words wisely,* Kennedy told herself.

Chloe took a deep breath, steadying herself for the revelation. "Nikki... told me she has feelings for me. Romantic feelings. It's... it's complicated."

"Chloe," Kennedy began, her voice soft and soothing. "I can only imagine how overwhelming and confusing this must all be for you. But you know what? Love is this wild and exciting thing; it doesn't neatly fit into boxes. It's messy and beautiful, and it challenges us to step outside of our comfort zones. So, feeling confused is completely natural. But remember, you're not alone on this journey. Bi-sexuality, lesbianism...it's the new normal these days."

"Kennedy," Chloe said, her voice tinged with newfound self-acceptance, "I've been thinking a lot lately. Maybe this is a part of who I am. Maybe my heart is open to loving anyone, regardless of what society expects. I don't even know how to begin navigating these uncharted waters," Chloe said as she recalled the strange message from her social media messenger page.

In response, Kennedy's voice brimmed with empathy and understanding, her words wrapping around Chloe like a warm embrace. Being in her second year of college, she had learned to tone it down a notch, as she was also engaging in her own journey of self-discovery.

"Chloe," she said reassuringly, "understanding ourselves and uncovering our truths is a journey we embark on. Mom may have a heart-attack, but I'm thinking about diving into the study of other religions, so it takes time, self-reflection, and the unwavering support of those who genuinely love us. You don't have to have all the answers right away. Trust your instincts and allow yourself the room to explore. Your happiness and well-being should always guide you."

Chloe breathed a sigh of relief, a wave of comfort washing over her. In the midst of her inner turmoil, Kennedy's laid-back approach was exactly what she needed. It gave her permission to explore her emotions without judgment and allowed her to accept herself fully.

~

Embarking on the path of self-discovery, Chloe sought peace and guidance in unexpected places, but one Sunday morning after a week had passed since Nikki's revelation, she found herself in the pews of the campus church, seeking spiritual clarity amidst the tumultuous revelations that had unfolded in her life. Church and God's Word were the one thing that she was always taught to rely upon.

As the hymns filled the air, Chloe closed her eyes, her heart heavy with the weight of her newfound truth. Amidst the fervent prayers and sermons, she felt a sense of conviction, a divine whisper urging her to embrace the truth of her past teachings, yet the inner turmoil returned, causing her to feel divided in her heart, but Chloe was bent on overcoming it.

After the service, Chloe mingled with the churchgoers, exchanging smiles and brief conversations. Random people, their faces glowing with kindness, offered words of encouragement and acceptance, unknowingly becoming beacons of hope in Chloe's journey of self-acceptance. Surprisingly, a familiar face from her high school, a non-binary individual, stood among the attendees, embodying the diversity of acceptance within the congregation. However, not everyone shared this acceptance, as evident disdain lingered on the faces of a few individuals.

As Chloe exited the church, the echoes of the hymns lingered within her, and she decided to delve into the depths of perspectives through a thought-provoking YouTube video by members of the Christian community. The various viewpoints presented in the video ignited a flame of perspectives, prompting Chloe to explore her authentic identity. The journey ahead seemed both daunting and promising, as the melodies of acceptance and disapproval continued to intertwine in the symphony of Chloe's evolving self-awareness. With that, she determined she needed an ice cream cone, as she exited the video and turned into a local restaurant.

Days passed, and as Chloe ventured out with Nikki, their once easy mutual friendship began to feel strained. They were no longer as close as when they first met. Chloe's eyes darted around the room, taking in the awkward silences between conversations that were punctuated only by forced laughter. Her mind raced as she tried to make sense of her tangled emotions; navigating this unknown territory was a struggle.

"Hey there, is everything alright?" Nikki inquired, noticing Chloe's uneasy demeanor. "You seem distant."

"I'm okay, I guess. There's just so much on my mind, but I'll manage."

"I've noticed you've been quite quiet since I confided in you concerning my sexual orientation, and I know that I was forward when I admitted that I was romantically attracted to you. I understand your hesitation, but there's something between us."

"I know, but it's also a bit awkward."

"I get it. I'll give you some space, but eventually, you'll have to prioritize your own happiness and not let others' expectations cloud your judgment. I'll leave you be for now, but we'll talk in the morning."

After Nikki left the room, Chloe was left to contemplate her words. While she acknowledged Nikki's advice as correct, Chloe was conflicted and uncertain about what to do next. Her heart was divided, and she was struggling with intense emotions. A passage from the book of James from the Bible came to mind, which discussed the instability of a double-minded person. The passage also likened this inner turmoil to being tossed back and forth like waves on the sea. Chloe understood the meaning of the passage, but she wished she didn't have to learn it through her own personal struggles.

As Chloe grappled with her inner conflict, a framed painting on the wall caught her eye. It depicted a turbulent sea with waves crashing against jagged rocks. The symbolism echoed the passage from the book of James that had come to mind, emphasizing the tumultuous journey of a double-minded person, tossed by the waves of indecision. But the more the painting pulled her into the turbulence, the more determined she pulled away from the chaos within her mind. So, the mysterious messages, shadows, and symbols that had started to weave their way into her life were about to offer both illumination and confusion on her path of self-discovery. Chloe told herself confidently…: I'm here for it…bring it on."

CHAPTER 15

I NEED AIR

"Hey, Cuzzo! What's on your agenda tonight?" Kennedy asked, her voice brimming with excitement, a familiar tone that Chloe used to shy away from during their childhood.

"I'm buried in reports for Nikki. She's been swamped with sales prospects lately," Chloe replied wearily.

"Clear your schedule, because tonight, you're coming out with me," Kennedy insisted.

"What?" Chloe questioned, taken aback.

"I said you're joining me and one of my friends at a party. I can't believe you haven't heard about it! The buzz has been going on for days," Kennedy explained with enthusiasm, since she decided she wouldn't take no for an answer.

"I'm always out of the loop. All I ever do is study and work," Chloe responded with a touch of dejection in her voice. It was true; Nikki had kept her busy lately, almost as if she didn't want Chloe to go out.

"Well, Miss Thang doesn't get to control your life. You're still a college student, you know. This party is happening right on your turf, and you're going. I'll swing by your place at eight sharp. Oh, and Chloe... please don't wear anything like that disastrous outfit you wore to your senior night party last year," Kennedy advised. Her words immediately resurrected a memory of a day when her mom had promised a mother-daughter shopping spree. Plans fell through as a work emergency arose, leaving Chloe wandering through the mall alone, picking out the outfit that Kennedy alluded to.

"Whatever. Nikki won't approve. She mentioned the other night that the workload has increased and she's been a bit stressed lately. I promised to work extra to help her catch up. Besides, I'm under contract to maintain my GPA, and partying is nothing but a distraction," Chloe sighed as she held to her strict diet of focusing on her new self.

"Partying can be a good distraction. Besides, I support whatever you're doing for Nikki, but again... she can't dictate your life. You need to step out of that house and explore different people and events. Nikki will come around. I'll pick you up; just send me a picture of what you plan to wear," Kennedy encouraged.

"Okay. You're right. A change of scenery might do me some good," Chloe said as she put away the paperwork and darted into her room to pick out clothing for a night out.

Eight o'clock arrived, but Kennedy was fashionably late as always. Chloe anxiously waited, feeling a mix of nerves and excitement. It had been a while since she had gone out with Kennedy. Suddenly, the door swung open, and Nikki entered, carrying her briefcase and a water bottle. She looked exhausted. "Hi, how was your day?" Chloe greeted her.

"A beast. I'm so tired. How are the reports coming along? I plan on reviewing them tonight before going to bed since I have a Zoom meeting at ten in the morning," Nikki replied, not noticing Chloe's attire, as she tapped her nail tips on the counter.

"I finished most of the reports. I only have three left," Chloe responded hesitantly.

"What? Wait... where do you think you're going? I need those reports tonight," Nikki exclaimed impatiently.

Not accustomed to this side of Nikki, Chloe swallowed hard, fidgeting with her hair. "Don't worry, I'll complete the remaining three as soon as I get back home. You can review the other seven for now and tackle the last three first thing in the morning," Chloe suggested. She couldn't help but notice the aggravation etched on Nikki's face. She perceived that Nikki might be gaining a bit too much control as she felt a surge of nervous energy coursing through her veins. *Why was Nikki acting so controlling?* Chloe questioned within.

"You didn't answer my question. Are you going somewhere?" Nikki's voice held a hint of suspicion, causing even more questions to arise within Chloe concerning Nikki's attitude.

"Yeah, I'm just hanging out with my cousin for a few hours," Chloe replied cautiously, gently biting down on her bottom lip.

"Oh."

"Is that okay with you?" Chloe asked, concerned, attempting to get a grip on her own emotions.

"Absolutely," Nikki responded, her expression subtly shifting. "Are you two heading to the big campus party?"

"How did you find out about the party?" Chloe inquired, surprised.

"Chloe, dear... I'm a mentor and a member of several college boards. I know everything that happens on that campus," Nikki revealed as she tossed her briefcase onto the table and kicked off her stilettos. Running her fingers through her hair, she tossed her empty water bottle into the recycling bin before grabbing another one from the fridge. Chloe marveled at how much water Nikki managed to consume.

"Yeah, Kennedy convinced me to go. It'll give me a chance to relax and clear my head. I've been feeling a bit off lately," Chloe confessed.

"Oh? Does that have anything to do with me?" Nikki's voice dripped with sarcasm, a side of her that Chloe wasn't familiar with, leaving her feeling uneasy.

"It's not just about you. Oh, I see car lights. I'm sure it's Kennedy," Chloe exclaimed as she rushed to the window, peeking through the blinds. "Yep! It's her. As promised, I'll finish those reports before going to bed tonight. Thanks for understanding," Chloe said, grabbing her crossbody bag and heading towards the door. As she took one more look in Nikki's direction, she could see that Nikki was clearly not pleased.

As she contemplated, she only wished she had mustered the courage to be as forward with her mother as she was with Nikki in the moment. Perhaps it was the fear of disapproval that prevented her in the past? Nevertheless, the gnawing feelings of fear and apprehension were swallowed up by a sense of confidence and stride as Chloe galloped out of the room behind her best friend and cousin.

Determined to have the last say, Nikki blurted out, "Remember, punctuality is something that will get you a long way in your professional career…take it from me, I know!" She cried out just as the sound of the door closing hit the atmosphere. A tinge of emotional betrayal began to run up and down her soul like a trained sprinter.

CHAPTER 16

A NIGHT OUT

The music thumped loudly, causing Chloe to feel overwhelmed. The room was packed with people from various fraternities and sororities. Multicolored lights flickered and danced across the packed space, casting shadows on the faces of the partygoers, all holding their red cups. Chloe scanned the room, The air was thick with a blend of laughter, chatter, and the faint scent of different perfumes and colognes. She couldn't help but wonder what was hidden in those red cups. Meanwhile, Kennedy and her friends were already dancing and enjoying themselves. Despite being there for only fifteen minutes, Chloe had been approached by four guys asking her to dance or go out. She felt uncomfortable but didn't regret coming.

Suddenly, Chloe heard a voice calling her "Little Miss Missing in Action." It was Chloe's wild and partying roommate Chelsea, who had snuck up behind her. "Hey there, what's up? I haven't seen you around lately," Chelsea said, her smile was crooked and the smell of alcohol was strong upon her breath.

"Just been busy with work and studying in a quiet place. Some of us need to concentrate while studying," Chloe replied sarcastically, noticing that Chelsea seemed to be drunk. Her blouse was twisted as if she had been in a wrestling match, and her cleavage bare.

Giggling, Chelsea said, "That's not what the grapevines are saying."

Confused, Chloe asked, "What do you mean?"

"Well, let's just say someone's not as innocent as they seem," Chelsea said before departing from Chloe's side, high stepping with a twist so exaggerated until she appeared to wobble. Shaking her head in disbelief, Chloe continued her attempt to blend in with the crowd.

"Hey, it's great to see you again!" a familiar voice called out to Chloe. She turned around to find Dan Dan standing before her.

"How have you been?" she asked him, happy to see him, but attempting to hide her enthusiasm.

"I've been good, really good," Dan Dan replied. "It's great to see you. Maybe we can catch up later?" Dan Dan asked as he awaited Chloe's reply. He watched Chloe's body language and facial expression intently, since he had not forgotten about the pain of the past break up between them. Although he moved on, Chloe was not one that was easy to forget. She still held a special place in his heart.

"Sure, I'll be around," Chloe said, settling into a chair and observing the partygoers as Dan Dan smirked and walked toward the other side of the room. She too held fast to the past issues between her and Dan Dan but her heart was genuinely glad to see him.

As she watched Kennedy, Dan Dan and the others chat and laugh, she couldn't help but feel like an outsider. She had always felt this way, even in other social situations. It made her wonder if there was something wrong with her.

However, Chloe remembered a Sunday school teacher who once told her that being unique was a sign of a special calling in life. She had yet to discover what that calling was, but she held onto the hope that one day she would.

Time seemed to slip away unnoticed as Chloe's eyelids grew heavy, her body shifting restlessly in the chair. The rhythmic move and flow of the music pulsed through the room, its melodic strains filling her ears as she fought off the sudden drowsiness. The remnants of three cups of punch lingered on her tongue, and she had made several trips to the restroom, the faint scent of soap still clinging to the skin of her hands.

As the clock struck eleven-thirty, a wave of sleepiness washed over Chloe, tugging at her senses. Just as she was about to succumb to its embrace, a familiar voice pierced through the haze. "Hey, remember this song?" Dan Dan's voice reached her, the sound drawing her attention as he approached from behind.

A spark of recognition ignited within Chloe, and her mind wandered back to the days when this love ballad had held a special place in her heart, especially on prom night. She had spent countless hours listening to it, allowing the heartfelt lyrics to paint vivid images of romance and longing in her mind. "Oh, yes. I do. It used to be one of my favorites," she replied, a hint of remanence lacing her words. The memories flooded back, a bittersweet melody from her past. The thickness of the memories temporarily causing her to forget the complexities of her current relationship with Nikki. Curiosity piqued as Chloe questioned Dan Dan's motives. "Why do you ask?" Her voice tinged with a mixture of wonder and anticipation, unsure of what his invitation might entail. Considering their past breakup and the timeframe it took her to finally move on, she desired to build a protective wall.

A mischievous glimmer danced in Dan Dan's greenish eyes as he playfully persisted. "Was hoping you'd join me in a dance," he replied, knowing he was taking a chance on being turned down.

Chloe hesitated for a moment, her initial instinct to decline, but something within her urged her to embrace the moment. She longed to break free from the constraints of the wallflower chair she had occupied for far too long. After all, she reminded herself of the journey she'd embarked upon and the excitement of developing a new identity. This moment would be worth the journal entry later. "No, thank you," she initially responded, but a flicker of longing crossed her face. The battle was tougher than she thought. *Why do I want to dance with him after the pain he put me through?* She questioned from within as the battle of the will and the heart wrestled.

Unfazed by her initial refusal, Dan Dan's smile widened, and he extended his hand towards her, an unspoken invitation. "Come on. One dance won't hurt. It'll be nice."

Caught in a whirlwind of emotions, Chloe's hesitation melted away as she found herself drawn to his energy. Tentatively, she reached out, accepting his hand. With a shared purpose, they ventured towards the center of the dance floor, their steps guided by the enchanting love song that resonated throughout the room. Other couples swayed in harmony to the romantic melody, their movements a testament to the power of music and love.

Chloe hummed the familiar tune under her breath, the lyrics etching themselves into her soul. The twinkle in Dan Dan's eyes mirrored her own joy as he guided her with a gentle hand resting on the small of her back. Their bodies moved in synchrony, gracefully navigating the dance floor. In that moment, the lighting seemed to soften, casting an ethereal glow upon the room, enhancing the enchanting atmosphere.

As Chloe nestled into the warmth of Dan Dan's embrace, memories of their high school days resurfaced, intertwining with the present. His familiar scent enveloped her, triggering a flood of emotions and recollections. The scent, once associated with carefree innocence, now mingled with a touch of confusion. Nearly a year ago, Dan Dan had shattered her heart into a million fragments, leaving her to piece them back together. Yet, here she was, leaning her head on his broad shoulder, while Nikki, her confidante or something more, awaited her return. Gently releasing from his tight grip with every thought of Nikki, but succumbing to the embrace even more with every memory from the good days of their past relationship.

Tangled thoughts swirled in Chloe's mind as Dan Dan's embrace tightened, blending comfort with longing. It felt both familiar and foreign, a juxtaposition that stirred conflicting emotions within her. The soothing mood threatened to lull her into complacency when suddenly, a commotion erupted, shattering the fragile tranquility that had enveloped them.

"You seem tense," Dan Dan whispered above the seemingly loud commotion.

"A bit tired. What's up with all the commotion toward the door?' Chloe asked as she peered toward the front of the room. Students seemed to be occupied with something in that direction and there was shouting but the music was loud, and it was hard to decipher exactly what was happening. Laying her head back upon Dan Dan's chest, she began to find contentment as Dan Dan assured her that everything was okay.

"Chloe!" The sharp voice of Nikki cut through the air, bringing the lively commotion in the atmosphere to a sudden halt. The pulsating music faded into the background, and laughter was replaced by tense silence. All eyes gravitated towards the trio of Dan Dan, Chloe, and Nikki, as if the world held its breath for what would unfold.

Chloe felt a surge of panic and embarrassment wash over her. "Nikki, I… I'll finish the reports once I get home, as promised," she stammered, desperation evident in her voice. "I just need to wait for Kennedy to be ready to leave."

Nikki's voice rang out, domineering and laced with an underlying threat. "No need to wait for Kennedy. Let's go," she commanded, her presence demanding compliance.

However, Dan Dan wasn't about to let Nikki dictate Chloe's actions. He tightened his grip on Chloe's hand and stood his ground. The crowd watched in anticipation, capturing the unfolding drama through their whispered conversations and eager video recordings. And just as tension reached its peak, Kennedy broke through the crowd, determined to rescue her cousin from this distressing situation.

In that moment, Kennedy marched alongside Chloe, offering her support. Chloe's eyes welled up with tears, grateful for her cousin's presence amidst the chaos that had enveloped her.

"Nikki, we're leaving. So why don't you stop causing a scene and save her from further embarrassment?" Kennedy's voice held a mix of defiance and concern, a resolute challenge to Nikki's authority.

Dan Dan, emboldened by Kennedy's intervention, stepped closer to Nikki, his anger evident. "Yeah, you old bat! Leave us alone," he spat, his words sizzled with defiance.

Nikki's response was laced with warning, a glimpse of a hidden power. "Watch your tongue, you little punk. You have no idea who you're messing with," she warned, her hand reaching out towards Chloe, The abrupt transformation in Nikki's demeanor left Chloe startled, as if a different person had emerged.

The exchange between Dan Dan, Nikki, and Kennedy continued, the bickering echoing through the venue. It lasted for another agonizing minute, until finally, Chloe, worn down and defeated, succumbed to Nikki's insistence, and left with her. As she left with Nikki, Chloe's shoulders slumped, and her eyes betrayed a mixture of confusion and resignation. Casting a gaze upon the once lively party, the colors that initially stimulated her senses, now only brought forth a dark shadow. She could see Kennedy and Dan Dan and others looking toward her direction with empathy.

Walking into the night air was a stark contrast to the warmth of Dan Dan's embrace only moments before the confrontation erupted. *What am I doing and how did I get here?* The question stalked her as she climbed into the vehicle with who was supposed to be her mentor and the source of her future success story.

The ripple effect of Nikki's entrance had transformed the once lively party into a stage for an unexpected confrontation, leaving partygoers on the edge of their seats, awaiting the next twist in the unfolding narrative. The once-promising night now lay in ruins, a night that Chloe would never forget.

CHAPTER 17

MAKING DECISIONS (CHLOE'S CONFLICTS)

Days passed in a whirlwind for Chloe, caught between the harsh realities and fleeting fantasies stemming from her newfound journey of self-development. The aftermath of that tormenting night at the party weighed heavily on her mind, and the conflicts with Nikki only added to the exhausting mix. She found safety in avoiding her dorm hall, knowing all too well that the majority of teasing and insults emanated from that direction

Amid her turmoil, Chloe became aware of the hurtful slang thrown her way by some of the girls. "Stud," "gold star," and "pillow princess" echoed in her ears in the cafeteria, the library, and other remote places, intensifying the sting of the rumors that had begun to circulate.

Overwhelmed, Chloe found herself on the receiving end of an unexpected phone call from her mother. It was not a good time to talk, as Chloe was exhausted from fighting the depression that continued to knock at the door of her soul. Mom, can I call you back?" Chloe's voice carried a weary tone, the weight of unspoken struggles evident in her words."

"Oh...not a good time? Studying?" Starla asked, a hint of disappointment in her voice. "The one time I surprise you with a phone call for no apparent reason but to say hello, and you're too busy to be surprised."

"Sorry, mom. You're right. I wasn't expecting a call. You're not sick are you?" Chloe asked, as she was genuinely concerned since her mom was always busy during the weekdays from morning until late evening.

"Of course not. I just had some things on my mind."

"Oh?" Chloe inquired, fearing her mom may have heard some of the rumors.

"Listen, don't concern yourself with me. You get back to your studies. We can visit later."

"Yes, ma'am."

"Chloe…", Starla continued, hesitancy in her voice.

"Yes?"

"Never mind. Enjoy the rest of your afternoon. Your dad and I…well, we're proud of you dear," Starla said and before Chloe could respond, she ended the call.

"Wow…now you tell me," Chloe muttered, shaking her head in disbelief. She felt uneasy by her mother's behavior. Something was off but she couldn't discern what it was.

"

After ending the call with her mom, , she decided to phone Kennedy but was not able to reach her. Phoning her Aunt Macy next, she sensed a cool breeze of refreshment when her voice chirped across the phone line.

"Hello, my baby girl! It's been too long. How are you?" Macy was excited to receive Chloe's call. They had not spoken but once since Chloe left.

"Hi, Auntie. I'm okay and you?" Chloe's voice sounded weak.

"I'm good. You don't sound like yourself, honey. Are you sure everything is good your way?"

"Yes, Ma'am. I phoned Kennedy and didn't get her, so I thought of you and how long it's been. Well, I'm gonna go, just wanted to hear your voice."

"Oh, no you don't. Take a deep breath and spill it. I mean it. I know you, young lady," Macy's voice was filled with determination to get Chloe to pour her heart out.

"You're right as usual, but I got it. I just miss home, is all."

"Aw, it's okay to be homesick sweetheart. I'll never forget when I went off to college. I cried at night for the first month, I know. Things were so different, but eventually, I was fine."

"Yeah, I'm optimistic that things will get better for me too. I love you, Aunt Macy."

"I love you more, and you dial my number anytime day or night, do you hear me?"

"I hear you. I'm gonna get back to work now. Bye now." Ending the call, Chloe fought to hold back a tear. Desperation to confide in her aunt pulsed through her, questioning whether the heaviness she felt was due to her closer connection with her aunt than with her own mother or something else entirely. Her thoughts began to swirl again, the buzzing of her phone catching her attention. It was Dan Dan. She had been avoiding his phone calls ever since that night. He would text when she wouldn't pick up the phone. The text message that he typed at that time was that he didn't care about her sexual preferences and that he only wanted to talk. He wanted to make sure that she was doing okay. Chloe continued to avoid him, as she felt she couldn't endure a conversation at this time. The only person that she had spoken with about the tangled web she was caught in with Nikki was Kennedy, who continued to be supportive. She honestly didn't believe she could handle explaining herself to Dan Dan, especially after their intimate dance and embrace at the party. Confusion persisted, threatening to erode the beautiful foundation she had painstakingly built on her journey.

Later that evening, Nikki arrived home, her usual routine

disrupted by the absence of water. Frustration laced her voice as she exclaimed, "Damn! No water?" Chloe couldn't shake the feeling that Nikki's frustrations reached far beyond the absence of a water bottle.

Chloe, being the problem solver, offered, "I can make a quick run to the market. We need a few other things anyway."

"Wait. We need to talk. Sit," Nikki commanded, her tone serious, with a hint of vulnerability

Curiosity tinged with nervous energy, Chloe complied, feeling her stomach knotting up as they delved into a discussion that had been a long time coming.

"I know you'll be turning nineteen soon, but... well, it's complicated, as we both know," Nikki began, her voice now even more vulnerable than at first. "Those brats from the party have been spreading rumors. Even though they can't prove anything, I think you might need to move back—temporarily, of course—into your dorm space until things blow over."

Chloe's eyes widened in disbelief. "No way. I can't go back there, Nikki."

"Just for the remainder of the semester, honey," Nikki proposed, her voice laced with a mixture of worry and resolve.

"You're serious?" Chloe's voice wavered, the weight of her tumultuous emotions hanging heavily in the air. Chloe's reaction intensified, a storm of emotions brewing within her as Nikki's vulnerability added a new layer to their complex situation.

"Yes, I can't risk the board hearing about these rumors and questioning me," Nikki explained, her vulnerability creeping into her words.

"It was your fault that night at the party. Nobody told you to come there!" Chloe retorted her frustration and hurt bubbling to the surface.

"Honey, you're right. I was aggravated and tired. Truth be told, I was missing you. When I saw you in that guy's arms, I went to a dark place I hadn't visited in a while. I'm sorry," Nikki confessed, her voice filled with remorse.

"Not as sorry as I am," Chloe choked out the words, her heart heavy with disappointment. Unable to bear the weight of her emotions any longer, she fled into her bedroom, collapsing onto the bed in a flood of tears. The intensity of Chloe's emotions surged as Nikki's confession resounded in her mind, leaving her grappling with a mixture of anger, hurt, and a profound sense of betrayal. The weight of disappointment and sorrow pressed down on her, breaking the dam of her composure and releasing a flood of tears that soaked the fabric of her bed.

Chloe's heart sank as her world seemed to spiral into darkness. Tears continued streaming down her face until Nikki's touch jolted her to life. The warmth of Nikki's embrace filled Chloe with a fire she had never felt before, and both terror and exhilaration coursed through her veins. Her lungs burned as she tried to catch her breath, yet Nikki demanded control with each word, pressing softer kisses onto her cheeks and forehead that expanded within Chloe like a tidal wave. With the strength of a goddess spell, Nikki pulled Chloe into an electrifying kiss that made every inch of her body tense in pleasure. "Let me guide you," Nikki whispered, "Look at me and see the truth. I'm here to show you who you are--you don't need to search anymore." Chloe melted under the comfort of Nikki's embrace, allowing herself to be guided by love for the first time in her

life. Chloe felt powerless against Nikki's alluring words and surrendered willingly to this newfound journey of self-discovery.

The warmth of Nikki's embrace provided Chloe with a sense of comfort as the morning sun slowly peeked through the curtains. After a lengthy discussion about how they would handle their newly formed relationship, they both agreed to honor each other's boundaries and keep it discreet.

"Am I ready to face the reality of embarking on a new relationship amid the chaos and pain from the past?' she asked herself as Nikki's departure found her alone to collect her thoughts. A cold chill coursed through her body as she remembered a saying from the elders of the church..."if you sow to the wind, you'll for certain reap a whirlwind" With a will to seek after any weapon in her arsenal of affirmations, she looked deeply within herself to pull on her faith and resilience. At the moment, she found little strength, but she spoke these words to her mind,

"God is in the midst of her, she shall not be moved; God shall help her, just at the break of dawn," and with that, she lay in a fetal position to rest her body and soul before tackling her day.

CHAPTER 18

MOVE OVER PAST...MY FUTURE IS COMING THROUGH

As Chloe settled back into her dorm room, the familiar scent of vanilla-scented candles and freshly laundered sheets surrounded her, but still did not provide a sense of comfort. The subtle sound of Chelsea's music, a genre Chloe found degrading, permeated the room. She tried to drown out the noise with her headphones, as she became more annoyed by the reality of her roommate not exhibiting the courtesy of turning off the music upon leaving. Even the fluorescent lights Chelsea chose over her desk conflicted with the softer lighting that she preferred. She knew she had to find ways to distance herself from Chelsea, who had taken a job at one of the bustling malls nearby, working late into the evening and well into the night. Chloe overheard her incessant whining about her GPA, a constant reminder of her own dedication to her studies. It was clear that Chelsea's priorities were vastly different from her own. Nevertheless, it was good to know Chelsea wouldn't be as present in the dorm room, and she hoped her loudmouth girl friends would not be hanging out. Chloe was accustomed to the quietness and meditation, which she was able to do quite often when living in one of Nikki's investment properties. "I'm going to miss being there," she whispered.

The sound of her phone breaking the silence jolted Chloe out of her thoughts. An echoing ding resounded in the small room as she answered the call. "Hey, how's it going?" Kennedy's voice, warm and familiar, greeted her on the other end.

Chloe scrambled to gather her belongings, her heart sinking at the reminder of her afternoon class. "It's going. I'm coping. This is day five, and I'm still standing," she replied, trying to inject a note of resilience into her voice.

Kennedy's voice crackled with concern. "Good. You'll be fine. Listen, you know I'm only half an hour away, and I can come over and whip Chelsea if necessary. In the meantime, you're going to have to take a stand for yourself."

A hint of a smile tugged at Chloe's lips at the mention of Kennedy's protective nature. She recalled how Kennedy always stood up for her during their childhood at school, camp, church, and it was pleasant knowing she still had her back. "Meaning?"

"Meaning, you need to set some boundaries with Nikki and you need to stand up to Chelsea," Kennedy emphasized, her voice firm. "Speaking of Nikki...what's the latest?"

"Nikki and I are being careful because so many people are talking about our... well, our living arrangements," Chloe confessed, her fingers tapping nervously against her backpack. "I've been praying and thinking along those boundary lines. For now, Chelsea is not around much,

Kennedy's voice lowered, laced with concern. "Living arrangements? I mean, you moved out, so there shouldn't be any heat about that. I can understand it, but don't you find something seriously wrong about Nikki's behavior at the party? I mean, she seems possessive and controlling. Those are warning signs that other issues are lurking inside of that head of hers."

Chloe sighed as she laced up her sneakers, her mind filled with images of Nikki's tight grip and condescending gaze at the party, which her recent love encounter smuggled any negativity that she may have had about this new lover of hers. "I don't know. She and I did have an agreement that I'd finish work, and it was getting late," she reasoned, attempting to justify Nikki's behavior while hiding the fact that she and Nikki had quickly taken their relationship to a new level. She affirmed within her mind she would protect her right to evolve on her new journey, though she felt she had experienced a setback and a horrible detour recently. She fought all the more to get back onto the main road of her path.

"Be careful, cousin.. I don't want you in harm's way, and I want you to enjoy your life," Kennedy's voice resonated with love and genuine concern. "You deserve to thrive. I've always seemed to be the adventurous one but this second year of college has taught me a thing or two. Life be 'lifing,' and being happy is a habit, not a condition. You've survived a lot of unhappy days when your parents were too busy for you. The best days of your life are still to come. You're my girl, and I love you."

"I love you too, and I'll be careful. I'm blown away by the wisdom you're speaking. You are growing, cousin. I'm proud of you. Look, I'll call you tonight. I'm heading to class now," Chloe reassured, her grip on her phone tightening as she prepared to face whatever challenges lay ahead. However, she did feel terrible about holding back on Kennedy. They had always shared their life secrets, no matter what, and to experience Kennedy's growth was amazing to Chloe, which proved that Nikki had a tight hold on her.

With a determined spirit, Chloe walked out of her dorm room, the weight of the world resting on her shoulders. She hoped she could get through her classes and the dorm life each day without dealing with insults, suspicions, or any other humiliation.

As Chloe navigated this delicate dance between secrecy and self-discovery, the tension between her, Kennedy, and Nikki simmered beneath the surface. Kennedy, protective and discerning, sensed Chloe's hesitation and the hidden layers of her relationship with Nikki, but decided to not press the issue for now. She knew her cousin better than anyone else, so she trusted Chloe to confide in her in her own timing.

~

So, throughout her first semester, Chloe made strides with the help of Kennedy's advice. She initiated boundaries in her relationships with Chelsea and Nikki, growing stronger by the week. After a few episodes of putting her foot down about cleanliness, the noise, and other issues, Chelsea finally started to respect Chloe's boundaries.

As she connected with other students on their own journeys of self-discovery, Chloe felt the tug of Nikki's love at the back of her mind, questioning her identity and purpose. The more time she and Nikki spent together, the heavier Nikki's influence became. By the end of the semester, Chloe's parents agreed to move her into her own apartment, giving her freedom to continue developing her identity but also opening her up to the avoidance of facing the hurt from her past summer camp pain. This pain still haunted her in her dreams and thoughts from time to time. But like a mighty warrior princess, she gripped tightly to the hope she affirmed. The scriptures and positive affirmations would continue to be her priority. She used her imagination to visualize herself in new and profound ways. She grew stronger day by day. The fight was fixed, and she determined that she would be the last woman standing.

CHAPTER 19

ORDINARY PEOPLE

Chloe's eyes widened as she watched Nikki place the sparkling crystals in their velvet-lined box. She had heard of new age spiritual practices but felt unnerved by them - especially since her pastor and family were so strongly against it. Taking a deep breath, Chloe squared her shoulders and politely declined Nikki's invitation to join her.

"No thanks," she said firmly. "One of the girls from our neighborhood was into that stuff. Kennedy and I were curious and did research once. Nope…not for me. I'll stick to reading my Bible devotion and praying."

Nikki shrugged and smiled. "Suit yourself, but if you're going to manifest your dreams quickly, I totally recommend it," Nikki responded, her voice full of persuasion Chloe listened intently, thought on the matter, but could not shake the restraint within her gut.

"Manifesting quickly is appealing, but as stated, I'm on a journey that I believe will get me to my destination in perfect timing," Chloe said, reclining on the Nikki's bed with plans of watching one of her favorite flicks.

"Get dressed. We're going out," Nikki said, gesturing at her overstuffed closet filled with all sorts of colorful clothing, from business suits to party wear, not to mention the numerous pairs of shoes that lined the floor like a tiny shoe store.

"But... I thought I told you I'd be heading back to my place," Chloe said, trying to stay true to the sensible advise her mentor Kennedy had given her about balancing fun and work. "We just went out last night. I've got two tests to study for."

"Oh, come on. This is a business thing…meeting with some clients. It will be educational for you," Nikki said as she gazed into Chloe's eyes, her expression a mix of annoyance and pleading. "Remember, your mentorship ends this semester so don't you want to make a great impression on your instructors? Besides, I need you to do a presentation of the mentorship program at the luncheon next month. The college needs to see how much progress my mentees are making so they will continue to allow me to work there. Oh, come on Chloe girl," Nikki's whining went up an octave as she spoke, her hands clasped together as if in prayer.

Chloe sighed deeply and rolled her eyes. "I guess," she said reluctantly. She didn't appreciate Nikki making plans without asking her first. Slowly, she dragged herself up from the bed to comply with Nikki's invitation. She told herself it was for her future.

~

Chloe arrived at the jazz bar, a popular spot amongst Nikki's clientele. Her eyes adjusted to the dimly lit room as she breathlessly joined them, barely having time to greet everyone before taking her seat. As they continued conversation, Chloe could feel her blood boiling. Not only did Chloe have studying to do, but she also had reports for Nikki as part of her mentorship program to complete. Feeling like she was invisible and as if Nikki was using her, she began to feel as if her feelings didn't matter much. With an almost inaudible huff, she rose from the table and said in a strained pleasant voice.

"If everyone will excuse me, I'm headed to the ladies room." Before anyone had a chance to reply, Nikki spoke up again calling over to the waiter to refill drinks as she linked arms with Chloe and steered her towards the restrooms. Once inside, Chloe let out all her pent-up frustration saying "What's the matter with you? You know I'm behind on your reports, and I told you I needed to study. I have two tests tomorrow that I don't feel comfortable with at all!"

"Don't whine like a baby," Nikki replied coolly. "You'll be fine. Just put the figures into a spread sheet, make your chart and bam – you've got yourself a report. As far as studying, I'm sure you'll do fine".

"But…"

"No buts!" Nikki said suddenly, her voice hinted with authority and seduction. Nikki's hand moved slowly and sensually down Chloe's back, her voice a low whisper of temptation. The other woman coming out of the restroom had a smirk on her face, as if she could sense what the two were up to.

"Stop it Nikki, not here! I think that lady saw us," Chloe said breathlessly. Despite her protests, there was a hint of excitement in her voice that made Nikki giggle. She pressed her lips against Chloe's ear and spoke softly.

"You and I both know you like it. This jazz lounge is full of people like us - ordinary people," she said with a mischievous twinkle in her eye before pulling away and heading toward the restroom. Chloe shook her head at Nikki's retreating form but followed close behind as if drawn by an invisible string. The more control that Nikki exerted over Chloe, the more her soul became intertwined with that control.

After rejoining the others at their table, Nikki and Chloe managed to get through the dinner and as usual, Nikki got what she demanded. The group loved all her presentations and feedback.

After settling in for the night, it was inevitable that they had moved from the casual days of working together to the nights when Chloe stayed at Nikki's place. Their relationship was escalating beyond what Chloe imagined at first. The sounds of a nocturnal Charlotte night echoed up through the open window, muffled by the heavy velvet drapes that kept out any prying eyes. Nikki loved an open window, while sweet jazz music played through the Bluetooth speaker. And so it was, their discreet relationship pulled Chloe deeper into Nikki's world and although there were the perks of Chloe basking in Nikki's vast knowledge of both real estate and finance, her soul became more knitted, until it became harder to keep breaking free of Nikki's control. Chloe often contemplated how to move back into a place of being that free spirit, making her own decisions...the independence she learned as a child. Where had it gone?

CHAPTER 20

STRANGE LOVE

The next day, both Chloe and Nikki overslept. The house was a mess as they both hurriedly refreshed themselves and started to catch up on the work that was incomplete. Chloe noticed an unusual change in Nikki. Everything seemed to bother her more than usual and the air around them felt heavy. She moved carefully, avoiding any sudden movements that might spark an argument. Hoping her coffee would give her enough energy to get through the morning, she worked on multiple reports for her clientele.

"I sent the first draft of Archie's report...finishing up the second one now," she said, eyeing Nikki with caution. The woman's expression was unreadable, and it was difficult to tell what she was thinking. "You okay?"

"Of course. Why wouldn't I be?" Nikki answered tersely, arms crossed as if steeling herself against impending criticism.

"Just asking. You seem a bit off since you got up is all."

"Since you asked, I wish you wouldn't act like a spoiled brat when you're among the clientele. It looks bad and frankly...I can't stand it. Pull yourself together and press through whatever challenge comes your way. Haven't you learned anything from me all this time?"

"What do you mean? I never act like a brat," Chloe responded indignantly, typing on her laptop with ever-increasing speed.

"I mean you pout too much and let things get to you without fighting back. That needs to stop."

"I disagree, but…let's discuss it later. I don't have time for this right now," Chloe said evenly as she kept her attention on the screen in front of her.

The bickering continued. Chloe, determined to complete the reports to get some study time in, insisted more sharply that she and Nikki discuss their differences later, which aggravated Nikki all the more.

"Are you dismissing me? Who do you think you are, missy?" Nikki said sternly, striding closer to Chloe's desk chair. "One would think someone would be more appreciative to someone who holds the key to their future."

"I do appreciate your mentorship, but you're suffocating me, Nikki. Like that business venture last night. I had no business there. It had absolutely nothing to do with me. Now if you'll excuse me…Jesus!"

"I've had quite enough of this attitude," Nikki fired off, moving closer to where Chloe was sitting.

Chloe's heart pounded, and her breath caught in her throat as Nikki's words hung in the air like a heavy cloud. The room seemed to shrink, and the air thickened with tension as she stood from her seat, fearfully taking a step back, her eyes widening with anticipation.

"I'm not the one with the attitude," Chloe said as Nikki's hand flew quickly in her direction. In an instant, the sting of her palm against Chloe's cheek spread across her skin. Her mind reeled in confusion, unable to comprehend what had just happened. The room blurred as tears welled up in her eyes, and she stumbled backward in shock, feeling the heat and throbbing pain on her reddening skin. The taste of salt lingered on her lips as she fought to hold back a sob, her hand instinctively reaching to soothe the assaulted area. In that moment, she felt small as she thought about the progress she had made on her journey to discovery. She felt as if she had been both physically and emotionally knocked back to the beginning of the journey.

"How could you do that? What did I ever do to you?" Chloe asked, her voice wavering with a combination of shock, fear, and confusion.

Nikki's posture shifted immediately as if a switch had been flicked. Her once fierce stance was replaced by one laced with desperation. "Come on...it was an accident. I didn't mean to hit you. I'm sorry."

But it was too late—Chloe already had her things and was out the door, racing away from Nikki's apology towards the safety of her apartment. As she drove off, Nikki yelled after her, "I love you! Don't leave!" But the car kept going, carrying Chloe farther away from the scene with each passing second.

Chloe pulled into the apartment complex, her heart sinking as Kennedy's car parked moments after. She nervously ran a hand across her tear-streaked face, taking a deep breath before stepping out of the car. Her cousin was standing there with her arms crossed and an expectant look on her face.

"Well, if it isn't my long-lost cuzzo," Kennedy said with a raised eyebrow. "What's up?"

Chloe refused to make eye contact, instead fumbling for her keys and trying to push past Kennedy. "Who said something was wrong?" she snapped, her voice wavering slightly.

Kennedy sighed and rolled her eyes. "I said what's the matter, not what's wrong," she said firmly, "which proves to me that something big has happened between you and you know who. I know something more is going on between the two of you, but I told myself not to press the issue until you're ready to talk to me about it. You know how we do, cuzzo. Spill it. What did she do?"

Chloe shook her head silently, pushing through the door of her apartment and refusing to answer. "Fine," Kennedy continued, stepping into the doorway and blocking her escape. "I've been blowing up your phone over the past few weeks - why haven't you phoned me back?"

"Been busy…okay?"

"Understood, but it's not like you to not get back with me. Now what's up with you? Hold up…your right eye is red and puffy. Chloe Marissa Rhodes…what the hell is up? What happened to your eye?" Kennedy asked, her face full of concern.

"Kennedy mind your business. I said I'm not talking about it!" Chloe yelled as she darted past her into the bathroom, slamming the door shut behind her. Kennedy could hear her stifled sobs from outside. Gently pushing open the door, she peered in. Chloe was standing in front of the mirror, a look of horror on her face as she saw her right eye, swollen and red. Knowing that something wasn't quite right between Chloe and Nikki for the last couple of weeks, she braced herself for what might come next.

"I'm calling mom if you don't tell me what's going on," Kennedy threatened softly, leaning against the doorway. Placing her hand gently on Chloe's shoulder, she continued to plead with her about the incident with Nikki.

"I shouldn't have picked an argument with her," Chloe sobbed, tears streaming down her cheeks.

"Don't do that. Don't dare blame yourself. I'm calling the cops. That controlling witch!" Kennedy said as she grabbed her cell phone from her cross-body bag.

"No! Don't do that. It was me. I started it. Kennedy please,"

Chloe begged desperately, lunging forward and gripping her arm tightly with both hands. "She doesn't abuse me—she's my lover," she blurted out suddenly as if a weight had lifted off her chest. She was relieved to finally be honest with Kennedy about her romantic relationship with Nikki.

Kennedy twirled a strand of her curly hair around her finger as she studied Chloe's bruised eye. "I'm not blind," she said, her voice thick with emotion. "Besides, people talk. The two of you have been seen a time or two in various clubs downtown."

"But...we've been meeting with her clientele. Gosh! Folks are so nosey!"

"Look, if you don't stop seeing her, I'm gonna call my mom."

"Kennedy! When do I ever get into your business? Huh? I've never called my mom when you tried smoking pot or the night you had sex after the football game," Chloe said, her tone filled with defensiveness. "It's my life."

"Yeah, it's your life but I'm worried about you. You're not just my cousin, Chloe. You're my best friend. I can't just..."

Chloe let out a long sigh as she brushed a tear away from her cheek. "Look, I'll text Nikki and tell her I need a break. I'll slow the relationship down."

"You'd better. I mean it. If I find out about her laying another hand on you, I'll take her down myself."

"Deal."

"I'm not playing around. I'd rather you be mad at me for caring about you than you someday regretting that I did not care enough." Kennedy pulled Chloe into a tight embrace.

"No text," Kennedy said firmly. "Let's go to her place together. That way she'll know that you are not some nobody with no family ties or someone in your corner." She paused before adding softly, "I know about psychos like this chick."

The two cousins left the apartment and headed to the pharmacy to pick up medication for Chloe's injury. Chloe was thankful to see the change in Kennedy. "You know you're starting to sound just like Aunt Macy," she said.

Kennedy gave Chloe a friendly wink as they left the pharmacy to discuss their plans for resolving the issue with Nikki.

The next day, Chloe and Kennedy arrived at Nikki's home. As soon as the door opened, a smoky aroma wafted into the air. Nikki was standing in the dimly lit living room, eyes glued to a muted TV screen. Kennedy stepped forward and stated their purpose for visiting. Her voice was firm and direct.

Chloe felt her stomach clench as she spoke up. She cleared her throat, trying to steady out her trembling voice, "Nikki, this is my decision...I need space to sort out my feelings."

Nikki regarded them both with a steely gaze before questioning why Chloe wouldn't finish the pending projects she'd already mastered. To that Chloe replied, "I won't be doing those, Nikki. I'm grateful for your mentoring and all the time you've spent showing me the ropes."

At that moment, Nikki softened and said she would respect Chloe's wishes. Before they left, she added one last thing: "And Chloe...I don't care what anyone thinks. I will always love you," She was emotionally wrecked, staring coldly at Kennedy, and contemplating her plans for getting Chloe back into her embrace.

Kennedy quickly grabbed Chloe's hand and the two exited the house. From the window, Chloe saw Nikki watching them leave with an expression colder than winter. Wondering what would happen next, an uneasiness settled deep in her stomach as they walked away. Images in her mind portrayed the whirlwind she had reaped by her decision to explore a romantic relationship with Nikki. The cold stare sent chills through her body.

CHAPTER 21

MY FUTURE

(Three Years Later)

As her senior year approached, Chloe had already secured a coveted position at one of Charlotte's esteemed real estate firms. Although it had been at least a year since she and Nikki's relationship had finally come to an excruciating halt, she never forgot any of the mentoring and finance training she had learned along the way. Three years ago, after the first incident of Nikki's physical abuse toward Chloe, Chloe took a break from the relationship but, against her better judgment, decided to give Nikki another chance. After another year, things began to spiral downward again. This time was worse than the former, thus Chloe, being afraid of what Kennedy would do if she found out, decided to threaten Nikki by going to the police for a restraining order. The word on the street was that Nikki had left Charlotte but continued to manage her properties from another location.

Despite fighting the thoughts of Nikki returning and her parents finding out about all the incidents, life seemed to be on a promising trajectory, that is until the eve of her graduation when a mysterious figure emerged from the shadows of the mall parking lot. A woman approached her, enveloped in the night's embrace.

"For you," a voice resonated, accompanied by an outstretched package. To Chloe's astonishment, it was Nikki. Gasping, Chloe struggled to compose herself before speaking.

"Nikki, hi. What's this?" she inquired, her voice tinged with a mix of curiosity and apprehension.

"I...I thought you left town."

"Now, come on, Chloe. You didn't think I'd forget about your momentous day tomorrow, did you?" Nikki replied, her words hanging in the air. Dressed in a sleek silk jumpsuit, her favorite stilettos commanding attention, she sported a fashionable hat that accentuated her beautifully styled hair, her eyes sparkling with an irresistible enchantment.

A year had elapsed since Chloe and Nikki had last exchanged words, their breakup leaving scars that had yet to fully heal. Nikki's once-controlling tendencies had escalated, surpassing the fateful night at the campus party three years prior, and that first incident of physical abuse. The toxicity had permeated Chloe's life, eroding her focus on academics.

"It's been quite a while since we last spoke, so I didn't expect to see you or hear from you. Thanks for the gift. It's thoughtful of you," Chloe ventured, attempting to lighten the weight of the cruel tension that hung between them.

"So, how have you been? Is there someone new in your life?" Nikki inquired, her gaze sweeping up and down Chloe's transformed appearance. "You've certainly revamped your style since the last time I saw you. When did miniskirts and heels become part of your wardrobe?"

"Well, change can be refreshing now and then," Chloe

responded, aiming to deflect the mounting unease. "To answer your question, I'm currently not dating anyone, but I've met interesting people and made new friends. I'm doing well. And what about you?"

"I've never been better," Nikki purred, her eyes lingering on Chloe's form. "Listen, I'd love to take you out or whisk you away for a short weekend getaway, celebrating your graduation... and, drum roll, your prestigious position at the real estate agency!"

Caught off guard, Chloe's bewildered expression betrayed her shock. "Wait, how could you know about the job? Only my family was aware. How did this reach you?" she asked, her voice a mix of confusion and concern.

"Do you really need to ask? I know more than you think, Chloe. Let's just say I have connections in high places," Nikki replied, her tone carrying an air of cryptic intrigue.

"High places? Look, Nikki, I don't want any drama. Right now, all I want is to get into my vehicle, drive to my apartment, and prepare for one of the most significant days of my life, okay? It's good to see you, though, and thank you again for the gift," Chloe exclaimed, her words punctuated by hurried steps as she reached her car. Swiftly unlocking the door with the kiosk, she slipped inside, aware of the lingering intensity in Nikki's gaze. Remaining in her presence any longer would have surely led to an unfavorable outcome.

"Okay, but it's important to acknowledge your identity, dear. Even if you don't feel like you belong to our community right now, it's something you'll have to face eventually, not to mention the love you know you still have for me!" Nikki shouted as Chloe's car drove away.

The next day was a beautiful but chilly December day, and Chloe couldn't help feeling a bit of excitement as she opened the double doors of her favorite mall. Her cousin Kennedy had agreed to go with her for an afternoon of pre-graduation pampering. As they strolled through the store, they eyed the discounts on clothes and makeup; Kennedy snatched several items off the racks while Chloe stuck to more affordable options. Excited chatter filled the air as they arrived at the cosmetics counters.

Kennedy turned to her cousin, her face already three shades darker than its usual tint. "Listen, I am always gonna be here for you. You've done the same for me. When I dropped out of college and ended up at the community college, you held my hand and didn't throw shade like most everybody else. I wouldn't have made it this far without you."

Chloe smiled warmly at her cousin's words and gave her a hug. "You're doing great things now! Soon enough you'll be a cheerleading coach at our old high school."

Kennedy nodded in agreement before her expression changed to one of concern. "By the way…rumor has it that your crazy ex is back in town, so be careful."

Chloe's smile faded, and she looked away. "It's not a rumor," she said sadly. "I saw her last night, but don't worry - I handled it." She forced a brave smile onto her face and grabbed hold of Kennedy's arm. "Let's keep going - graduation is only six hours away!"

"Wait. You better be careful. Nikki is a lunatic, I know you set boundaries a while back, but I don't trust her at all."

"I got this...I made it quite clear last night that I wasn't interested in a relationship with her. But you're right, she has some mind issues." Chloe said as she nervously chewed on her bottom lip and shifted her weight from one foot to the other.

"That's putting it lightly," Kennedy added.

"I'm a little concerned that she knew about my new job. I only told the family about it," Chloe said, looking away for a moment and taking a deep breath before continuing. "Said she had friends in high places."

"It could be that she has connections with the company somehow,"Kennedy replied, eyebrows furrowed in worry. "Who knows, but again, don't let your guard down. I wouldn't be surprised if she's been stalking you."

"I don't know about stalking, but I agree that she may have connections with the company," Chloe replied with a sigh of resignation. She thought back to how Nikki used to appear wherever she went - always smiling slyly, almost as if knowing something Chloe didn't know. "After all, she is affiliated with lots of people in that industry." Taking a deep breath of resolve, Chloe continued: "Anyway, like I said, let's finish our venture. Graduation is tonight and I don't want anything spoiling my moment of bliss!"

CHAPTER 22

MY IDENTITY...MY TIME

"Mom, where's dad? Is he coming to the ceremony tonight?" Chloe asked, confused.

"Yes," Starla replied calmly as she continued to get ready.

"But why isn't he here? You both agreed you'd take either a full or half day off work today, right?"

"We did," Starla responded, her voice still even.

"Mom, something's going on. Are you and dad fighting again?"

"Darling, there's no need to worry about us right now; this night is all about you."

"I know, but I can tell when something is wrong. You might as well tell me, mom."

"Good grief. Alright then, we're separated. We've been apart for the past two weeks and thought it best to wait until after tonight's ceremony to tell you. When it was decided, you were studying hard for finals," Starla's words cut deep like a knife as Chloe stood in her parents' bedroom, motionless.

"What? How could you not mention that you were separated? That's so wrong," Chloe whimpered.

"Honey, life is complicated and has its challenges. Your father and I have been struggling for years now."

"You should have talked to me about it though," Chloe murmured softly as the news of her parents' separation sunk in. "So, are you guys getting divorced?"

"Let's talk about this together later; it's not an appropriate time for discussing this now."

"But it is. I should have a say in something for a change in this nightmare of a family!" Chloe exclaimed, her face red with rage and eyes shimmering with unshed tears.

"Chloe, watch your tone honey and stop being overly dramatic. Now, your father and I are figuring out what to do; we have been seeing a therapist for two weeks. Give us time sweetheart...just a bit more time," Starla pleaded softly as she took slow steps closer to her daughter.

A tear streamed down Chloe's cheek as she slowly turned around and headed toward the door, feeling exhausted. She paused, peering into the mirror to glance at her mother's reflection before reluctantly taking a step toward the doorway. Another tear hugged Chloe's cheek as she slowly turned her body around to view her mother in the mirror again, she wondered if she was right to be angry at her parents for not being honest with her when she had been keeping secrets for years.

~

It had been a year since Chloe's graduation and subsequent new job at the real estate agency. Despite an ongoing divorce between her parents, they had started spending more time together. Kennedy had found success working in education, and Macy and Broderick still played large roles in Chloe's life.

At church, Chloe was able to use her American Sign Language skills to interpret sermons and songs for the Deaf community, which often resulted in people coming to the altar after experiencing her ministry.

Chloe picked up the phone with a shaky voice. "Chloe Rhodes speaking, how may I be of service to you? Hello, this is Chloe Rhodes…hello" She knew it was her ex-lover on the other end of the line; each call this week ending with a silent hang up or disconnection before she could even get a word out. Her thoughts were interrupted by the company's secretary Matilda who entered the office carrying a mysterious envelope. Placing it on the corner of Chloe's desk, Matilda cleared her throat as if to gain Chloe's attention.

Matilda stood at the threshold of Chloe's office, glasses sliding down the bridge of her nose and a scrunched expression on her face. A thick envelope she held in one hand clutched to her chest was exuding an unfamiliar scent that made it difficult for her to breathe properly. "You know, I wished that folks would respect others' in that not all of us can endure certain scents," Matilda spatted as she cleared her throat before letting out a huge sneeze. "This envelope reeks some exotic scent that I'm sure most would love, but it's killing my sinuses."

Chloe looked up from her desk and took notice of the envelope with puzzlement. "I smell that. I can't imagine who this could be from or why it smells the way it does," said Chloe, a hint of embarrassment washing over her like a breeze. She moved around her desk and approached Matilda with outstretched hands for the envelope before adding, "Thanks for bringing it."

Matilda hesitated, her eyes scanning Chloe's face intently. Then, with a polite nod and slight shrug of her shoulders in resignation, Matilda handed Chloe the letter. She turned away to leave, but Chloe quickly roused herself to make small talk. "So how has your day been?"

"Productive," came the blunt reply as Matilda slowly moved towards the exit door. Once outside Chloe's office, she paused briefly to listen for any disturbance from within before silently shutting the door behind her.

Sitting back down at her desk, Chloe ripped open the envelope and gasped as she saw what was inside: Photographs of her and Nikki in her apartment in compromised positions caused a nauseating sensation to grip her abdomen. A note inside read, "Reminiscing" along with an imprint of a lipstick kiss beneath it; the very same shade Nikki always wore. Chloe felt dizzy as she processed what had just happened – sickened by this unexpected development as if someone punched a hole through her stomach. Rising from her desk, Chloe crossed over to the window and peered into nature - trees swaying gently in the wind - searching for answers no one seemed to have.

The wind stirred, sending the crisp red and orange leaves skittering across the sidewalk. Normally, she would be filled with a sense of joy at this sign that fall was here, but today she only saw grey clouds hung low in the sky, and distant thunder rumbled through the air. She grabbed her briefcase resolutely and tucked the manila folders inside. A ray of hope flickered inside her chest; perhaps tonight her devotional would have something comforting waiting for her—some verse written just for her on that very page. She looked forward to the sense of peace and comfort that attending church on Sunday usually brought her, yet at the same time she often worried that someone would corner her regarding her lifestyle as bi-sexual or non-binary. Keeping the secret from her parents and other relatives was hard enough. She prayed during her commute home that this week's sermon would bring the sense of inspiration that she craved.

CHAPTER 23

"HE GIVES POWER TO THE FAINT-HEARTED"

Walking into the sanctuary early one Sunday morning, Chloe prepared her garments and gloves and spent time in meditation before the start of the service. She always had nervous energy before the service, although she'd participated in the ministry for a while.

"Good morning. "You look like you're in deep thought," a voice gently interrupted as Chloe sat on a small pew next to a window in the music room.

"Good morning. I'm sorry, are you visiting? Our service time begins at ten," Chloe said, attempting to be hospitable to this stranger who was interrupting her quiet time.

"Right. I was giving myself a bit of a tour. Hi, I'm Aaron, I'm Pastor Conner's nephew," the young man answered with an extended hand.

"Oh hi. I'm Chloe Rhodes. I'm a part of the music and drama ministry. I usually arrive about an hour early on Sundays. Pastor Conner talks of you a lot. It's good to meet you," Chloe said as she entertained Aaron's handshake.

"Well, don't let me stop you from continuing your meditation.

You looked like you were really connected with heaven," Aaron said, his words were charming yet sincere. "Hope to talk with you again, Chloe," he said, offering a warm smile that showcased his perfect white teeth before gracefully exiting the music room. Of medium height and dressed in a well-polished suit, Aaron gave off a distinguished presence. His clean-cut and handsome appearance was complemented by a personality that shone like a ray of sunshine. Chloe couldn't help but notice that he reminded her of a younger version of her father.

As Chloe's thoughts lingered on Aaron, a peculiar sensation washed over her. These thoughts collided with the lack of peace within herself, stemming from her brief encounters with Kimyatta, a woman she had dated on a couple of occasions. Nevertheless, Chloe had decided to discontinue the relationship and continue embarking on a personal journey of self-discovery.

She knew continuing her journey of self-discovery and embracing her identity would not come without potential judgment and misunderstanding from those around her, especially from some members of her church and even her own parents. Her stomach twisted with fear every time she contemplated facing potential backlash from those closest to her, as if a physical weight were draped over her shoulders in an effort not to reveal too much. Yet still, she trudged onwards, determined to find happiness in being unapologetically herself. As awful as things were between she and Nikki, Chloe credited Nikki with helping her to become the young woman she'd evolved into over the past four years.

Refocusing her attention, Chloe delved deeper into her meditation, determined to set aside these swirling thoughts, at least for the time being. She sought peace in the serenity of the moment, immersing herself in the spiritual stillness of the sanctuary. There, within the hallowed walls, she could find balance and clarity.

"Good morning," one of the choir members called out as folks started to fill both the music room and the sanctuary. Chloe was shocked at how quickly the time had passed. As everyone on the team gathered and joined together for prayer, Chloe felt a warm sensation of peace wash over her. Quickly moving to the sanctuary, her anticipation heightened as she awaited what the service would bring.

As the melodies of worship began to fill the air, Chloe's hands gracefully moved in sync with the lyrics, her ASL skills breathing life into the sacred words. The congregation gathered, their voices rising in harmony, blending with the gentle strumming of guitars and the resounding notes of the keyboard.

After the service concluded, Chloe remained in the sanctuary for a while, her spirit refreshed by the shared devotion of the congregation. Glancing at the time, she realized she had some spare moments before the next engagement on her agenda. She and Macy had planned to meet with Kennedy at a nearby coffee shop when she heard her mom calling out to her.

"Chloe," Starla exclaimed, her voice brimming with excitement, "look who's here! It's your old college mentor, Miss Witherspoon. What a delightful surprise!"

To Chloe's astonishment and disbelief, standing in the grand foyer of the church was none other than Nikki Witherspoon, the one who had been her first female lover. A jolt of memories flooded back as Chloe tried to gather her composure.

"Nikki? What on earth brings you here?" she managed to utter, her voice laced with a mix of curiosity and disbelief.

Nikki's reply carried the same magnetic charm that had once captivated Chloe. "Hello, Chloe. I happen to have a client who resides in this city, and she has been insisting on brunch for some time now. I remembered you mentioning your home church, so here I am."

Chloe's surprise mingled with a tinge of skepticism. Nikki, clad in a bold, hot pink bodycon dress adorned with a delicate gray necklace and open-toe shoes, seemed out of place. Chloe had expected her to be in her beloved stilettos that exuded confidence and attraction.

"Really? I must admit, I'm surprised you remembered," Chloe confessed, her voice tinged with sheepishness as she struggled to maintain her composure. Nikki had been trying, unsuccessfully, to contact Chloe for weeks via texts and Facebook messages. Now here she was, standing before Chloe in an unexpected moment. Nikki had a knack for appearing in the most unexpected moments, and Chloe knew deep down inside that her sudden appearance meant trouble.

"Guess what, darling? I've invited Nicole to join us for a fabulous brunch," Starla exclaimed, her eyes sparkling with excitement as if she had just stumbled upon a hidden treasure.

"But Mom, I was supposed to meet up with Kennedy and Macy today, remember?" Chloe protested; her voice filled with a touch of childish disappointment.

"Well, why not invite them along or reschedule? It's not every day that you have the chance to mingle with someone as remarkable as Ms. Witherspoon. This could be an incredible opportunity for both of you to share insights about your careers," Starla suggested her unwavering dedication to work evident. Chloe couldn't help but feel a pang of annoyance at her mother's insistence on this brunch, oblivious to the complicated history between Nikki and Chloe.

"Fine, Mom. I'll text Kennedy and postpone our plans," Chloe conceded, her tone tinged with resignation. She reached into her purse to grab her cell phone and sent a message to Kennedy. As Chloe glanced in Nikki's direction, an unwelcome chill crawled up her spine at the expression etched on Nikki's face.

CHAPTER 24

DON'T JUDGE ME

The brunch unfolded precisely as Chloe had envisioned, a heap of tangled emotions and simmering tension. Her mother, a forceful presence, commanded the conversation, while her father, who was only hanging around for appearance's sake, remained ensnared by his phone and the flickering television mounted on the wall. Nikki, with a plastic smile etched upon her face, disguised her inner demons with every uttered sentence. And then, in a dramatic twist, both Kennedy and Macy unexpectedly arrived, injecting an extra dose of chaos into the gathering. Chloe found herself caught in a whirlwind of thoughts, exclaiming silently, "What a mess!"

"Macy… Kennedy… what a surprise," Starla exclaimed with a pretentious smile. Her words dripped with underlying disdain. "Chloe, you neglected to mention that they would be joining us," she continued, her tone filled with passive aggression. Starla wasted no time in summoning the waitress, ordering an additional chair with an air of entitlement.

Macy, undeterred by Starla's words, greeted the assembled company with a cheery disposition. She wore a delightful sundress adorned with a springy overlay, tastefully concealing her exquisitely sculpted physique. Kennedy, wearing a similar dress but without the overlay, shared her mother's tall and elegant stature, though their physical resemblances ended there.

"Well, well, well, if it isn't Nikki Witherspoon," Kennedy remarked, a hint of surprise mixed with suspicion in her voice. "What a surprise indeed. I never imagined our paths would cross again." Chloe shot Kennedy a silent plea, a look urging her to temper her words. Kennedy, catching the drift, cleared her throat and flopped down onto the extra chair the waitress had hastily brought in.

Meanwhile, Starla attempted to steer the conversation back on track, asserting her control over the situation. "We've been engaging in some rather intriguing conversation," she said, her tone commanding attention. "Nicole here has been enlightening us with her expertise in housing and finance. She's even acquired property in our city and is currently managing out of a lucrative piece of property a mile from our church. I've been telling Reginald how fortunate Chloe was to have her as a mentor." Starla's gaze bore into her husband, who had long since detached himself from the ongoing conversations. Chloe shook her head, exasperated, and mustered the courage to interject.

"Excuse me, I need to visit the ladies' room," she announced, rising abruptly from her seat and escaping the pandemonium. Kennedy, sensing her cousin's unease, excused herself as well and swiftly followed Chloe's path.

Once within the confines of the cramped restroom, Kennedy couldn't contain her curiosity any longer. "What in the world is going on? Why is Nikki here?" she inquired urgently, her voice tinged with concern.

"I don't know," Chloe replied, her frustration evident. "I didn't even know she remembered anything about our church."

"Wait... she came to church?"

"Yes, she did! I only found out afterward. Mom and Nikki bumped into each other near the foyer area, and that's when my mom invited her to brunch. I'm on the verge of losing it. This woman is cunning, rubbing her toes against my ankle."

"Disgusting. Look, Chloe, you need to act before Nikki's shenanigans escalate once again."

"What do you mean, 'escalate'? I set boundaries before, and they worked. I have not had any connection with her in over a year."

"You managed things well, but you still allowed Nikki access to your life and your bedroom after you broke things off. Especially since she was abusive. You made a huge mistake. I tried to tell you. She's quite persuasive. Seeing her show up out of the blue has me worried, cousin."

"I hear you. It makes me nervous too, but… it also stirs up conflicting emotions in me. I'm feeling lost once more," Chloe confessed, her hand absentmindedly scratching her forehead. She had come to terms with her sexuality, accepting her truth, yet she wasn't ready to thrust it upon anyone just yet. The Kimyatta incident was enough. The sight of Nikki had thrown her emotional equilibrium off-kilter, an uncomfortable place to be, especially when other aspects of her life seemed to be falling into place.

"Are you suggesting that you still have feelings for Nikki? Perhaps it's time for some soul-searching," Kennedy proposed gently, placing a comforting hand on Chloe's shoulder. "Personally, she wouldn't have a snowball in hell chance if it was me. She hit you more than once."

"She did."

"You didn't answer my question…do you still have feelings for this psycho?"

"I don't know. What I do know is that I am who I am. I was born gay. I find joy in the company of women. Men simply don't hold the same appeal for me. Women are more nurturing and trustworthy."

"I understand, and it's your prerogative to discover your true self. But can you handle keeping your identity hidden?"

"I don't know that either. It's challenging to conceal the truth, especially with my mom idolizing Nikki like some sort of god."

"Well, Nikki is far from divine. You know you can talk to Mom about this whole situation, right?"

"Yes, I've contemplated it countless times. Aunt Macy has always been easier to confide in than my mom," Chloe admitted as she grabbed a damp paper towel, pressing it against her forehead. Determination welled up within her. "I'm going to do it. I'm going to tell my parents."

"Right now…?" Kennedy's voice wavered with apprehension. She yearned for Chloe to step out of the shadows, but she wasn't sure if the middle of brunch was the most opportune moment.

"If I don't do it now, I never will. I've grown a lot over the past few years. Besides, it'll give me a chance to put Nikki in her place. Right now, she feels she has the upper hand because my parents are oblivious, but once I shine a light on the truth, darkness will no longer be her ally," Chloe declared resolutely, striding out of the restroom with unwavering determination. Kennedy trailed behind, astounded by this newfound side of Chloe she had never before witnessed.

"Mom, Dad…I…I've been wanting to say this for a while now. I know it's not the appropriate timing, but I've got to unload before I explode. I was born unique…"

Reginald finally tore his attention away from his phone, his eyes meeting Chloe's troubled gaze. "Of course, you were, honey… I've always said that" he said, concern lacing his voice. "But you look pale like you're not feeling well. Are you okay?" He rose from his seat, closing the distance between them.

"She's fine. Chloe, why are you standing? Sit down," Starla

commanded, her voice tight as she tried to maintain control of the situation.

"Obviously she's not fine. Sweetheart, go ahead with what you were about to say," Macy interjected, reaching out to touch Chloe's hand, offering comfort and support.

"Excuse me, but who asked you, Macy? She addressed me and her father, and you are neither," Starla retorted with anger in her tone. The room fell into an uneasy silence, all eyes fixed on the tense exchange. Nikki wore a devious smirk, her gaze fixed on Chloe. Starla's words were like venom, meant to sting.

"No, I have always been in a place to take up your slack when you were too busy to notice your daughter's needs," Macy struck back, her voice firm and resolute. She had reached her limit and refused to stay silent any longer.

"Mom, don't. This is not the place for a family argument. Let's go and allow Chloe and her parents the time to talk," Kennedy interjected, rising to her feet. "And that includes you, Nikki. You should leave and give them the space they need."

"By all means. I'm in agreement if that is what Chloe and Starla want," Nikki said, her voice laced with false innocence as she glanced around the room.

"Mom, Dad, I'm gay. I was born that way… I'm sorry if you don't agree, but it needs to be out in the open," Chloe revealed, her voice trembling with a mix of fear and vulnerability.

"What?" Reginald asked, his dismay evident in his voice. "What in the world are you saying?" He was shocked, unable to find the right words, while Starla, for the first time, was left speechless.

"I'm sorry, Daddy. Mom…say something…look, that isn't all," Chloe's voice faltered as she locked eyes with Nikki. She felt her strength waver as if her tongue had become glued to the roof of her mouth. "I had… I had a relationship with Nikki. It was during my first year of college, and…it continued into a romantic relationship."

Macy and Kennedy embraced Chloe, offering their support, and then they gathered their belongings, preparing to leave the restaurant. "Give me a call when you arrive home, okay?" Macy said softly before she and Kennedy departed, leaving Chloe to face the aftermath.

"Okay, let's not cause a scene. Everyone, please, let's discuss this," Reginald said, his tone calmer now as the waitress cleared the table. "Miss Witherspoon...what do you have to say for yourself?"

"I can explain. Chloe and I spent time together... look, I'm going to leave you all alone. This doesn't really involve me," Nikki responded with a mix of guilt and resignation.

"What the hell do you mean? Huh? It has everything to do with you. I ought to have you arrested or fired, or something," Starla erupted, her words a volatile blend of anger and disgust. "All this time, you've been parading around us like you had our daughter's best interests at heart, but you were turning her out?"

"Starla, let me handle this... let me—"

"No, Reginald. You've never handled anything. This is your fault. You've never scolded or talked to Chloe about these things," Starla accused, her eyes filling with tears.

"Mama, that's not fair. It's nobody's fault. It is what it is. I was wrong to keep all of this from you, and I'm sorry," Chloe's voice trembled, her vulnerability laid bare, yet there was empowerment within.

As silence settled around the brunch table, Nikki made her exit. With Reginald, Starla, and Chloe left alone, the three finally had a chance to hold a brief conversation before parting ways. The family faced a long road ahead, with the next hurdle being Chloe's acknowledgment of her identity to her church. While Reginald disagreed on its necessity, Starla had won the battle, insisting that Chloe speak with the Pastor immediately, given her prominent position in the ministry.

CHAPTER 25

NOBODY TOLD YOU IT WOULD BE EASY (STARLA'S POV)

Starla stormed ahead of Reginald as they burst through the front door of their home, still simmering with the tension that had hung heavy in the air during their silent car ride. Without a word, she slammed the door shut, shutting out both the world and her husband. The two had agreed to remain separate, but to spend time on Sundays, until they were ready to make a final decision. Now this incident threatened to strain their relationship even more.

In the solitude of their bedroom, Starla felt the weight of her world crashing down around her. Chloe's revelation had blindsided her, sending her spiraling into a whirlwind of emotions she could not begin to untangle. She stripped off her clothing with a forceful motion, shedding the burdens of the day and slipping into the comfort of a pair of soft shorts and a cotton t-shirt.

Reginald, finally breaking the uneasy silence, approached her tentatively. He began to unbutton the cuff of his shirt, a nervous gesture belying the gravity of the situation at hand. Starla paid him no mind; her silence spoke volumes.

"Why did you choose to speak up when you did?" Starla's voice was laced with a mixture of frustration and hurt. "You seemed so disconnected during brunch. And then, when Chloe spilled her unsweetened tea all over the place, you decided to speak, but without any authority."

Reginald's brow furrowed, confusion etching lines on his face. "I didn't want to cause a scene in a public restaurant. I understand you're embarrassed and overwhelmed, but we can't ignore this. We aren't exempt from these kinds of issues. Many parents are grappling with similar challenges."

Starla took a deep breath, her eyes red and puffy from unshed tears. "Do you think we failed our daughter?" The weight of those words hung heavy in the air.

Reginald's gaze softened, and he reached out to take Starla's hand. "I believe we did everything we could to provide for Chloe. Looking back, though, I can't help but wonder where the time went. Other fathers in my department talk about the amazing things they do with their daughters, and I can't help but feel like we fell short in time management."

Memories flooded Starla's mind, the hardships she had endured as a bank teller, the constant battle to balance work, studying, and raising Chloe alone while Reginald went out of the state to college. Grabbing Reginald's handkerchief, she wiped away a stray tear. "I remember all the sacrifices I made, the long nights of studying while managing work and taking care of our child. Everything I did, I did for us."

Reginald's arm found its way around Starla, offering a small solace in their shared pain. "You're right, it was never easy. I remember the struggles of juggling college and a demanding job."

A bitter edge crept into Starla's voice. "And then there was the constant comparison to Macy, the perfect neighbor. She had it all together, and Chloe adored her. Macy's perfect life - a clean house, hot meals, fresh laundry. She had to flaunt her perfection in my face, while Chloe worshipped the ground she walked on."

Reginald nodded, acknowledging the tense relationship between Starla and Macy. "True, but we can't deny the bond Macy and Chloe share. And Kennedy…they're more like sisters than cousins."

Starla paced the room, unable to contain her frustration. "Yes, but I wish Macy wouldn't rub it in. It's not her place."

Reginald rose from the bed, walking over to Starla and guiding her back into his embrace. Concerning the traumatic tension between you and Macy, I equally share in the tension. Broderick had never been one to speak up, but oftentimes I could sense how he viewed our family dynamics, causing me to feel somewhat less than a father when he shared about he and Kennedy's milestones… the tooth fairy moments to the driving lessons. Things I missed with Chloe. But I pressed on. After you became pregnant in our senior year in high school, my entire life changed. My focus became different. This mindset still drives me today, and Chloe somehow got lost in the shuffle between fulfilling the call of duty to succeed in a career versus succeeding as a father."

"True. Macy and Broderick never walked in those kinds of shoes," Starla responded to Reginald's remarks.

"We'll take this one day at a time. We'll stand by Chloe, no matter what." Reginald affirmed.

A glimmer of hope sparked in Starla's eyes, mingled with deep concern. "But we can't ignore the reality that not everyone shares the same views on same-sex relationships. We need to protect Chloe from the judgment and shame that may come. Remember what happened to Mario? Rumors spread about him being gay, and our former pastor forced him to resign. I heard it through the grapevine."

Reginald's hold on Starla tightened as the weight of their daughter's journey became even more burdensome. Even his own emotional concerns began to surface, as he recalled how certain key people from his family felt about same sex relationships. He grappled with how he would answer if anyone would question his stand. "You have a point. We'll navigate this carefully. One step at a time. But ultimately, we'll stand by Chloe, no matter what the church or anyone else thinks."

Starla welcomed Reginald's embrace, finding comfort in his touch. They were in this together, facing the challenges that lie ahead with unwavering determination and love.

As Starla and Reginald stood wrapped in each other's embrace, their hushed conversation was interrupted by the shrill ring of a phone. Starla quickly reached for her cell, seeing Chloe's name flashing on the screen. She answered with a smile, grateful for the distraction.

"Hey, sweetheart," Starla said, her voice filled with warmth.

"Hi, Mom," Chloe replied, her voice tinged with concern. "I just wanted to check on you and Dad. I hope everything went okay after I left. I know you two are trying to work on your marriage and I don't want to be a burden."

Reginald took the phone from Starla and spoke into it, "Hey, Chlo. Yeah, we're home now, just having a talk about everything."

Starla watched her husband's expression soften as he listened to their daughter on the other end. Chloe's voice had always held a special place in his heart, and Starla could tell he was glad to hear from her.

"I'm sorry for the way things went down," Chloe said, her voice carrying a mix of sorrow and determination. "I didn't want to ruin the brunch. I just couldn't keep it to myself anymore, you know?"

"We understand, sweetheart," Reginald replied gently. "Sometimes things happen, and we must find the right time to talk about them. Although we've not shown it too well, we're here for you, always."

Chloe's gratitude was present in her voice. "Thank you, Dad. That means a lot to me."

Regardless of her anger toward Nikki and the shock that Chloe had caused, Starla felt a surge of pride for her daughter's bravery, and she couldn't help but chime in, "You don't need to apologize for being true to yourself, Chloe. We love you, and we're proud of you. I'm sorry it had to come to something like this for us to engage in a family conversation."

Chloe felt relieved. "I love you both too, more than you'll ever know."

The conversation continued, and they spoke for a while longer, catching up on lighter topics to ease the tension that had hung in the air. Reginald couldn't help but share some of his classic jokes sometimes shared with his country club colleagues, making Chloe laugh, and Starla shared a funny anecdote from work. After all, this was all the couple knew, work and community events.

As they laughed and connected as a family, Starla felt a renewed sense of hope. Their bond had not been strong, but they would face whatever challenges together. After ending the call, she turned to Reginald with a soft smile.

"I'm glad she called," Starla said. "It's a good reminder that we're in this together."

Reginald nodded; his eyes filled with love for his wife. "You're right. And we'll navigate this journey together as a family, even if it means missing out on some of the community events. Also, it'll give us time to fix us. I still love you," Reginald said.

With that, they embraced once more, cherishing the love and support that held them close. No matter what the future held, they knew they could face it with strength, unity, and the unbreakable love of a family.

CHAPTER 26

I'M HERE FOR IT

Whispers of secrets and gossip permeated the air, swirling like dark shadows in the depths of people's minds. It took just a week for the scandalous tale of Chloe's supposed gay lifestyle to spread like wildfire, leaving her vulnerable and exposed in the judgmental eyes of the community. And if that wasn't enough, the news of Nikki, the infamous black sheep who had acquired an investment property just a mile from the sanctity of the church, only added fuel to the ever-blazing fire.

"Ion know what this world coming to but these young people need Jesus!" Sister Lula exclaimed as she and one of the other women wobbled out of the market as Chloe hurried into her vehicle to escape the hurricane from their piercing words. One of the women had been her Sunday School teacher many years ago, she was not the one speaking, but her stare pierced a hole into Chloe's soul. A day or so prior, it was told Chloe that some of the younger people were proud to take a stand that it was Chloe's choice to love whom she wanted and were disappointed that their church leadership did not support the non-binary ideology.

Settling into her car seat with the belts buckled into place, a vibration from her phone startled her out of the deep sea of thoughts.

With tension thick in the air, Nikki's voice came through the phone, her tone nonchalant as if oblivious to the turmoil she had stirred. "Hi, Chloe. How's it going?"

Chloe's voice was sharp and icy, desperation fighting against her composure. "You," Chloe blurted out, her frustration barely contained. "Stop calling. I won't change my phone number just because of this. I've had it for eight years."

"No need to worry about that," Nikki reassured, her voice dripping with a mystery that piqued Chloe's curiosity. "Look, this is a business call, in case you were wondering."

A sense of unease settled upon Chloe, her heart pounding in her chest as she tried to make sense of Nikki's intentions. She seemed to have a split personality, and Chloe no longer felt the connection she had prior. "What kind of business?"

"I'm staying at the property I recently acquired, just a mile away from your beloved church," Nikki revealed, her words mysterious and intriguing. "But things have gone south, and I thought maybe you could handle it. Now you know me. I don't like to fail at anything I set out to accomplish."

"Why would you want to do that?" Chloe couldn't help but be suspicious, memories of past controversies were still fresh in her mind. Like possessiveness and weird mood swings.

"Because, despite everything, I still believe you're the best person for the job," Nikki confessed, her words filled with regret and longing. "I bought it for you as a graduation gift, intended to surprise you. But then, well you know...things happened between us, and I decided not to mention it. I told myself to move on, but honestly, I don't know of anyone else I want to trust with such an important business venture."

Chloe struggled to process Nikki's unexpected offer. Conflicting emotions surged within her, clouding her judgment and making her tread cautiously. "Why are you telling me this now?"

"Because I can't manage it with my schedule, and since it's near your home, it just seemed like the perfect opportunity to make things right," Nikki reasoned, her voice tinged with vulnerability. "Let this be my way of apologizing for all the trouble I've caused. I never meant to hurt you. And, Chloe, I have to say it… I love you. I can't control how I feel."

Silence hung heavy between them, the weight of their shared history and unresolved emotions consuming the atmosphere. Chloe struggled to find her voice, her heart warring against her mind. She knew the turmoil that awaited her if she allowed Nikki back into her life. She was well aware of the kind of control and difficulty that Nikki's presence brought. But at the same time, a part of her could not deny the lingering feelings that churned deep inside her.

"Nikki, it's thoughtful of you to offer me the property," Chloe finally spoke, her words laced with gratitude and caution. "Thank you for thinking of me. But I can't accept it."

Confusion filled Nikki's voice; her determination unyielding. "I don't understand why not. Let's meet tomorrow over a cup of coffee. I'll bring the paperwork. All it needs is your signature. It can be yours. I've already started the process. What do you say?"

Searching for clarity within the chaos of her emotions, Chloe couldn't help but feel the echoes of her past self, the young freshman swept up in the mighty whirlwind of Nikki's influence. "Okay, let's meet at one of the downtown coffee shops, tomorrow morning. Say, seven-thirty. Does that work for you?"

"Perfect," Nikki confirmed, and as the call ended, Chloe's mind raced with swirling thoughts. *Why had she agreed to this? What had compelled her to disregard her own reservations and engage with the person who had caused her so much pain?*

After settling into her apartment later that day, her hand reached for her well-worn Bible and notepad, seeking comfort and guidance. With a myriad of contradictory thoughts competing for her attention, Chloe prepared to read and reflect, hoping to find clarity before she surrendered herself to the unknown. She was about to turn to a specific verse in her Bible when her attention was drawn to words from another passage. They read, *"The LORD will guide you always; he will satisfy your needs in a sun-scorched land and will strengthen your frame. You will be like a well-watered garden, like a spring whose waters never fail."* These words spoke to her deeply and she realized she had never noticed them before. She had been feeling drained and exhausted lately, like a plant in a desert with no water. "Wow, what an impressive promise. Lord, please rejuvenate my mind and give me the grace to know Your will in all things, in Jesus Name...Amen."

With that, she decided to call it a night and trust God for the satisfaction and the fuel to face her tomorrow.

CHAPTER 27

I'M ON MY WAY

"I'm on my way," Chloe declared, her voice exuding both determination and uncertainty as she ended the call with Nikki. The phone had been ringing constantly, and Nikki's concern as to whether Chloe would show up was evident. Through her morning routine of exercising, showering, and styling her hair, Chloe couldn't escape the thoughts that raced through her mind. "I'm on my way, but where am I going?" she pondered, her voice trailing off like a gripping suspense movie.

As she prepared to leave, Chloe knew she needed to talk to someone she could trust, someone who would provide wisdom and understanding. Dialing her Aunt Macy, she felt a sense of relief wash over her just by hearing her chipper voice on the other end.

"Hello, sweetheart. How's your morning going?" Macy greeted, her warm tone wrapping around Chloe like a comforting embrace. Gathering her belongings, Chloe took a deep breath before confiding in her aunt.

"Hi, Auntie. My morning is going okay. I'm headed out the

door," Chloe replied, gratitude washing over her for a moment to spend with Macy.

"Okay. What's on your mind?" Macy inquired gently, her caring tone encouraging Chloe to share her inner turmoil.

"Auntie, things have been going great so far with my job, the ministry, and even my relationship with my parents, but..." Chloe's voice wavered, uncertainty tainting her words.

"But you're worried about your sexual preference and how others will perceive it," Macy interjected, her intuition keenly attuned to Chloe's emotions.

"So, you and Kennedy have been discussing this, huh?" Chloe remarked, half-jokingly, knowing her aunt's intuition was almost uncanny.

"Nope. I sense it in your voice. I can hear the conflict in your heart. I may hold certain beliefs, but that doesn't mean I won't stand with you in love and support of your decisions," Macy assured her. "You have the right to choose, but you must be prepared for the consequences of every decision you make, whether it's about your sexual preference, your career, your home, or anything else."

Chloe nodded, absorbing her aunt's wisdom. "I thought I had it all figured out, but... Nikki's presence here has thrown me off, and..."

"Are you in love with her?" Macy asked gently, probing deeper into the core of Chloe's emotions.

"That's the issue. Sometimes I feel I am, but at other times, I don't know," Chloe admitted, her inner turmoil laid bare.

"Honey, I know how much you love devoting yourself to the scriptures. Look within yourself. What does God's word say about confusion?" Macy prompted, urging her niece to reflect on her faith.

"A lot, I'm sure. But it's more than just confusion. Nikki has been there for me in so many ways. She helped me through housing issues in college, guided me through financial troubles, and supported me in my major…not to mention she's partly responsible for the empowerment I've gained over the years." Chloe recounted, gratitude mingling with her uncertainty.

Macy offered a fresh perspective, "Think about it. Were those tangible contributions a part of her mentorship services? If the answer is yes, then Nikki was merely fulfilling her commitment to you as she would with any mentee."

Chloe's eyes widened as she considered her aunt's words. "I never thought of it that way. But…there is the reality that we crossed the mentorship line. Auntie, I'm almost at my destination. Our talk has shed some light, though."

"I'm glad to hear that. Before you go, remember to consider what's healthy for you, and be true to the life you've chosen as a gay woman," Macy advised, her love and concern evident in her parting words.

"Yes, Ma'am. I hear you. I love you," Chloe replied, a newfound sense of clarity settling within her.

"Honey, I love you too," Macy said, her affectionate tone resonating even after the call had ended.

~

Nikki stood at a corner table; her smile bright as the sun as she signaled for Chloe to join her. The cozy coffee shop was crowded, filled with the hustle and bustle of people placing orders and hurrying on their way. Chloe noticed the subtle tension in the air as she walked towards Nikki, wondering what awaited her.

As they faced each other, Nikki's smile transformed into a somber expression. She had already ordered Chloe's favorite latte, a small gesture that brought back memories of their past. "How was your drive over?"

Chloe took a sip of her latte, trying to steady her nerves. "It was good. I had an enjoyable discussion with my aunt prior to leaving home. She always makes me feel better," she replied, attempting to deflect the growing tension.

"Are you okay?" Nikki asked, her voice carrying a mixture of intimidation and frustration. She leaned forward, her eyes fixed on Chloe. "Did your aunt tell you to turn me down?"

Chloe sighed, feeling the weight of the situation. "No, I didn't discuss that with her… listen, what are we doing? We ended things a long time ago, and I think it's best to leave it in the past. I don't want to reopen our case, so to speak. A romantic relationship isn't what I want right now."

Nikki's eyes narrowed with a hint of challenge in her voice. "I see you're still the detailed, black-and-white Chloe. But life isn't always so neatly packaged. If I've taught you anything, it's to follow your heart. Your heart, Chloe, not someone else's."

Chloe hesitated for a moment. Nikki's words struck a chord within her, but she had her reasons for wanting to move on. "I am following my heart. I love my job, living apart from my parents, and my church ministry… all of it is what I have in my heart. I'm eagerly awaiting the next phase of my life, and I don't think God intended for you to be a part of that phase. I'm sorry."

Nikki's gaze softened, disappointment mingling with shock as she began to notice the change in Chloe. "Don't be sorry, especially if you believe God doesn't want me in your life. But here," she said, reaching into her briefcase and pulling out an envelope. "Take these and read them over. Sleep on it, give it some extra thought. If you still feel that you don't want to manage this property, then I'll pass it on to someone else. Fair enough?"

Chloe nodded, accepting the envelope with a mix of curiosity and caution. As she opened it, a sense of unease crept over her. She knew Nikki wouldn't give up easily, and the stakes were higher than ever.

At that moment, a familiar voice broke through Chloe's

thoughts. "Chloe?" the voice called from behind her. She turned, surprised to see Aaron, the pastor's nephew, standing there dressed in a sharp suit. His smile was warm, and his voice carried a distinct charm.

"Good morning, Aaron. Do you have an early morning conference or a funeral or something?" Chloe asked, her curiosity piqued.

Aaron chuckled; his voice filled with warmth. "No, this is just how I typically dress. It's a Conner tradition, you know? Both my father and grandfather would scold me if they caught me downtown without a suit on. Silly, I know, but it's a preacher thing."

Chloe smiled, finding his adherence to tradition endearing. "You're right, it's silly. But I admire that you hold onto the traditions of your family. I never got to know either of my grandfathers; they both passed away when I was young."

Interrupting their conversation, Nikki interjected herself. "I'm Nikki, a long-time friend of Chloe's. Would you like to join us?"

Aaron introduced himself, shaking Nikki's hand politely. "I'm Aaron Conner. Thank you for the offer, but I'm just going to grab a coffee and head to a meeting. I'll take a rain check, though," he said, his eyes lingering on Chloe with an intensity that didn't go unnoticed.

As Aaron left, Nikki's voice dripped with suspicion. "Well, looks like somebody is crushing," she commented, her voice loaded with insinuation.

Chloe dismissed Nikki's comment, trying to keep her emotions in check. "That's absurd. He's just friendly because of our connection at the church."

Nikki stood to depart, leaving Chloe feeling like the aftermath of a storm. The emotions stirred by their conversation, and the unexpected encounter with Aaron, weighed heavily on her.

Taking one last sip of her beverage, Chloe planned to leave but to her surprise, Aaron had stepped back into the coffee shop.

There was a man following close behind who looked to be in distress. Chloe's eyes followed hard after Aaron. There was something about his mannerism that caused her senses to stand in attention. From the way he moved, to the way he spoke, to the way he stood at the counter, paying for a cup of coffee and a croissant for someone who looked to be in need.

"Change your mind about your meeting?" Chloe asked as Aaron turned from the counter.

"Nope! About to head on over. Hey, what about me taking you up on that raincheck for lunch today...right here?"

"The raincheck actually belongs to Nikki," Chloe said as she smirked. Talking with Aaron brought out her natural personality. Only a few people had ever been able to do so.

"Right. But...you witnessed it, so what do you say?' Aaron continued.

"I don't think so. I have piles of work to get done and probably won't do lunch today, but thanks for the gesture."

"Where is work, if you don't mind me asking?"

"Typically, I would mind, but since you're Pastor Conner's family, it's KW's."

"Impressive. I've heard great things about that firm. Was thinking of checking you all out for my next venture," Aaron replied.

"We'd be delighted to assist you. So...see you at church on Sunday," Chloe said as she looked into Aaron's deep brown eyes before dashing toward the door.

"See you around," Aaron said as he watched Chloe exit. The entire atmosphere appeared to change for both individuals as they resumed their morning routines. Chloe shook the melancholy chill from her heart as she entered her vehicle while Aaron began to quote "Jesus keep me near the Cross!"

CHAPTER 28

NO RESPECT (NIKKI'S POV)

In the luxurious space of her Victorian-style vacation home, Nikki paced back and forth, her heart ached with every step she took. Seeking solace in the memories of her connection with Chloe, she scrutinized every conversation, replaying them in her mind like a broken record, desperate to find lingering traces of affection. With a tight grip on her water bottle, she mused, "Well, she did show up for coffee, didn't she?" as if engaging in a conversation with an imaginary friend. That simple affirmation fueled Nikki's determination to draw Chloe back into her life like a spider skillfully weaving a web to ensnare its prey.

Stepping out onto the sunlit patio, her glimmer of hope was shattered by the unwelcome intrusion of her phone. As she glanced at the caller ID, she crinkled her face with reluctance at the thought of speaking with her mother. "Nicole Witherspoon," Nikki greeted halfheartedly, pretending to be busy with work.

"Hello Nikki, dear. How are you?" came her mother's concerned yet nosy voice, a touch of worry creeping into her words.

"Oh, good, just swamped with work. What is it? What do you

need, Mom?" Nikki replied with an edge of frustration, prancing from the patio back into the living area.

"Why... do I always have to need something from you when I call?" her mother's voice sounded hurt, her passivity seeping through.

"That's how it usually goes," Nikki sighed, her patience wearing thin.

"I haven't heard from you in a while, and I just wanted to make sure you're doing alright," her mom's voice carried genuine concern, a rare moment of sincerity in their complicated relationship.

"Been busy, Mom," Nikki replied dismissively, her mind still preoccupied with thoughts of Chloe.

"Well, how are all those fancy houses and the beautiful young people you're helping on the college campus?" her mother inquired, attempting to bridge the distance between them.

"Everything's fine, Mom… Look, if you're okay, I really have a ton of work to get back to," Nikki hurriedly responded, her words dripping with haste.

"Dear, are you still taking your meds? Have you visited with Dr. Crokard recently?" her mother's worry spilled through the phone.

"Is that why you're calling me and interrupting my work? To be nosy?" Nikki snapped, her frustration bubbling over.

"No… that's ridiculous," her mom defended herself, hurt by Nikki's accusation.

"I believe it is. You're lying," Nikki shot back, her emotions unrestrained.

"Nikki, I'm your mother. I'm concerned. The doctor's office called the other day… they say you've skipped your last couple of appointments. I'm worried, dear. You shouldn't jeopardize your health. It's important to keep your appointments and take your medication. You remember what happened—"

"Why are you always bringing up the past? Look, Mother… I'm

fine. If I tell you that all is well, then believe it. Stop being nosy. Pay attention to your own health," Nikki abruptly ended the call, the pain of unresolved issues lingering in the silence that followed.

Disturbed by the conversation, Nikki reached for her empty prescription bottle of Rexulti, realization washing over her like a wave. Her mother was right; she hadn't taken her medication in quite a while. Dismissing the need for it, she continued to sip her water, lost in contemplation of her plans to rekindle her relationship with Chloe. Taking decisive action, she decided to contact Chloe's employer and arrange meetings with her immediate supervisor, hoping to explore real estate investments together – anything to remain connected to Chloe's world.

In her well-arranged home office, bathed in the soft glow of warm lamplight, Nikki crafted an email to one of her former colleagues, a person with valuable connections to Chloe's real estate company. The email carried a client proposal, meticulously composed to catch the attention of the executives. With her undeniable influence and charisma, Nikki was confident she could secure an appointment to meet with them, but she yearned for it to happen sooner rather than later, as her impatience gnawed at her like a persistent ache.

As she plotted her strategy, Nikki's mind turned to the vulnerabilities she knew existed in Chloe's personality. Deep in thought, she pondered ways to manipulate the situation, convincing Chloe that she misunderstood her actions, and that no one loved and cared for her the way she did. A cunning plan formed in her mind - she would target Chloe's relationship with her mother. If she could drive a wider wedge between them, she believed she could exploit Chloe's emotional vulnerabilities and draw her back into her orbit. "Yes, you were broken when I found you, abandoned in your soul… and I can continue to shape you," she murmured to herself, staring into the void while clutching her phone, fixated on an old photograph of Chloe.

Summoning the courage to execute her scheme, Nikki composed a text message to Chloe, inquiring whether she had decided on the property offered the day before. The phone's soft glow illuminated her intent gaze as she pressed the send button, her heart pounding with anticipation.

A response from Chloe appeared on the screen, and Nikki's breath caught for a moment. "Hi, Nikki. I have decided not to accept the property. Thank you for your generous heart. Take care."

The words hit Nikki like a sucker punch, leaving her momentarily breathless. Unbeknownst to her, she had clenched her teeth so tightly that her bottom lip was now bleeding, a physical manifestation of her frustration and disappointment. Her carefully crafted plan had hit a snag, but Nikki was not one to give up easily. She knew she needed to adapt and find another angle to reel Chloe back into her grasp.

Taking a deep breath to steady herself, she wiped the blood from her lip with a tissue, her mind already racing with new schemes and tactics. If she couldn't convince Chloe with gifts and offerings, then perhaps she could appeal to her emotions in other ways. Nikki's determination only grew, and she vowed to leave no stone unturned until she achieved her desired outcome – to have Chloe once again within her grasp, entangled in a web of her own making.

Nikki's heart raced as she clicked on Chloe's social media profile, her fingers trembling. She watched the pop-up tab take over her screen and imagined what they would talk about. Minutes dragged by without a single response. A lump formed in her throat as she logged off and reached for a bottle of wine, desperately trying to distract herself from the pain with one of her favorite movies.

CHAPTER 29

CHLOE'S NEW NORMAL

Speeding through the swarming traffic, Chloe's heart raced in rhythm with the anxious beat of her pulse. She had to make it to the church thirty minutes early for her meeting with Pastor Conner, and the rush was taking its toll on her composure. As she pulled into the parking area, a few fellow choir members exchanged warm smiles, unaware of the turmoil within her.

"Sister Chloe, so glad you could make it. Have a seat," Pastor Conner's authoritative voice greeted her, drawing her attention. He was a middle-aged man with distinguished salt-and-pepper hair, and his presence commanded respect. Despite her best efforts, nerves tightened her stomach, rendering her rehearsed lines a blur. Trying to find some sense of normalcy, she asked, "How was your day, Pastor?"

"Busy as usual. Seems like some issues never arise until Sunday or Wednesday, the days when I need as few fires to put out as possible. Thanks for asking. I'll get right to the matter at hand," Pastor Conner replied, his gaze fixed on Chloe's face. The gravity of the conversation weighed heavily upon her, and she accepted the bottled water he offered with a grateful nod.

"It seems there are rumors floating in the air concerning a certain woman from your past and… well, your sexual preference," Pastor Conner addressed the delicate topic with measured caution. "The Bible warns against busybodies, so I don't typically pay attention to gossip. I like to speak directly to the people involved."

Chloe cleared her throat, trying to steady her voice as she admitted, "Yes, Pastor, the woman they are speaking of is Nicole Witherspoon. We knew each other during my college days, and she recently reappeared when she attended our church. She's managing some properties here for her real estate business."

The moment of truth hung heavy in the air as Pastor Conner pressed on, "Do you engage in romantic relationships with those of the same sex?"

Chloe's breath caught, and beads of sweat formed on her forehead. Summoning courage, she answered, "Yes, Pastor. I have in the past, and I do prefer women over men. It's just who I am, and I believe I was born with this tendency. Is this a problem?"

Pastor Conner's demeanor remained composed as he replied, "Sister Chloe, it is a problem with God, so that makes it a problem with me. But I cannot judge you. The scriptures are clear on the matter, but my philosophy is to let the wheat and tares grow together and let God separate—no judgment from me. However, I'll need to discuss your situation with the Board of Trustees at our next meeting. You understand."

Chloe's heart sank at the prospect of her personal life becoming the subject of church scrutiny. "Honestly, I don't understand. What does my preference have to do with my church attendance? I'm currently not in an active relationship, by the way."

"The fact that you have confessed to being gay is enough for me to bring it before the Board due to your position on the drama ministry team. We usually arrange counseling sessions for these situations, not out of judgment, but out of love and guidance based on God's word," Pastor Conner explained, trying to strike a compassionate tone.

"It still feels like a judgment call if my ministry responsibilities are at stake," Chloe said, determined to stand by her truth, even in the face of uncertainty. "Besides, aren't there laws to protect people's sexual orientation choices?"

"There are laws, but we also have documented By-laws specifically for our ministry. Now, these by-laws are subject to being revised from time to time as the board sees fit. I do understand what you are saying about your current situation. Feel free to remain a part of the ministry until the board meets, and we schedule the counseling sessions. Is that agreeable to you?" Pastor Conner offered a temporary resolution.

"Certainly, Pastor." Chloe said tightly, her knuckles white as she clutched the edges of the chair. She had steeled herself to accept the challenge that stood before her, yet she still felt a wave of apprehension coursing through her veins. "I…so how often are these counseling sessions?"

"Shouldn't be no more than four sessions over a space of five to six weeks…give or take. I'll be in touch with you soon to let you know when these will start," Pastor Conner replied calmly, before getting up and reaching for his tablet and Bible. Chloe forced a nod of affirmation, thanked him, and hurriedly exited the room, her heart heavy with dread.

~

The week had flown by in a whirlwind, leaving Chloe grappling with the weight of recent events—the unsettling meeting with Nikki and the disheartening conversation with Pastor Conner. Now, her mother's unexpected text message demanded her attention. Phoning Kennedy, Chloe knew she was busy with her after-school cheer squad but needed to talk.

"Hey, Cuzzo...what's up?" Kennedy's voice sounded cheerful, but Chloe could sense her busyness.

"It's been bananas! Everything's been so crazy," Chloe replied, her emotions still raw.

"I've heard all the talk about you and Nikki. People can be so messy," Kennedy chimed in, getting straight to the point.

"That's an understatement. She's practically moved here, managing properties, and offering me one as a gift. It's overwhelming," Chloe explained, feeling the weight of the situation.

"Sounds like she's trying to reel you back in. You must have made quite an impression on that woman. What did you two do? Just saying," Kennedy teased, trying to lighten the mood.

"Kennedy!" Chloe said, "Not in the mood for humor."

"Sorry, sorry. It's just... it's been years, Chloe. She's still pursuing you even after you've made it clear it's over. She's obsessed," Kennedy stated, her concern evident.

"I think we had something special once, and maybe she just needs understanding and counseling or something," Chloe reasoned, trying to find a compassionate perspective.

"You might be right, but that's not your responsibility. She needs to move on and respect your boundaries," Kennedy asserted, supporting her cousin.

Changing the subject, Chloe shared her recent meeting with Pastor Conner, where he had inquired about her sexual preference and was now planning to bring it before the board and arrange counseling sessions. Kennedy wasn't surprised, as she had warned Chloe about this possibility after college.

"I've always encouraged you to live your truth, Chloe. It's your choice, and I respect that. I'm not into dating women, but everyone should be free to make their own choices," Kennedy affirmed.

Chloe expressed her frustration at having to go through counseling and how she felt it was unfair. Kennedy empathized but mentioned that if it was part of the church's procedures and bylaws, there might not be much Chloe could do unless she wanted to consider leaving.

"You remember Tina Culpepper? She used to be on the usher's auxiliary board. She was a lesbian, and when the board found out, she refused counseling and eventually left," Kennedy recalled, providing another perspective.

Chloe was taken aback, realizing that others had faced similar situations in the past. As the conversation continued, Chloe's thoughts shifted to the trauma she had experienced years ago at camp, particularly involving Ms. Monet. The memories had rarely resurfaced since college, but now they thundered in her mind like an amplified boom box.

"Kennedy… I might need to talk about something from the past…about what happened at…" Chloe hesitated, unsure if she was ready to confront those memories.

"I'm here for you, Chloe. We can talk whenever you're ready. Take your time," Kennedy reassured her, offering support and understanding.

"Thanks. I need to go now. My mom wants to see me before I head home. I don't know what's waiting for me there," Chloe said, feeling a mix of anxiety and apprehension.

"Alright, we'll talk soon. Take care, girl," Kennedy bid her farewell.

Ending the call, Chloe's mind was fraught with dread, not only from the impending meeting with her mother but also from the resurfacing memories of her traumatic encounters with Ms. Monet. She knew she couldn't keep avoiding these issues; they demanded to be acknowledged and addressed, no matter how difficult it might be.

CHAPTER 30

CHLOE'S WEB

As Chloe walked up the path to her mom and dad's porch, the familiar scent of her aunt's cooking across the way wrapped around her like a warm embrace. But her headache and the weight of the day's events dulled her senses. She knew she had to confront her mother's urgent matter, yet her appetite was nonexistent after forgetting to eat lunch amid the turmoil.

"Mom! I'm here... Mom!" Chloe called out, seeking her mother's presence to address the impending issue.

"Coming! I'll be right there," Starla's voice rang out, as Chloe sank into the cozy couch, resting her head on the arm, trying to find some respite from her pounding headache.

"Hi Sweetheart," Starla greeted with concern, leaning in to give Chloe a tender kiss. "You don't look so good," she added, gently placing her hand on Chloe's forehead.

"I'm fine. Just forgot to eat lunch, and it's been a long day. Anyway, you sounded like you have something urgent to discuss?" Chloe replied, trying to shake off her discomfort.

Sitting on the adjacent end of the sofa, Starla fumbled with her hair before facing Chloe. "Yes... I heard from Miss Witherspoon today. She tells me you've turned down a lucrative investment opportunity?"

Chloe sighed, feeling annoyed by Nikki's relentless persistence. "She never knows when to stop. I turned down her offer, yes."

Starla's face grew serious. "She also mentioned something about some secret traumatic incident you had at camp. And she somehow implied it was my fault?"

Chloe's headache intensified, her heart pounding in her ears. "She told you that? Wait…what exactly did she tell you?" Chloe asked, stunned by Nikki's audacity.

Starla's eyes welled with tears, her hurt evident. "She said something about you experiencing a traumatic incident at camp and that because I wasn't in your life, you're struggling to make important decisions. Chloe, you had no right to confide in a perfect stranger about something traumatic and not talk to me." Starla expressed, her voice trembling.

Chloe's heart sank as she realized her mistake. "Mom, I didn't mean to hurt you. I couldn't talk about it with anyone… the words wouldn't come."

"But you told her. Why didn't you talk to me? What happened at camp that was so traumatic?" Starla demanded, her emotions simmering with anger and hurt.

Chloe's throat felt constricted, her words caught in a web of pain and fear. Tears welled in her eyes as she struggled to find her voice. "I was… I… Mama, one of the counselors took advantage of me. I was so scared… I asked if I could leave, but you had meetings all week and refused to pick me up," Chloe confessed, her voice trembling with raw emotion.

Starla's face paled; her anger momentarily forgotten as she absorbed her daughter's painful revelation. "Chloe… I didn't know…how exactly were you taken advantage of? I didn't know," she whispered, her heart aching for her daughter's pain, but shifting back into feelings of betrayal, she scolded once more,

"Nikki knows something intimate about you and I didn't know makes me angry. Now, Nikki didn't give any detail, so what was it?"

Chloe felt a coldness in her mother's response, one she hadn't experienced before. "So, you're angry because Nikki knows something you don't, but what about being angry because someone took advantage of me? You don't care about me!" Chloe's voice cracked with hurt and frustration as she rose from the couch, seeking to escape the suffocating atmosphere.

"Get back here! Chloe! That's not it. I do care about you, and that's why I'm asking. Chloe!" Starla's voice echoed, as the weight of her daughter's pain settled heavily on her heart.

The air felt tense with unspoken emotions, leaving both mother and daughter in turmoil. Chloe needed space to process her feelings, and Starla grappled with the knowledge of her daughter's trauma and the guilt of not being there when she needed her the most. Not to mention Nikki's involvement. The evening turned into a battleground of emotions, and the road to healing would require both understanding and empathy.

Chloe's cheeks were wet with tears, and her hands shook as she tried to avoid eye contact with her mother. A knot in the pit of Chloe's stomach tightened as she spoke. "It had to do with the ASL lessons," she said with a quivering voice. She reached for her keys, desperate to escape the conversation.

Starla stepped forward and blocked the door. "I'm your mother and I demand you to tell me," Starla said, anger radiating from her crossed arms. The knot in Chloe's stomach tightened further. She knew that telling the truth would only lead to more hurtful comments about how young she was when it happened. Guilt weighed on her shoulders like an oppressive fog. "I felt like she always put me on the spot, and I got teased a lot, most called me a goody two shoes," Chloe lied, desperately trying to make her exit.

As the night settled in, Chloe found herself in the quiet solitude of her own apartment. The turmoil of the day had left her emotionally drained, and she longed for a moment of rest. The soft glow of her bedside lamp offered a gentle comfort as she curled up on her bed, wrapped in a cozy blanket.

Her mind wandered back to the memories of that fateful camp experience, the wounds of the past now resurfacing like relentless waves crashing upon her shores. She had carried the weight of that trauma in the depths of her soul for so long, burying it beneath layers of silence and pain. But Nikki's audacity had torn open those old scars, exposing them to the rawness of the present.

Chloe knew that counseling was desperately needed, but the emotional journey ahead felt overwhelming. There were three pressing issues that demanded her attention, each pulling her in different directions like a deadly storm.

First, she needed to confront her true feelings for Nikki. The memories of their past relationship lingered like ghosts in her heart, and she couldn't deny the connection they once shared. However, she also recognized the toxic and possessive nature of Nikki's pursuit, which left her feeling suffocated and unsettled. Chloe knew she must find clarity within herself before she could move forward.

Second, the imminent possibility of her ASL ministry coming to an end at her beloved church weighed heavily on her mind. For years, the ministry had been her sanctuary, a place where she found purpose and community. The thought of it dissolving left her heart aching with a profound sense of loss. She questioned whether she could stay connected to the church in any other capacity or if it was time to seek a new spiritual home.

Lastly, her relationship with her parents needed healing. Chloe longed for the opportunity to pour out her pain in words, to express the loneliness and hurt she felt as a child. The camp incident was just one layer of her deeply rooted emotions, and she knew there was a load of untold feelings that needed to be explored and addressed.

Just as she was lost in her thoughts, a text notification snapped her back to the present. It was Pastor Conner's secretary, informing her of a counseling session scheduled for Saturday morning with Minister Aaron Conner. While her initial instinct was to ignore it, Chloe decided to entertain the message and respond with a hint of sarcasm, trying to mask her anxieties.

With a tub of her favorite ice cream in hand, Chloe settled in for a night of reflection and self-care. She allowed her emotions to flow freely, acknowledging the pain and fear she carried within.

As the moon cast its soft glow through her window, Chloe whispered affirmations of courage and resilience to herself, vowing to face her fears and embrace her truth. The journey ahead would be tough, but she was ready to embark on the path of self-discovery and healing. With each passing moment, she grew more determined to reclaim her voice and find the strength to face whatever lay ahead. After all, she found joy in knowing that even though things looked bad, she had been empowered and was not the same fearful freshman college student. At least she had mastered something from her past relationship with Nikki.

CHAPTER 31

CHLOE'S CAREER POV

Stepping briskly through the parking lot of her real estate firm, Chloe rehearsed the details of the agenda items for the executive committee meeting scheduled to start in a half hour. She typically preferred early morning meetings over afternoon ones, but this one involved her making her first real presentation. Being nervous was an understatement. Walking into her office, logging into her laptop, and pulling out her portfolio, she began to affirm her courage, boldness, and ownership of the situation at hand. "You've got this. You've spent the last three weeks preparing, praying, and planning. You cannot fail," is what she uttered as she took a deep breath, hoping to calm herself.

Just then, the office door creaked open, and Matilda peeped her head in. "Chloe, Mr. Stephens wants a word with you before the meeting."

Chloe's heart skipped a beat, wondering what Mr. Stephens could possibly want. "Absolutely. I will be right there," she said with confidence, though her heart still raced as she proceeded to Mr. Stephens' office. Dontavious Stephens was one of the most aggressive executives in the company, but at the same time, the youngest on staff. He was all about business and professionalism, and everyone had great respect for him. As Chloe entered his office, she noticed the walls adorned with framed accolades and certificates, and the light of a desk lamp illuminating the room. It seemed to hum with an invisible force, reflecting Mr. Stephens' energy.

"Good morning, Mr. Stephens. You wanted to see me?" Chloe said, trying to steady her nerves.

"Yes, Chloe. Good morning," he said, his focus still on the papers in front of him. "Have a seat. I'll be right with you."

Sitting down, Chloe couldn't shake the faint pain in her gut - a normal reaction to her nerves. She wondered what Mr. Stephens wanted to discuss with her.

Finally, he set the papers aside and looked directly at her. I wanted to tell you personally that we are quite pleased with your progress. You've only been with the company for a short period of time, and your portfolio is quite impressive, which leads me to wonder why you would turn down such a lucrative property that we've been attempting to secure for some time now."

"I beg your pardon?" Chloe said, confused as she stared at the document that Mr. Stephens waved in her face. Taking hold of it to inspect the property, she was taken aback to discover that it was the very same property Nikki had offered her a week prior. Feeling faint, she prepared to speak, "Oh, I…I did not know that our company was interested in the property or I…" Chloe cleared her throat, deciding to go on with an explanation, "I must have overlooked this, Sir…I am happy to reconsider. When the offer was presented, I did not have my portfolio nor any other material in front of me."

"I see. So, are you saying that you are reconsidering your decision, or should I discuss the matter with another agent?" Mr. Stephens asked, raising an eyebrow.

"I am absolutely saying that I would love to manage this property for our firm."

"Are you certain? Because there is another agent who joined us a few months after you who is quite interested in gaining more responsibility."

"No troubles at all, I can manage the property."

"Sounds great."

"Will that be all, Sir?"

"That's it. And Chloe, the company that we will be working with on this property is one that we are interested in partnering with. Nicole Witherspoon's real estate company has shown to be quite profitable, and she and her team are the type of clients that we take pride in working with. Are you sure you can handle this?"

"Yes, Sir, absolutely," Chloe said, her mind now buzzing with mixed emotions. Excitement and resentment swirled within her at the thought of partnering with Nikki, but she knew she had to remain professional.

With that, Chloe walked back into her office, her thoughts racing. She needed a moment to herself. Sitting down, she pulled out her handkerchief and dabbed her forehead. Her mind was a whirlwind of emotions. Nikki had managed to manipulate the situation once again, and Chloe felt both excited and 'duped' at the same time. *Nikki strikes again,* she thought, as she contemplated the upcoming partnership.

Taking a deep breath, Chloe decided to find peace in one of her favorite Bible verses: "Be still and know that I am God." However, the verse didn't activate serenity in her thoughts as quickly as it normally would. She knew she had to find her inner peace amidst the chaos and prepare for the challenges that lay ahead.

As the minutes ticked by, Chloe reminded herself that she had faced challenges before and always emerged stronger. The journey ahead would be daunting, but she was determined to reclaim her power and embrace her true self, no matter what obstacles Nikki or anyone else threw her way.

The meeting went more favorably than Chloe could have ever anticipated. As Mr. Stephens announced that she would be handling the new property acquisition, a sense of pride and excitement swelled within her. The junior partners around the table raised their eyebrows in surprise. Climbing the corporate ladder at Chloe's firm was known to be a slow and difficult process, so naturally, most of her colleagues were taken aback.

"Congratulations, Ms. Chloe. You are the epitome of a rising star," Kory Adams said as the group made their way back to their offices. Kory was that guy that the few women in the office gossiped about. Slick, handsome, and witty, he had worked for the company much longer than Chloe but didn't seem to be as aggressive in his career pursuits.

"Thanks for the encouragement, but this all comes as a huge surprise. I'm excited to keep learning and growing," Chloe responded, maintaining her trademark humility. She was never heady or boastful, but always attentive to detail and dedicated to demanding work.

As the day continued, Kory approached Chloe again with a different kind of proposition. "Look, I've been meaning to ask... would you like to grab a drink after work or a bite to eat sometime? I'd really like to get to know you better," Kory asked, his charming smile radiating warmth.

"Oh, how nice, but...I don't think so," Chloe answered, feeling a bashful blush creeping up her cheeks. While she wasn't familiar with any explicit rule against dating within the company, she didn't want to risk any potential complications. Besides, deep down, she knew she had no romantic interest in men.

Kory seemed undeterred; his confidence unwavering. "No problem at all. The offer still stands if you change your mind," he said with a wink before returning to his office.

Chloe chuckled softly to herself, appreciating Kory's persistence and charm. As the workday drew to a close, she couldn't help but feel a mix of elation and relief. Taking charge of the new property acquisition was a significant step in her career, and she was determined to excel in her new role.

After work, Chloe decided to treat herself to a quiet dinner at her favorite local cafe. The soothing atmosphere and delicious food provided the perfect opportunity for her to unwind and reflect. She replayed the events of the day in her mind, realizing that despite Nikki's manipulative schemes, she had managed to turn the situation in her favor.

As the evening sun painted the sky, Chloe's mind drifted to her upcoming counseling session with Minister Aaron Conner. While she wasn't thrilled about discussing her sexual orientation with others, she understood the importance of facing her truth and finding her inner peace.

She knew there would be hurdles and doubts along the way, but she was ready to embrace her journey fully. Her heart swelled with gratitude for the support of her friends, like Kennedy, who had always encouraged her to live her truth.

CHAPTER 32

CHLOE'S HURDLES

Walking down the long hallway to the Associate Minister's office felt like traversing an endless corridor. With every step, Chloe's heart pounded louder in her chest, and her mind held a mixture of anxiety and determination. Throughout the day, she had wrestled with herself, almost talking herself out of keeping this meeting at least four times. But each time, she mustered the courage to face it head-on, knowing it was essential for her personal growth and journey ahead.

She had spoken to Kennedy twice about the upcoming counseling session, and their conversations had brought her comfort. Both of them agreed that no matter the outcome, Chloe would come out of it stronger and more self-aware.

Approaching the door to the Associate Minister's office, Chloe's thoughts swirled like a tempest. She took a deep breath, trying to steady her nerves before knocking on the door. Just then, Aaron jetted out like a bolt of lightning.

"Excuse me, I'll be right back, Sister Chloe," Aaron called out as he darted into the restroom. Chloe couldn't help but chuckle at the comical timing. Dressed in a formal suit on a Tuesday evening when the church was deserted, Aaron did look a bit out of place.

As she waited in the hall for him to return, Chloe took a moment to observe her surroundings. The church's corridors were quiet, the dimmed lights casting a serene shadow on the walls adorned with religious artwork and inspirational quotes. The familiar scent of polished wood and candles comforted her, evoking memories of countless services and moments of inspiration.

A few minutes later, Aaron emerged from the restroom, looking a bit more composed. "I apologize for the brief delay. Thank you for waiting, Sister Chloe," he said warmly, his sincerity putting Chloe at ease.

"No problem at all, Minister Aaron. I appreciate you taking the time to meet with me," Chloe replied, returning his warm smile.

With a sense of determination, Chloe followed Aaron into his office. The room exuded an air of tranquility, with soft light filtering through the window and casting gentle patterns on the floor. The shelves were adorned with books, symbols of wisdom and guidance that had shaped Aaron's journey as a minister.

Seated across from Aaron, the counselor's presence was calming and reassuring, showing his years of experience guiding others through challenging moments. Even though he was a young minister, Chloe immediately sensed she could trust him with her most vulnerable thoughts.

Aaron leaned forward, his gaze filled with kindness and understanding. "So, Chloe, how do you feel about today's counseling session? Is there anything specific you'd like to discuss or any concerns you'd like to address?"

Taking a deep breath, Chloe mustered her courage. "Well, there are some things I've been grappling with for a while now. I understand that Pastor has filled you in on my sexual preference. I've been exploring my true self, my identity, and my past experiences."

"Correct. He did fill me in; however, I want to hear your heart. This session is about you releasing whatever you want to release.

"There's something I need to share with you, something that's been a source of pain and confusion for me. I used to be involved with an older woman, and now she has resurfaced...she's possessive and controlling."

"What seems to be the source of your confusion?" Aaron asked.

"Well, I cannot seem to understand why I sometimes feel I still have feelings for her, or that I need her."

"Are you saying you still love this older woman," Aaron asked as he loosened his bow tie and relaxed in his chair.

"My heart is telling me that I miss her, but I'm not sure if I know what love is," Chloe responded.

"It's okay. The best way to discover love is to first discover God's love that He has for us, then learn to love ourselves and our fellow man. That's where we start. But listen...this is your time to release any and all pain. Feel free to speak your heart and mind. As I stated previously, I'm here to listen."

As the words flowed from her lips, Chloe felt a sense of liberation, as if a weight was gradually being lifted off her shoulders. She was surprised that he had not once preached or tossed scripture passages to explain why her sexual preference was wrong or an abomination to God like other ministers she'd heard about. Kimyatta, her most recent female encounter, had mentioned how most church leaders only stressed scripture passages, without further explanations or without hearing her side.

As the time ticked by, Chloe found herself engrossed in a conversation that felt both healing and transforming. With each passing moment, the bond of trust between her and Aaron grew stronger, and she knew that she was in the hands of a compassionate counselor who would help her navigate this complex journey of self-discovery.

With a deep sense of gratitude, Chloe left the office feeling lighter, as if a burden had been lifted from her spirit. As she stepped back into the quiet church hallway, the weight of her day seemed less heavy, and she embraced the journey that lay ahead with a newfound sense of hope and determination.

Walking her to her vehicle, the night's air seemed crisp and refreshing. "Good night, and I look forward to our next session," Aaron said as Chloe entered her vehicle.

"Same here. The session was helpful," Chloe responded.

CHAPTER 33

IT KEEPS HAPPENING

Chloe's alarm buzzed promptly at 6:00 AM, signaling the start of a new day. She knew it was time to take a step she had been contemplating for a while now – reaching out to her mom. Determination filled her as she hoped this small gesture would bridge the gap that had long separated them. Brushing and flossing her teeth, she picked up her phone, took a deep breath, and dialed her mom's number. It would be their first time communicating after that evening of chaos when Starla had demanded Chloe speak about her camp experience, which she refused to do after sensing her mom's anger.

"Hi mom, how's your morning going?" she asked, trying to sound casual while her heart raced.

"I'm rushing as usual. You know me, I multi-task first thing in the mornings, and then when I'm done doing my 'me' time, I'm almost late for work," her mom replied in a hurried tone.

Undeterred, Chloe continued, "I was just calling to wish you a good day," Chloe said, attempting to cover up their last brawl and to distract her mom from bringing it back to surface. "And...also to let you know I had my first counseling session with Minister Aaron last night."

"Oh, no. How was it? Are you okay, dear?" her mom's concern now evident in her voice.

"It was nice, mom. Minister Aaron was down to earth and mostly listened to what I had to say," Chloe responded, trying to continue with a conversation that normal daughters have with their normal mothers.

"That's surprising, but I'm glad, honey. Now, don't get your hopes up, I heard that the board of trustees is divided on the issue. Some say to let you keep your ministry position, some say to dismiss you."

Chloe chose not to dwell on that for now. "I'll deal with that in time. But…are we okay, Mom? I know our last conversation didn't end on a pleasant note."

"No, it didn't. I'm still hurt, but I believe you'll talk to me about the camp experience when you feel you are ready. How's everything in the real estate world? You know the Fed has dropped the prime rate twice this month! Business is booming on our end," Starla fired off. She often masked her pain by hiding in the shadows of career and innovation.

"Things are good, as a matter of fact…never mind, I'll tell you about it later. I know you need to get to work," Chloe said, her disappointment evident in her voice. Starla's firing off about her job immediately after asking her about Hers didn't settle well within Chloe's heart. Chloe also knew that her mother was still resentful toward her for not sharing the camp incident with her instead of Nikki.

"Right. I'm already five minutes late. Talk to you soon, stop by tonight if you want", her mom rushed to end the call.

With a shake of her head, Chloe decided not to let her mom's dismissive attitude affect her day. "Always a workaholic," she mumbled as she finished getting ready. Determined to make the best of the day, she treated herself to a latte at the bustling coffee shop before heading to work.

As she waited for her order, engrossed in reading a news article on her phone, a familiar voice broke her concentration. It was Nikki, and she wasted no time in offering her congratulations on the successful meeting. Nikki had played a part in Chloe landing the opportunity, but Chloe knew she had worked hard to earn it too.

"Thanks, Nikki. I'm sure you had a hand in it," Chloe acknowledged with gratitude.

"A little, but you have worked and held your own. You should be proud. What about dinner tonight on me?" Nikki proposed.

Chloe hesitated, thinking of spending time with her mom and attempting to clear the air, but Nikki's persistence won her over. "Okay, what time and where?", Chloe asked with resignation.

"Let's do Olive Garden. I know how much you love their salads," Nikki suggested with a smile.

"K…I'll meet you at the Olive Garden on Commons Boulevard at seven," Chloe agreed as she grabbed her latte and left the shop. Doubts began to creep in as she pondered if she was making the right decision.

On her way to work, Chloe's phone rang, and she saw Aunt Macy's name on the screen. Answering the call, she smiled, "Auntie, good morning. What a pleasant surprise."

"Just checking in. Wanted to see how the session went last night with Minister Aaron," Aunt Macy inquired.

"It went…I wanna say phenomenal," Chloe replied, her excitement evident.

"Well, did it go phenomenal or not?" Aunt Macy chuckled on the other end.

"Yes! Unbelievable. He is so approachable. The words seemed to automatically roll off my tongue. It was nothing like I imagined," Chloe exclaimed.

"Great to hear that. I hope everything works well with it," Aunt Macy responded, picking up on Chloe's hesitancy.

"I believe it will. Just don't know if the other side of the situation will go as smoothly," Chloe confessed.

"You're talking about the crazy mentor woman," Aunt Macy said, understanding the situation.

"Yes, she's resurfaced, and it appears she's not going away anytime soon. She has properties here and has also helped me land a huge assignment at work," Chloe explained, her concern could be discerned.

"Honey, be careful. Everything that glitters is not pure gold. That's what I used to hear my mother say. I know it's exciting to get promoted but be cautious with this woman. You hear me?" Aunt Macy warned.

"I hear you, Auntie. Just need to sort out some feelings," Chloe acknowledged, grateful for her aunt's advice.

"I get it, and you will. I believe in you," Aunt Macy reassured her.

"Thanks, Auntie," Chloe said, feeling a bit more reassured as she ended the call. She knew she had some decisions to make and emotions to untangle.

As Chloe drove to work, her mind was in a constant whirlwind. The conversation with her mom and the upcoming dinner with Nikki had left her with conflicting emotions. She needed a moment to collect herself, so she decided to turn on the radio for some distraction. As she tuned into a local station, a familiar song started playing, instantly transporting her back to her college days when she and Nikki were inseparable.

The melody triggered memories of carefree laughter, late-night adventures, and the feeling of companionship she had with Nikki during those years. But mixed in with the happy memories were fragments of something else – memories of control and mood swings. Chloe also dealt with the haunting memories from the summer camp issue that had taken place when she was twelve. The trauma had left its mark on her, and even now, it still lurked in the corners of her mind.

As the song played on, Chloe's grip on the steering wheel tightened, her heart racing. She had spent years burying that painful incident, trying to move on and focus on her accomplishments and career. However, the past had a way of resurfacing when least expected, and today seemed to be one of those days.

Trying to shake off the unsettling feelings, Chloe took a deep breath and reminded herself that she was no longer that young, vulnerable girl. She had grown and found strength through the challenges she had faced in life. The counseling sessions with Minister Aaron would help her navigate the complexities of her emotions and past trauma, and she knew she had the support of Aunt Macy and Kennedy.

The drive to work seemed longer than usual, as Chloe's mind alternated between the song's nostalgic feelings and the echoes of her past. Finally, she pulled into the office parking lot and turned off the car engine. For a moment, she closed her eyes, allowing herself to feel the emotions and memories swirling within.

As Chloe opened her eyes with newfound determination, she knew she couldn't change the past, but she could shape her present and future. Perhaps this is the attitude that gave her the courage to share her past pain with Nikki, rather than her parents. Gathering her resolve, she stepped out of the car and walked towards the office entrance, ready to face the day and whatever it may bring. The song's melody faded away, but the strength it awakened within her remained, propelling her forward with hope and courage.

CHAPTER 34

I CAN DO ALL THINGS THROUGH CHRIST (AARON'S POV)

Gathering his belongings and planning to head out, Aaron's mind buzzed with reflections on his meeting with Chloe, eagerly anticipating their next session. The stark contrast between the chilly atmosphere at the beginning and the warmth that enveloped them by the end sent a shiver of excitement down his spine. He was convinced that he was on the right path to help Chloe find inner peace on her self-discovery journey.

As he packed up, the familiar voice of Pastor Conner called out from his adjacent office, breaking Aaron's train of thought. The bond between them ran deep, with Aaron being the pastor's only nephew and having followed in the footsteps of his father and grandfather as a devoted servant of the church.

"Hey, Son, let me see you before you head out," Pastor Conner beckoned, removing his glasses to look directly at Aaron. "Tell me, how did the session go the other night with Sister Chloe?"

"For the first meet-up, I'd say it went remarkably well. I have no doubt that Sister Chloe is destined to find the path God has laid out for her," Aaron responded, pride and certainty lacing his words.

Pastor Conner's surprise was evident in his raised eyebrows. "Oh yeah? That's good to hear," he said cautiously. "But you should be aware that half the board isn't pleased with her continuing in a leadership role, and there's plenty of gossip going around in the church and community. We need to ensure that we're following the Spirit of the Lord and not succumbing to emotions."

"Absolutely, Uncle. I understand the importance of being cautious," Aaron assured him earnestly. "I am deeply invested in Chloe's progress. She's an exceptional young woman with numerous ambitions, but she also carries hidden scars that she's bravely starting to reveal. It's a work in progress, but I truly believe she'll be alright."

"Is that so?" Pastor Conner observed, studying Aaron's face closely. He did this because his nephew referred to her as *Chloe* rather than *Sister* Chloe. "Well, tread carefully, my boy. We don't want a repeat of what happened before. You know what I mean, right?"

Aaron's expression remained steady, showing both determination and respect. "I assure you; I've learned from the mistakes I made with Lillie. I went too far with her, and her suicide after all those counseling sessions nearly crushed me. But I've healed, Uncle. I've grown stronger through God's grace."

"Good to hear," Pastor Conner said with a hint of relief. "I don't bring up the past to shame you, but I know the devil can be cunning, trying to drag you down with guilt. You did your best for Lillie, but, her decision was her own. You've come through it all, and I'm proud of you for that."

"Thank you, Sir," Aaron replied gratefully, touched by his uncle's understanding.

As they exchanged a firm handshake, both men prepared to leave the church building. Aaron couldn't help but wonder as he walked out into the cool evening air - was his growing sense of concern and compassion for Chloe merely a professional attachment or something deeper, something that could stir his heart in ways he hadn't anticipated? The uncertainty lingered in his mind, leaving him pondering the boundary between professional duty and personal emotions.

As Aaron entered the dimly lit garage, he found himself unable to move from his car seat for several long moments. A flood of memories washed over him, bringing back the haunting image of Lillie, a young woman whose face eerily resembled Chloe's. He could still hear the echoes of his own voice, desperately preaching every verse of scripture he could muster in a fervent attempt to heal her. Back then, he was determined to make his father and grandfather proud, to prove his worth as a counselor, but the weight of those memories had haunted him for three long, agonizing years. It was only through God's Word and a complete restructuring of his thinking that he finally found peace. Now, with Chloe in front of him, he couldn't shake the fear that history might repeat itself.

As the mental turmoil churned inside him, Aaron couldn't ignore the nagging doubt gnawing at his heart. Could he truly handle this situation better than the previous one? Would he risk getting too invested again? After the incident with Lillie, his counseling experience had been limited to male congregants, but now with Chloe, things would be different. She stirred something in him that he couldn't explain, and he grappled with the fine line between professional boundaries and the feelings tugging at his soul.

Taking a deep breath, he finally stepped out of the car, determined to face his internal struggle head-on. He needed to be honest with himself about the emotions that were surfacing, even if it meant confronting the painful memories of the past. Deep down, he knew this was going to be a test of his strength and faith, one that would challenge the very core of his being.

Turning to one of his favorite verses, "I can do all things

through Christ, who strengthens me," Aaron encouraged himself before spending time in prayer. Soon after, he retired for the night.

CHAPTER 35

IT'S MY LIFE BUT...

As the days passed, Chloe found herself thriving at work, thanks to the valuable pointers she had received from Nikki during their recent dinner date. They had also agreed to be friends, or at least that was Chloe's intention. She felt indebted to Nikki for the significant role she played in her professional success, and while some of her coworkers genuinely celebrated her accomplishments, others seemed envious and resentful. Nevertheless, Chloe remained resolute in her determination to push forward.

Yet, amidst her achievements, a lingering emptiness tugged at her heart. She couldn't shake the disappointment she felt towards her parents, Starla and Reginald, who seemed oblivious to her achievements. All they did was focus on their own past accomplishments and how they had sacrificed their own dreams during their early twenties to care for her. It was as though they blamed her for their lost opportunities and unfulfilled desires. Chloe oftentimes wondered if she was the main reason for their marital issues.

One Sunday morning, Chloe was startled by a knock on her

door. Opening it, she found Nikki standing there with a wide grin on her face.

"Knock knock," Nikki chimed, her enthusiasm contagious. "Sorry to barge in, but I wanted to surprise you. Guess who's gracing the church edifice today?"

Chloe's eyebrows lifted in surprise. "Oh, so you're going to church?" she asked, taken aback by the unexpected visit. Nikki never showed interest in church, although she never discouraged Chloe from attending.

"I am. Don't look so surprised," Nikki said playfully. "Listen, I think it's best if folks see us together if we're going to be genuine friends. Isn't church where love and care are supposed to be?"

Chloe pondered Nikki's words for a moment, recognizing the truth in her friend's reasoning. "Yes, it is. But—" she hesitated, unsure about the prospect of walking into church with Nikki.

"Nope, no 'buts.' We are connected. We mean something to each other, and both your parents and your church congregation need to accept your choices," Nikki asserted, her voice brimming with conviction.

Chloe felt torn. While she agreed with Nikki's sentiment, she also wanted to avoid unnecessary gossip and judgment. "I tend to agree, but I don't think we need to walk into church together," she said, trying to find a middle ground. "Let's wait on that, okay?"

Nikki's face contorted into a playful pout. "Just when I thought you were growing into a mature woman, you pull this on me. Okay, I get it. I'll see you there," she said, teasingly turning up her nose before heading towards the door.

As Nikki left, Chloe felt a mixture of emotions. On one hand, she admired Nikki's boldness and authenticity, but on the other, she couldn't shake the fear of judgment and the lingering doubts about her own maturity after Nikki's remarks. Sitting down, one shoe in hand and the other on her foot, she couldn't help but question whether she was truly living life on her terms or merely trying to appease those around her. She liked to stay focused on the fact that she was much stronger than she used to be.

Despite the looks, whispers, and nervous flutter in her stomach, Chloe let herself go and used her ASL to express both songs and Pastor Conner's sermon. The entire congregation was enveloped in the presence of God as Chloe's face, hands, and body language seemed to flow with a newfound grace. It was as if she had surrendered herself to an audience of one - her Heavenly Father. Tears welled in the eyes of many, both hearing-impaired and those without hearing impairment, as they flooded the altar, seeking prayer or embracing the Christian faith. Chloe's parents, Kennedy, and her Aunt Macy stood on their feet in awe of the powerful moment.

"Sister Chloe, what an anointed demonstration of the song 'Shine on Us'," a congregant said, approaching Chloe and her family after the service. With a grateful smile, Chloe thanked the woman, feeling a profound calm within her soul compared to the restlessness she had felt earlier that morning.

However, amidst the praises, there were whispers circulating among some members of the congregation. Minister Aaron overheard a group speculating on how someone from Chloe's past lifestyle could move under such a divine anointing. The congregation appeared to be divided in their opinions about Chloe's lifestyle choices.

"Sister Chloe, I was blessed by your ministry today. What an outpouring of the Spirit. We had a number of people rededicate their lives to the Lord, and many found salvation through Jesus Christ," Aaron shared with a smile. "Pastor Conner is so joyous; I don't think he's come out of his office yet," he added with a hint of humor.

"Thank you, Minister Aaron," Chloe replied, feeling her heart soar with joy. Her passion for ministry had always burned bright, but today's experience was different - it was like encountering God's Spirit in a way she had never felt before.

"Please, call me Aaron—" he began to say as his eyes flickered with emotion, the impact of the ministry from Chloe earlier that day still flowing through his veins. He was divided; a small part of him wanting to remain professional and help her find healing inside, while the other half desperately wanted to get to know her.

"Call you Aaron? Is that appropriate for a man of the cloth to insist on congregants using their first names?" Nikki interrupted; her voice laced with sarcasm. Both Aaron and Chloe jolted as they realized Nikki had been standing there.

"Minister Aaron, you remember my friend, Nikki Witherspoon. She's also been a beneficial part of my profession," Chloe said, trying to hide her embarrassment. However, she couldn't ignore the concerned looks from her family who stood far off, watching and worrying about Nikki's presence.

"Sister Witherspoon, it's a pleasure to see you again," Aaron greeted, extending his hand, which Nikki blatantly refused to acknowledge.

"Ahh, so... Sister Chloe, I was going to invite you to lunch, but if the two of you have plans—" Aaron said politely before being interrupted again.

"No plans that cannot be changed. We'd love to go out to lunch, Aaron," Nikki said assertively, wearing a look that troubled Chloe.

"Thank you, Minister Aaron. I'll take a rain check on that, but I look forward to our upcoming session," Chloe said, attempting to regain control of the situation.

"Sounds good. I look forward to seeing you then. Sister Witherspoon," Aaron responded, disappointment etched on his face as he walked away.

"Nikki, you cannot do that," Chloe spoke up, her frustration evident. She glanced toward her family on the other side of the room, worried about their reaction.

"Do what?" Nikki feigned innocence.

"Interrupt my conversations, act rudely to the ministers... you know what you did."

"It's obvious that the good preacher is trying to do more than counsel you. Does he know that you like the same thing he likes?" Nikki taunted sarcastically before giving off a high-pitched giggle.

"Stop it. I'm going to join my family now. I'll talk with you later," Chloe said, growing uneasy as she moved away from Nikki's presence.

But Nikki couldn't resist her old ways, grabbing Chloe's arm as she continued to provoke, "Why are you dismissing me like this? You act as if we don't have anything going, but we both know it's a lie," Nikki's lips pressed tightly together in a mixture of anger and desperation. Chloe could feel her family's concern as Starla reached out to hold Reginald's arm.

"Nikki, please let go. Nikki, you're causing a scene," Chloe said calmly, trying to handle the situation gracefully.

Finally, Nikki let go, and Chloe quickly distanced herself from the situation, rejoining her family. As Nikki realized she wouldn't get her way, she hurriedly left the church sanctuary. In a matter of minutes, the glow of the service dissipated from Chloe's soul upon encountering the toxic presence of Nikki.

"What was that all about? The nerve of her coming here?" Starla snapped.

"I'm good, mom," Chloe said, standing tall with chin up, demonstrating a confidence she didn't have. Her inner self felt bewildered, lost, and as if she was losing control.

Reginald's gaze fixed on Starla; his concern etched into his features. "Looks like someone needs to be confronted. I've tried to keep my distance and let you handle this, but what I saw just now doesn't look safe," he voiced, a tone of worry in his words. Even though he could see positive change in his daughter, he couldn't turn a blind eye to the potential dangers.

"I know how it must have looked, but Nikki gets like that when she doesn't get her way."

"A woman of her success and pomp? I don't get her," Starla retorted, shaking her head in disbelief. "One thing is for certain; I've lost all respect for her."

Silently acknowledging Starla's comments, the trio proceeded towards the foyer exit. No words lingered in the air; the weight of Nikki Witherspoon's actions hung heavy in the air, leaving a sense of tension. Nikki had struck again, and as always, she left behind an aftermath of residue that compelled one to scratch their head and think.

CHAPTER 36

THE ELEPHANT IN THE ROOM (CHLOE'S POV)

The family gathering after church service at Macy and Broderick's' home usually echoed with joy, laughter, and lively conversation. However, today, an unsettling cloud of silence hovered over the atmosphere. It wasn't linked to her parents' impending reconciliation, despite their previous separation. As they gathered in the cozy living room, a weighty concern filled the minds of the entire family. Nikki's outburst following the church service had cast a lingering unease over everyone present, and they couldn't brush aside the toxicity that seemed to radiate from her. The congregation's eyewitness accounts only intensified the difficulty of ignoring the unsettling incident.

The room was filled with tension as they tried to avoid discussing the elephant in the room. Chloe, sensing their unease, finally broke the silence. "I'm sorry about Nikki's behavior after the service today," she said softly, her eyes downcast.

Starla reached out and gently squeezed Chloe's hand. "Honey, you don't have to apologize for someone else's actions. We're just concerned about you," she said, her motherly instincts kicking in.

Macy, who typically stepped into that role was somewhat shocked by Starla's words.

"I know, Mom, but I feel responsible for her. I want to help her, but it's like she always drags me down with her," Chloe admitted, her voice tinged with sadness.

Kennedy chimed in, her voice firm and supportive. "Chloe, we love you, and we know you have a big heart. But sometimes, you need to protect yourself from people who drain your energy and positivity."

Reginald nodded in agreement. "Your cousin is right. We've seen how Nikki affects you, and it worries us. We want you to chase your dreams and achieve your ambitions without any negative influences holding you back. This woman is the main reason people are talking against you."

Chloe's Aunt Macy, usually the life of the party, interjected with a somber expression. "Chloe, dear, you have so much potential, and we all believe in you. It's time to prioritize your own well-being."

Chloe felt the weight of their concern, and a tear trickled down her cheek. "I know you're all right, but I can't just abandon Nikki. She's been there for me in some tough times," she confessed, torn between her loyalty to Nikki and the need to protect herself.

Kennedy leaned in closer to Chloe, her eyes filled with empathy. "Chloe, no one is asking you to abandon Nikki completely, but you need to reset those boundaries and take care of yourself too. You can't pour from an empty cup."

Broderick, who is usually a man of few words, with a demeanor like his brother Reginald, also chimed in with words of wisdom concerning Nikki's need to seek counsel to drive out the root embedded within that causes her behavior patterns.

Chloe nodded, feeling a mix of emotions. "You're right. I'll talk to Nikki and explain how her behavior affects me. I need to protect my dreams and ambitions."

The family nodded in agreement, acknowledging Broderick's wise insight. They knew that toxic people often carried deep-rooted issues that required understanding and compassion. Starla admired her brother-in-law's calm and measured wisdom, grateful for his presence in this moment of support for Chloe.

As they continued in conversation, showing solidarity, the doorbell's chime cut through the air, breaking their introspective moment. Broderick questioned if anyone was expecting a visitor, but Kennedy replied in the negative. Macy, with an air of excitement, stood up and headed for the door. There was a glimmer of intrigue in her eyes, as she had a surprise for Chloe and the entire family.

"Hello, and so glad you had the time to swing by," Macy's voice chimed out, welcoming Minister Aaron into the home. The family sat in anticipation in the living area, curious about this unexpected visit. "Everyone, it's Minister Aaron. I invited him to swing by for a few moments. I thought it would be nice to have an extra prayer for Chloe and our entire family."

The room filled with a mix of surprise and warmth as Aaron stepped into the living room, looking as dashing as ever in his debonair suit. His countenance was calm and carried a kindness that put everyone at ease.

"Afternoon, everyone. Hope all is well this time around," Aaron greeted, his voice soothing and comforting. He made his way towards Chloe, who felt a flutter in her heart at his nearness. Their eyes met, and a subtle spark passed between them that both baffled and excited her.

"Thank you for coming, Minister Aaron," Chloe said, her voice slightly breathless as she stood to greet him.

"It's my pleasure, Chloe," he replied, his voice gentle and sincere. "Again, your ministry today touched many hearts. I could feel the Spirit moving through you."

A blush-colored Chloe's cheeks at his praise. "Thank you. I'm grateful for your support and encouragement."

The family members watched the interaction between Chloe and Aaron with keen interest, noticing the growing connection between them. Kennedy exchanged knowing glances with Macy, who held a twinkle of delight in her eyes.

Broderick spoke up, addressing Aaron with a welcoming smile. "We appreciate you taking the time to visit, Minister Aaron. Your presence brings a sense of peace to our home."

"Thank you, Mr. Rhodes. It's always a pleasure to be among good company," Aaron replied, his charisma evident as he engaged in conversation with the family.

As they settled into a cozy discussion, Chloe felt a sense of ease and comfort in Aaron's presence in a greater way than during their first session. His attentiveness and genuine interest in her well-being made her feel special, understood, and valued. She couldn't deny the growing fondness she had for him, and she wondered if he felt the same or if all the chaos from the day had her focus off balance.

Throughout the afternoon, the family enjoyed Aaron's company, exchanging stories, laughter, and prayers. Chloe's heart swelled with gratitude for the support and love surrounding her. As they shared the joys and challenges of life, she felt a newfound sense of belonging.

As the day drew to a close, Aaron bid farewell to the family, leaving with a promise to pray for Chloe's upcoming session with him. The lingering warmth of his presence stayed with her, igniting a hopeful excitement within her heart.

Retreating to her home later that evening, Chloe found herself lost in contemplation about the day's events. The warmth of her family's love, coupled with Aaron's comforting presence, reassured her that she wasn't navigating her journey of self-discovery alone, despite the unsettling incident with Nikki. Her musings were interrupted by a call on her phone, its unfamiliar number initially urging her to ignore it. However, a sense of curiosity prompted her to answer.

"Hello," she responded with anticipation.

"Chloe?" Aaron's familiar voice echoed through the line.

"Yes, this is Chloe Rhodes."

"This is Aaron. I... wow, this is a bit awkward," Aaron stumbled over his words, carefully explaining the reason for his unexpected call. "I was hoping you'd made it okay and...had you in my thoughts, Chloe. Wanted to wish you sweet sleep."

"Sweet sleep…huh? Do you always phone the people you counsel to wish them sweet sleep?" Chloe teased.

Chuckling on the other end of the line, Aaron admitted that it was not the norm. "I know it's strange, just had an urge I couldn't shake. Would you like to join me for an early morning coffee or an early morning run or walk?"

"Wow. So many choices. So, you remembered that walking early in the morning before my latte and work was one of my morning routines. Impressive," she said, stroking her hair while lying across her bed. "I think I'd like to beat you down in a power walk."

"Oh, beat me down, huh? I think I'm down for the challenge. So…we're meeting in the park at six for a thirty-minute power walk…correct?" Aaron reiterated; a certain joy evident in his voice.

"Yep! Make certain you have your best shoes. I'm known for knocking out two miles in thirty minutes time," Chloe bragged.

"I'll be ready. See you at your favorite park."

Excited, Chloe decided to call it a night. As the moonlight gently bathed her room, she drifted off to sleep with a contented smile, one of her favorite verses of scripture dancing in her head: *"Trust in the Lord with all your heart, lean not unto your own understanding, acknowledge the Lord in all you do, and He will direct your paths."*

CHAPTER 37

FIRE AND DESIRE

The next morning brought forth excitability as Chloe and Aaron both indulged in moments of freedom from responsibilities from both the secular and spiritual realms. It felt nice being themselves…laughing like children and not ashamed to be vulnerable. The walk went from being a competition to being a time of transparency for both parties. Aaron expressed painful disappointments from his past as well as Chloe expressing some of the issues she had struggled with from her past.

"I don't want you to be shocked by my past relationship with Nikki. At first, I brushed it off as curiosity and a fling, but we had something deep."

"How so?" Aaron asked with curiosity, causing their walk to come to a brief halt.

"Well, for one thing she made me feel safe, and I was able to express my pain and share some of my deepest secrets with her. Things that I had suppressed as a youth, somehow came spilling out of me."

"You must feel safe with a person to show that kind of vulnerability," Aaron agreed.

"Right. I mean I told her about an incident that I was never able to tell Kennedy, and I've always shared my secrets with her."

"What about romance?" Aaron asked, being forward sent a bit of a chill up his spine. He hoped that Chloe wouldn't take offense.

"She was my first sex encounter if that is what you mean. I can't lie and say that I didn't feel a strange, yet close connection to her. She guided me, took care of me."

"I see."

"Well, where are the scriptures…the speech?" Chloe said jokingly but Aaron could tell she was dead serious.

"All of that is excluded. Just think of me as your secret keeper, your diary…so to speak. Just like when we were in our counseling session. I want to hear your heart, Chloe."

"Thank you, I appreciate your kindness."

"I also have hopes of being more than a counselor to you. I hope we can spend more time together," Aaron's voice was sincere, his eyes begged for a certain response.

"I'm flattered, but…I don't know if I was made to be in a romantic relationship with males…just so you know. I mean I'm not trying to lead you on, I…"

Before Chloe could finish her sentence, Aaron's lips clung to hers, gently, yet forcefully. She wanted to pull away, but it was like they were stuck together by some invisible force. The heat between them felt electric and tangible as their sweat mixed and their embrace lasted long after it should have been broken. When she finally stepped back, Chloe could see a mixture of fear and desire in Aaron's eyes. "What are you doing?" she asked in a breathy voice, confusion began to surface as she felt the same heat throughout her body as she felt for Nikki on that first night of intimacy.

"Forgive me, please. I shouldn't have, it's just that…"

Chloe reached out for Aaron, and he pulled her close, enveloping her in his strong arms. Her heart pounded against his chest as they held each other for what felt like a lifetime. Their brows connected in sweat-soaked desperation, and both were afraid to let go; their hug was an admission of guilt, a plea for forgiveness and mercy.

"I…I've got a nine o'clock meeting…I…may I call you later," Aaron asked, both determination and a hint of shame covering his face.

"Sure."

Hour upon hour, Chloe's mind spun with questions as she sat at her desk. *Is this what it looks like to be in control of life? Are you bipolar or what? You like men now?* Before she had time to sort out the thoughts and questions that were controlling a great part of her day, her phone lit up with a text from Nikki. It sparked an intense wave of fear within Chloe as she read about Nikki being determined to end her own life. Without hesitation, Chloe put on her coat, grabbed her purse, work files, and her briefcase, informing Matilda she was stepping out for an emergency. She quickly glanced over the calendar: thankfully, no meetings or appointments. Adrenaline pumping through her veins, she raced through the city towards Nikki's home where her vehicle was parked. She pulled into the extra space and breathed deeply as apprehension coursed through her body. Dialing Kennedy, she braced herself before going into the resident.

"Thank God you picked up. I'm at Nikki's place. Listen, I'm forwarding you a copy of a text she sent about twenty minutes ago.

"Slow down. Okay, I'm opening the message now. "Girl, what in the world? Look, I don't believe this chick. Chloe where exactly are you?"

"I'm on her front lawn," Chloe said as she peered toward the windows of the house; beads of sweat pouring down her forehead as she scrutinized the neighborhood. "I'm almost afraid to go in," she added, her voice trembling.

"Think about it...if she were serious about hurting herself, she wouldn't have texted you. Trust me. Leave." Kennedy was a year older and had taken on the role of big sister from when they were children, even though Chloe was always more mature.

But Chloe wasn't the type to back down from something so uncertain. She slipped her hand into her pocket and felt the cold metal key between her fingers—reciting a prayer in her mind gave her strength to move forward with her plan. "I can't just leave. Look, I have a key, so I'm going in."

Kennedy let out a frustrating sigh before responding: "Chloe, don't. Just call her and I'm sure she'll pick up."

"I tried that twice from the office and four times in the car over here. Something is not right," Chloe groaned in frustration. "Nikki always picks up on the first or second ring. Don't worry about me," she reassured Kennedy before ending their call and stepping out of the car. Taking a deep breath, she made her way up the porch steps until finally standing at Nikki's front door.

Closing the door behind her, she carefully stepped through the house, keeping her eyes peeled for any signs of Nikki. Every creak of the floorboards sounded like thunder in her ears. She passed Nikki's phone resting on the bed as she entered the master bedroom, where makeup was scattered across the dresser and clothes were strewn across the floor. Swallowing hard, Chloe tentatively crept toward the bathroom.

"Nikki?" she uttered in hushed tones as she pushed open the door, only to be met with a terrifying sight—Nikki lay motionless in a large bathtub, an empty champagne flute and an opened bottle of prescription pills beside her.

Chloe shouted her name again as she stumbled forward and grabbed Nikki's wrist, checking for a pulse. Fear surged through

Chloe as she felt Nikki come back to life, grabbing her tightly in an embrace that seemed too tight to be real. Chloe's fright slowly left as she returned Nikki's embrace and realized what had happened. Gently pulling away, Chloe quickly grabbed the pill bottle from the plush mat and saw that it was half-empty and past its expiration date. Panic swelled inside Chloe again as she stared at Nikki—her eyes were swollen and red, and her breath reeked of alcohol and something else. "What did you do? Oh my God, Nikkk! Did you overdose? Answer me! I'm calling an ambulance!"

"Calm down. I haven't taken them yet. I passed out from drinking. Good thing, huh?" Nikki's eyes looked wild, her body trembling in its drunken stupor. "So…I was feeling suicidal. I was about to take those pills. Something stopped me. It was like a powerful force."

Chloe exhaled a deep breath of relief and helped Nikki out of the tub. "Okay, well, Thank God you're okay," Chloe said as she guided Nikki into her bedroom. "I need to get to work but we'll talk about this later."

"Do you think you love him? Because there is a difference between love and lust you know," Nikki said as she continued to rub Chloe's arm.

"Wait…you were there weren't you? You were stalking me earlier this morning," Chloe accused with suspicion, her heart fluttering in fear as thoughts of Nikki hiding somewhere at the park flooded her mind.

"Nope. I was about to get coffee, saw your vehicle and was going to join you for a morning stroll, and lo and behold...what did I see?" Nikki's voice sounded strained as she stared at Chloe with an intensity that made her feel uncomfortable.

"Stay away from me. You're crazy. You need help. Please get the help you need," Chloe's warned.

Nikki moved closer and grabbed Chloe forcibly, her body pressed against Chloe's as she spoke in a low whisper: "Not until you own your truth." In an instant, Chloe felt paralyzed by the power of Nikki's words, wanting nothing more than to escape this wild situation. However, her body betrayed her; before she knew it, they had both fallen back onto the bed and started making passionate love, their bodies moving in sync until finally both collapsed in exhaustion.

Chloe was not sure if the love making was a result of relief in knowing that Nikki was still alive, or if it had something to do with the fire Aaron had started earlier that morning, but never put out.

CHAPTER 38

A TASTE OF YOUR OWN MEDICINE (MINISTER AARON)

Aaron felt a mix of emotions as he sat in his office, contemplating the upcoming Harvest Day celebration. The opportunity to preach in front of his father and grandfather filled him with both excitement and nervous fear. He wanted to impress them, but the weight of their expectations felt like a heavy burden on his shoulders. Perhaps he could find a way to avoid the spotlight altogether and let another associate take on the task.

Lost in his thoughts, Aaron was startled when he heard a voice at his doorway. It was Chloe, and her presence instantly brought a smile to his face. They had played phone tag over the last couple of days, so no conversation about their Monday morning park incident. He tried to compose himself, straightening his tie, and gathering his scattered thoughts.

"Earth to Minister Aaron...hello, are you available now or should I come back later?" Chloe asked playfully, standing in the doorway. She was somewhat ready for their session; however, the thoughts of their kiss and embrace in the park the other morning had her thoughts jumbled, not to mention the whirlwind that her Nikki incident was causing.

Aaron chuckled, feeling a bit embarrassed by his distraction. "Chloe..., come right in," he invited, trying to regain his composure.

As she settled into the chair, Chloe's eyes held a genuine concern as she noticed the troubled expression on Aaron's face. "Are you good? Looks like you were in deep thought...troubling thoughts at that," she observed.

Aaron hesitated for a moment before confiding in Chloe. He shared the pressure he felt from his upbringing as a pastor's son and grandson, the strict rules that governed his every move, and the anxiety he had about living up to their expectations.

Chloe listened attentively, her wisdom and understanding shining through her eyes. "We all have our struggles," she reassured him, making him feel understood and supported.

Her empathy put Aaron at ease, and he found himself loosening up in her presence. When Chloe pointed out his habit of adjusting his tie, he couldn't help but chuckle. "Just a habit, I guess," he replied, appreciating her attention to detail.

Their conversation flowed effortlessly, and Aaron felt a deep connection with Chloe, sensing that she had a unique ability to see through his exterior. He found himself sharing more about his internal battles, including his desire to follow his own calling in ministry rather than conform to the traditional expectations of his family.

Chloe's insight and vulnerability encouraged him to open up even more. As the topic shifted to her own struggles, Aaron realized the importance of their mutual support. He admired her courage in confronting her past and her determination to understand her identity and sexuality.

"Let's pray about the both of us gaining the grace and courage to manage our business...what do you say?" Aaron suggested, rising from his chair.

Chloe stood up, facing him with gratitude in her eyes. "I've always heard that prayer changes things. But I'm dying to ask you something," she hesitated, her voice tinged with uncertainty.

"Ask away," Aaron encouraged, genuinely interested in hearing her thoughts.

"Why haven't you given me your honest reflection on same-sex relationships? I mean, I appreciate you not judging me or being preachy about the subject. I understand the sensitivity of it all, but you have not once said anything about all the gossip, uproar, and division within the board about the whole thing."

Aaron gently took Chloe's hand, looking deeply into her eyes. "God has directed me to listen to your heart and assist you on your road to the destination that he has in front of you," he explained, hoping to reassure her that he was there to support and guide her, regardless of the controversy surrounding her life choices. "Also, Chloe…look, about the other morning, I want to apologize for crossing the line the way I did. I honestly appreciate you keeping your appointment and behaving as if it didn't happen, but I think we need to address it," Aaron explained with empathy in his voice.

"No worries. I agree that we need to set the record straight on what happened between us. The two of us were lonely or just tempted…it happens. Since we're speaking on the subject, I believe I have found my truth as far as discovering myself. This may not be what you wanna hear."

"No, it's okay. Go ahead and release whatever is on your heart."

"So…Nikki and I are an item. I can no longer hide the truth. It is what it is, even though the relationship is toxic. Nikki needs help, but you know…some in the church also need help. Some say God only approves of male and female romantic relationships, some agree that some people are born to have affection for someone of the same sex…it's so controversial."

"I get that. It is a controversial matter and I've not openly discussed all this with you because I wanted to be fair and let you speak your peace," Aaron gently explained. "Rest assured, my stand on same-sex relationships goes beyond opinion, since I take the approach from what I interpret the Holy Scriptures teach about the matter."

"Regardless of all that, I want you to know that I am gay. Sometimes I wonder if I may be bi-sexual, but...none of that erases the reality of Nikki and me. Our relationship is real. I know in my heart that I cannot turn off my feelings, but I do need to convince her to get the help she needs."

"I hear you. I respect you for standing up for what you believe, so...well," Aaron took a long breath before continuing. "Let's continue our session. So, what other questions do you have for me?"

Chloe's next question made his heart skip a beat. Her sincerity and vulnerability were captivating, and he felt an overwhelming urge to protect and cherish her.

"Why is it that folks say that same-sex relationships are a sin when it was God who gave me the tendency that I have to love a woman in the manner that a man loves a woman?"

"That answer is already in your heart. If you must ask, you already know," he responded, hoping to encourage her on the journey. "Listen, I have a few verses of scripture I'd like to text you. Read and ponder these. We will discuss your question during our next session. Fair enough?"

"Fair enough," Chloe answered with a gentle smile.

As they continued to talk, Aaron continued to feel drawn to Chloe's presence, finding her not just intriguing but enchanting. He sensed a growing fondness for her, one that went beyond their professional relationship. The connection between them felt like a divine plan, so he felt trapped in a maze, since Chloe had openly admitted that she had no interest in men.

"So, you wanna tell me why you're staring at me like that?" Chloe asked.

"Because you are intriguing. You ask questions that will set so many people free," Aaron's voice held a purity that caused Chloe to feel light.

The meeting concluded, and Aaron walked Chloe to her car. As they said their goodbyes, he could not help but feel a swirl of emotions within him. Driving home, he found himself praying for strength, wisdom, and guidance in his interactions with Chloe.

"Father, God, I'm in deep with this one," he prayed, pouring his heart out to the heavens. "Help me to do your will and help Chloe find her path to discovering the true path that only You have ordained for her to walk upon."

The night air offered a soothing embrace, calming the turmoil within Aaron's heart. However, his peace was abruptly shattered when he sensed a presence creeping up behind him. Startled, he turned to find Nikki standing there, clad in a dark gray jogging suit with a hoodie, her eyes reflecting an unsettling intensity.

"Oh, Jesus! Ms. Witherspoon, is that you? You startled me," Aaron stammered, trying to regain his composure. His voice was tinged with both surprise and concern. "Can I help you with something?"

Nikki's demeanor seemed confrontational as she took a step closer to him. "You can start by leaving Chloe alone," she demanded, her words laced with a mix of defiance and accusation. "Why lead her down a pathway that we all know she is not determined to tread on?"

Aaron's confusion deepened. "What are you talking about?" he asked, genuinely puzzled by her cryptic words.

"She's a lesbian, Aaron," Nikki declared bluntly, as if exposing a well-hidden secret. "It's time you church people get off her case about it and let her live the life of her own choosing."

"Listen, I don't know what you're trying to accomplish tonight or what's going through your mind right now, but we love Chloe, and we're not going to leave her alone unless she requests that we discontinue our counseling sessions."

Nikki's response was filled with a sense of defiance. "We'll see about that."

Refusing to be swayed, Aaron stood his ground. "Go home, Ms. Witherspoon. Safe travel. Oh, and hope to see you in church on Sunday."

Her laughter echoed through the cool atmosphere. "I see straight through you," Nikki taunted. "You don't fool me. It's in your eyes. You want her body, don't you? Well, she's mine."

"Go home, Ms. Witherspoon. You shouldn't be here."

"She and I had sex the other day. Yep, the same day you attempted to seduce her in the park. Did she tell you that in your little counsel session?" Nikki admitted as she retreated into the shadows.

Her words left Aaron feeling both insulted and appalled. "Look, I've got lots to get done before retiring for the night, so if you don't mind, I'd like for you to leave my property now."

Nikki seemed to get the message and begrudgingly left, leaving behind an eerie feeling in Aaron's gut. He couldn't shake the unsettling encounter.

Retreating into his home, Aaron contemplated the strong connection he sensed with Chloe. The unspoken understanding between them hinted at a journey filled with challenges and uncertainties. Thoughts of the infamous Nikki lingered, a gloomy presence in the background. Navigating the emotional roller coaster triggered by the incident outside his home would demand a steadfast exercise of faith.

With these contemplations, Aaron retired for the evening. In the quietness of prayer, he sought comfort, placing his trust in the belief that God would intricately guide both him and Chloe along their intertwined paths.

CHAPTER 39

CHLOE...STAY FOCUSED

The morning escaped Chloe like a fleeting breath as she navigated a flurry of phone calls and virtual client meetings. Time slipped through her fingers like grains of sand until an unexpected knock on her office door interrupted her busy schedule. Kory Adams, the suave and handsome colleague from down the hall, poked his head in with a playful grin.

"Do you ever eat?" Kory teased, his voice carrying a hint of concern.

Chloe blinked, realizing that it was already noon. "The time got away from me. I didn't realize it was already lunchtime."

"Want me to grab you something? I'm heading out," Kory offered.

Before Chloe could respond, Nikki pushed her way into the office with an Olive Garden bag in hand. Her sharp, cold gaze fixed on Kory, and an awkward tension filled the room.

"Got her favorite. A nice, healthy salad just the way she loves it," Nikki said with a hint of venom in her tone, as she presented the lunch to Chloe.

Kory gave Nikki a puzzled look and excused himself. As the

door closed behind him, Chloe felt the need to address the situation.

"Nikki, you shouldn't have. I was planning to grab a sandwich," Chloe said, trying to hide her annoyance. "But I want to talk to you about the help you promised to get."

"Listen, if this is about last Sunday or even the pill thing...look, I want to apologize. I got a bit carried away. None of it will happen again," Nikki said, attempting to brush off both incidents.

Chloe hesitated before speaking, aware of Nikki's toxic nature. "Thanks for the apology, but we still need to set boundaries. It's best if we keep our relationship strictly professional until the tensions at the church settle."

Nikki stood with the bag still in hand, her expression unreadable. "Chloe, are you leading me on? You told me you loved me when we made love the other day...this is confusing."

"Not here, Nikki," Chloe replied, hoping to avoid a scene at her workplace.

Ignoring her request, Nikki persisted. "You are here because of me. Don't you forget it."

Chloe felt a twinge of dismay, realizing that Nikki was not going to back down easily. "Nikki, we need to focus on work and keep our relationship separate from church matters and definitely not have it out here at my place of employment."

But Nikki seemed unfazed, delving into another topic. "Mr. Stephens will be back tomorrow. If I were you, I'd make sure the preliminary report is ready for his review."

As the conversation veered in different directions, Chloe's stomach growled, reminding her that she was hungry. She reached for the salad as Nikki continued probing her feelings.

"You didn't answer my question. Do you love me?" Nikki insisted, her eyes glistening with emotion.

Chloe's heart raced as she struggled to find the right words. "I care about you, Nikki."

"Care about me? You know it's more than that. Whatever happened to the love and respect we once had for each other?" Nikki's voice wavered, and her eyes welled up with tears.

"Can we discuss this later?" Chloe asked, trying to divert the conversation back to work.

"No, I want to settle this now," Nikki insisted. "Look me in the eyes and tell me you don't love me."

Chloe's heart pounded. She couldn't deny the complex feelings she still held for Nikki, and it left her feeling conflicted.

Nikki's triumphant smile suggested she had already won. "You do love me," she declared, her voice filled with satisfaction. "When all this chaos settles, the two of us are going on a cruise."

Chloe forced a smile, hoping Nikki would leave her office soon. "Sure, let's talk more after things settle down. Thanks for the salad."

With a final touch on Chloe's cheek, Nikki left, leaving Chloe to grapple with her emotions and the unresolved tension between them. As she sat there, her mind was a whirlwind of conflicting thoughts, but no matter what, she refused to succumb to the way she used to be. From now on, she would call the shots in her life...regardless.

~

As the day ended, Chloe found it difficult to gauge her productivity amidst the numerous interruptions. Battling a sense of homesickness, she resolved to visit Aunt Macy, but not before making a brief stop at her parents' home. Her mother would have a fit if she knew that Chloe was at Macy's but didn't stop by.

Parking in the driveway, Chloe noticed an unfamiliar vehicle next to her mom's. *Company on a Thursday?* she mumbled within, shutting off the engine before entering the house. Following her routine, she called out to Starla. In the dining area, a woman with a familiar face sat at the table with her mother.

Oh, hi honey. What...what brings you by? Starla asked, her expression betraying surprise, as if caught in the act.

"Just dropping by for a few minutes before going to Aunt Macy's. Who's this?"

"Ahh, an old friend, dear."

As Chloe studied the woman, a peculiar feeling washed over her. Recognition dawned. "Wait, this is her! The woman who ruined my prom. What is she doing here? Mom, is she still seeing Dad or something... why is she here?" Chloe's voice grew loud and frantic.

"Hold on, calm down. She's an old friend... remember? Your father and I explained that to you years ago," Starla explained sternly, rising from the table.

"I'm not that same naïve teen. I can't stand how everybody thinks they can live the way they want and then shelter me and tell me what to do," Chloe, arms folded, felt empowered to stand up to her mother.

"What in God's name are you talking about?" Starla responded.

"Star, we can catch up later. Looks like the two of you need time alone," Henrietta said with the same tone Chloe remembered from the night of the prom when everything exploded.

"Star? Is that your pet name for my mom? Have a pet name for dad as well?" Chloe said with defiance. Fed up, she continued, "You were with my father in that restaurant at the mall. I know it was years ago, but I recall it like it was yesterday. You were holding his hand, he kissed yours. You two were clearly an item, and my parents both lied about it."

In response, Starla slapped Chloe across her face. Shocked and ashamed, Starla covered her mouth before apologizing. "Oh, baby girl, I'm so sorry. I lost control," Starla said in tears, with Henrietta equally stunned.

"No worries. I've got tough skin," Chloe's voice trembled as she turned to leave, with Starla trotting behind, apologizing once more before the door slammed.

"I told you something like this would happen. You're going to have to eventually tell her… you know that don't you?" Henrietta remarked as they stood in the dining room, where the aftermath of the incident lingered in the air.

"I'm not ready to tell her something like this," Starla said, sinking into a chair in dejection.

CHAPTER 40

FAMILY DRAMA (STARLA'S BREAKDOWN)

The next day Starla rushed out of her meeting to take time for her lunch break, her mind swirling with thoughts, most of them revolving around the situation with Chloe on yesterday, not to mention Chloe's relationship and ministry issues. The gossip circulating about her daughter's life had begun to bother her, especially when it reached her colleagues on the bank's board. Maintaining their reputation in both their careers and the community had always been essential to Starla and Reginald, and she was determined to handle this situation discreetly. Having to deal with multiple issues was taking a toll on her emotionally.

Spotting Macy retrieving the mail, Starla decided to take a moment and address her concerns with her sister-in-law. She parked her car and approached Macy, determined to have a heart-to-heart conversation before continuing with her day.

"Can we talk?" Starla said, her expression serious yet tinged with a hint of vulnerability.

"Of course, is everything alright with Chloe?" Macy replied, her concern evident as she regarded her niece, who had always held a special place in her heart.

"I wanted to discuss your invitation to Minister Aaron a couple of weeks ago. Was it about prayer, or were you trying to play matchmaker?" Starla asked, getting straight to the point.

Macy paused for a moment, choosing her words carefully. "It was about the prayer, but I won't deny that I've noticed how Minister Aaron seems fond of Chloe. As for playing matchmaker, that's not my intention. We have the Lord for that," she responded, trying to be respectful of Starla's position as Chloe's mother.

"I've so much on mind right now, so I'll get right to the point. I made it clear years ago that I'm the one who should be making those decisions for Chloe, not you," Starla said, her frustration evident as she gestured with her hands.

Macy nodded, acknowledging Starla's feelings. "I understand, and I didn't mean to overstep any boundaries. I just wanted to bring some positive energy into Chloe's life during this challenging time."

"Why can't you just mind your own business? It feels like you're always there, acting like some kind of bodyguard or advocate for her. If you truly knew what was best for Chloe, you would have stopped this chaos a long time ago, I'm talking about this gay relationship she started with Nikki! I'm sure you were aware long before me!" Starla said with a stern and angry tone, causing the nearby neighbors to glance curiously at the heated exchange.

Macy lowered her voice, trying to diffuse the situation. "Let's not involve the whole neighborhood in this conversation. I only want what's best for Chloe."

"They may as well be a part of it. Everyone is talking about my gay daughter who is now flirting around with the most eligible bachelor in town, and they are also talking about the possessive and jealous lover, who, by the way, happens to be a female. I'm done with walking in your shadows Macy Rhodes.

Starla's frustration continued to rise. "Everyone is talking about my daughter and I won't allow you to contribute to this any further. From now on, stay away from Chloe's life and don't do anything without discussing it with me or Reginald. Is that clear?"

Macy took a deep breath, trying to remain composed, but she broke down. "Okay, let's talk about this! I don't think your anger is just about my inviting the minister over for prayer the other day. That may have gripped you a bit, but the root of this entire shenanigans today is the fact that Chloe is closer to me as a mother than she has ever been toward you! You are the one who left Chloe with me time and time again when you were busy chasing dollar bills and dreams," Macy said angrily, tears forming in her eyes.

"How dare you bring up my past struggles to justify your unacceptable actions! What I did all those years ago, I did for Chloe. Chloe has never lacked anything. Both Reginald and I made a sacrifice so that we could offer the best for our daughter!"

"But you didn't offer her you. She needed you more than she needed materialistic things," Macy responded in a much calmer voice. She wanted to address the issue by standing her ground but deep down she felt Starla's pain and suffering and wanted to resolve their differences once and for all.

Starla felt the sting of Macy's words, and tears began to well up in her eyes. She tried to respond, but her voice faltered, and she found herself struggling to find the right words.

Macy's anger softened, and she reached out to her sister-in-law, embracing her gently. "It's okay. Everything will work out for Chloe. She's a remarkable young woman, and the favor of God is upon her life. She'll triumph in the end, you'll see."

Feeling the warmth and comfort of Macy's embrace, Starla couldn't help but break down completely. Macy's words touched a deep part of her heart that had been longing for reconciliation.

"Thank you," Starla whispered, tears streaming down her cheeks.

"You're welcome, Starla. I meant every word," Macy replied, her own eyes misty with tears.

"No, I mean... thank you for taking care of my little girl all those years I was absent," Starla said, her voice filled with emotion. "I don't even believe I've ever told you before how I appreciate you."

"You are welcome."

"Also, Chloe came by yesterday and saw me and Henri...well, she and I had a fight yesterday, and I slapped her. It was awful. All the past mysteries that Chloe held onto concerning Henri, her father's relationship with her after seeing them together years ago, and for her to walk in on us..." Starla's pause made way for her embarrassment and vulnerably. "It was just awful."

"Oh, no," Macy's hand rested gently over her mouth before continuing. "No wonder she didn't come by. She texted and said she'd changed her mind about coming over. I could tell she was upset but thought she was tired from work. May I offer advice," Macy asked tenderly.

"Sure, be my guest. You wouldn't be wonder woman Macy if you didn't," Starla said, using humor in hope to lighten the load of her own burden.

"Chloe is tougher than you think. I believe if you and Reginald will have a conversation with her about the past, it will clear up a lot of questions and confusion that has hung in her mind."

"I'm sure you're right and Henri says the same...I'm not ready. Pray for me, Macy. Pray that I gain the insight and strength to deal with this along with all the other earth-shattering things going on in my daughter's life. It's so hard right now!" Starla was emotional and allowed herself to release her heart to the sister-in-law that she formally resented.

"What is Reginald saying about it all?" Macy asked.

"Reginald is being Reginald. He had agreed to save face and attend church together to keep the congregation out of our business. At one time it felt like we were going to be able to live under the same roof again but that soon proved wrong. We live a fake life to keep up our status in the community."

The two women continued to hold each other, their hearts pouring out years of buried emotions. Slowly, they began to heal the wounds that had kept them apart for far too long. As the neighbors retreated to their homes, leaving the two women to their conversation, Starla and Macy knew that this moment of emotional healing marked a new beginning in their relationship.

With a renewed sense of understanding and compassion, they parted ways, ready to face the challenges that lay ahead. Sometimes, it takes a breakdown to lead to a breakthrough.

CHAPTER 41

IT'S NOW OR NEVER (CHLOE'S DECISIONS)

As the morning drifted by, Chloe found herself grappling with the decision to meet with Nikki after work. She needed Nikki's help with some of the management issues for the new property. The burden of her job pressed on her shoulders, each responsibility a heavy stone she couldn't afford to drop. The air in her office felt tense, and the soft hum of the air conditioning unit accentuated her dilemma. Mr. Stephens valued self-starters, and Chloe was determined to maintain her position in the company. Yet, the counseling sessions with Aaron were also taking a toll on her emotions, especially the conflicting feelings she experienced whenever she was near him. The scent of freshly printed paperwork settled through the office, mingling with the aroma of coffee from her morning cup.

She made up her mind to meet with Nikki after work. Discussing her work-related issues in conjunction with the issues in their relationship needed to be sorted out. The looming church board meeting held the keys to her ministry position's fate, and she dared not risk further complications from her tangled relationship.

Amidst the chaos of her busy day, her phone rang, and she answered without checking the caller's ID. It was Aaron, sounding pleasant yet anxious.

"Hello, Chloe Rhodes speaking, how may I assist you?"

"Hello, Chloe. How's your day going?"

"Aaron…hi. What a surprise. I'm busy as usual, drawing for straws as they say…what about yours?"

"About to meet with my father and grandfather."

"You sound nervous," Chloe said as she continued to multi-task between talking to Aaron and reading a proposal.

"I am, but I've got to get some things off my chest. They want to talk about the Harvest Day celebration. I already know how it's going to go down."

Stopping, Chloe felt compassion for Aaron. She recalled their conversation a while back and how Aaron always walked in his father and grandfather's shadows when it came to the traditional styles of preaching that they held. Aaron always felt bound and uneasy, but never seemed to be able to muster up the courage to discuss his true feelings with them. "Well, you know what you've told me about standing my ground. Now it's your turn."

"Young lady, you are so right. I knew I was moved to call you for a reason. Oh, and by the way, we didn't get around to addressing that challenging question you posed a couple of sessions ago, but no worries…we'll address it at some point in time if you're still up for it."

"No problem. I understand. I'll wait," Chloe said as she resumed reading through her paperwork. Listen, you're going to be fine. Just speak your heart. I'm sure that all will be well."

"Thanks, I'll let you get back to it. Just wanted to hear your voice. Listen, Chloe. Your questions about God and how he feels about same-sex relationships is not all we need to discuss."

"I know, but untangling the knot in our personal emotions right now is not the best route to take."

"You mean because of Nikki or because you sense a connection with me?" Aaron asked, feeling a bit off about being too forward.

"Something like that," Chloe answered, taking her glance away from the paperwork she held in her hand. "But for now, you are going to deal with your issue with your dad and grandfather. I'm sure they will hear you out. You got this."

"Okay. Enjoy the rest of your day."

As she hung up, she found herself lost in thoughts. The stress of her job, Nikki's behavior, and the uncertainty of her future all weighed heavily on her mind. Amidst her musings, she found herself haunted by memories of Miss Monet, who had caused her immense pain during summer camp. The buried pain from that incident resurfaced at unexpected times. Once again, the memories came crashing in like waves, their emotional intensity threatening to drown her.

Her focus was interrupted by Mr. Stephens, who entered her office and found her preoccupied. The faint smell of his cologne, mixed with the scent of coffee and paper, filled the room. Embarrassed by the coffee spill she had caused, she tried to compose herself but couldn't hide her disarray.

"Miss Rhodes, is everything alright? You seem a bit distracted today," Mr. Stephens said with genuine concern. His deep voice vibrated in the small office.

Chloe took a deep breath, trying to regain her composure. The soft sound of her exhale echoed in her ears. "I'm sorry, sir. It has just been a busy day, and I was lost in some thoughts. I assure you; I'm fully focused on my work."

Mr. Stephens raised an eyebrow, studying her for a moment. The clicking of his pen provided a steady rhythm in the background. "I understand that the demands of your position can be overwhelming but remember that it's important to maintain a balance. Don't hesitate to ask for support or delegate tasks if needed. We believe in your potential, Miss Rhodes, but taking care of yourself is equally vital."

"Thank you, sir. I'll keep that in mind, also...I sent the executive summary portion of the report for the upcoming meeting," Chloe replied. Her heart rate began to slow down as she appreciated Mr. Stephens' understanding nature. She felt a sense of reassurance, like a gentle breeze on a warm day, knowing that she was valued as an employee.

"Miss Rhodes...I received the report...just wanted to have a brief discussion. How well do you know Nicole Witherspoon?"

A lump formed in Chloe's throat as she attempted to swallow. Rather than the lump conforming it choked her as she suddenly began coughing uncontrollably. Reaching for bottled water, she paused as she took a drink, holding up her finger to indicate for Mr. Stephens to give her a moment.

"Take your time," he said gently.

"I know her, quite well, sir. I met her when she became my finance mentor during my freshman year in college. After the mentoring, we became...we remained friends after my college years...sir."

"Be careful. There have been reports from a negative standpoint to come across my desk recently. I want to make sure that your duties and responsibilities are not compromised by something that is of a personal matter. Feel free to discuss anything you feel we need to know concerning our new client."

"Yes, sir. I..." Chloe froze. Her words would not come out. She was stifled by the fear. Her heart was panting.

"You have something you want to say, Miss Rhodes?" Mr. Stephens asked once again.

"Yes, I...I promise to ensure that my job is not compromised by my personal relationship with Nicole Witherspoon, sir,"

"Thank you. That is appreciated. Why don't you go out for a

moment? It's a nice sunny day...yes? Get you a bite to eat. The work will be here when you return."

"Yes, sir...I will and thanks again. Counting her blessings, she was happy to take the needed break suggested by Mr. Stephens. Grabbing her belongings, she spoke peace to her inner storm.

As she stepped out of her office to clear her head, she encountered Kory Adams, who was eating from a fast-food bag. The enticing aroma of fried food filled the air, making her mouth water.

"Exercising?" Kory asked with a teasing grin. His warm smile lit up the environment.

Chloe chuckled, relieved to have a light moment amidst her hectic day. "No, I was just thinking before heading over to the coffee shop to grab a sandwich. I see you have picked up a little something."

Kory laughed, "Yep, I have to have my all-time favorite meal since high school every now and then. My mom, who is a holistic practitioner, warns me about eating from fast-food restaurants, but I can't resist."

"I know. I like it too. I'm going to head on over there now," Chloe said as she started walking, trying to escape the mounting pressure of her day. The sound of their footsteps echoed softly across the pavement.

"Why do you always run from me?" Kory asked playfully, catching up with her.

Chloe blushed, "I don't. I'm always busy, and you always pop up at the most inconvenient times."

Kory's laughter was like music to her ears, lifting her spirits. "Okay, I see. Anyway, see you later, Miss Chloe Rhodes, future top executive."

"I receive it," Chloe replied, feeling a bit lighter from the brief exchange. The gentle warmth of Kory's teasing reminded her that there were people who cared for her and believed in her potential.

Each step towards the coffee shop fueled Chloe with a renewed determination, a fire kindled within her despite the mounting pressure of the day. She knew that addressing her issues with Nikki and confronting her past traumas were essential steps toward taking control of her life. With God's guidance and support from unexpected sources like Kory, she believed she could overcome the obstacles in her path and find brighter days ahead.

CHAPTER 42

GETTING TO THE ROOT (CHLOE)

Finishing up the final load of laundry, Chloe couldn't help but feel a mix of anticipation and anxiety as she tidied up her home in preparation for Nikki's arrival. Nikki, always punctual, was about to walk through that doorway any moment now. As Chloe sliced fruits and opened a package of cheese squares, her mind couldn't help but wander off into a sea of questions and doubts. *Was she in love with Nikki? Or was she just clinging to her because of the help she could offer with her new role at the real estate company?* It was time to confront the truth and make some tough decisions for her own mental well-being, especially after her discussion with Mr. Stephens.

Throwing the garbage bag into the outdoor dumpster, she heard a distant voice approaching her. Startled, Chloe turned around to see a young woman walking towards her. The woman had a natural Afrocentric hairdo and was dressed casually in jeans and sneakers. She looked about the same age as Chloe.

"May I help you?" Chloe asked, trying to hide the tension in her voice.

The woman introduced herself as Lisa Kelley and explained

that they had attended the same university. She wanted to speak with Chloe, but it had to be quick because Nikki was on her way over.

"Nikki?" Chloe asked, realizing that no one else was expected to arrive at her home.

"Yes, I wanted to warn you about her," the young woman looked frightened as she clutched her hands together.

"She's toxic," Lisa said, glancing over her shoulder nervously. "I've been in and out of relations with Nikki over the past couple of years, and I'm concerned about your well-being."

Chloe was puzzled and didn't fully understand the situation. Lisa continued, revealing her history with Nikki and the toll it had taken on her mental health. She had been stalked and manipulated by Nikki, who even sent her text messages whenever Chloe and Nikki were together.

"I'm sorry to inform you that she was doing the same thing when she was in a relationship with you during your freshman year," Lisa said, her voice filled with empathy.

Chloe was stunned by this revelation. It seemed that Nikki's destructive behavior extended far beyond their current situation. Lisa also shared that Nikki was supposed to be on anxiety medication but hadn't taken it in some time, which could explain her erratic behavior and also the half empty pill bottle that Chloe had found with the past expiration date.

As Lisa hurriedly left, Chloe stood silently in front of her home, tears welling up in her eyes. She felt overwhelmed by the information she had just received. Looking up at the stars, she turned to God for guidance and thanked Him for sending Lisa to warn her but whined that she was simply tired of dealing with it all.

With newfound determination, Chloe knew she had to act. Grabbing her phone from her pocket, she dialed Minister Aaron's number.

Chloe's heart raced as she spoke to Aaron on the phone,

desperately trying to convey the urgency of the situation with Nikki. His voice carried genuine concern, and she knew he would be there in a heartbeat if she needed him. "I don't think she's dangerous," she assured him, trying to quell her own fears as well. "But I'll call you if anything changes."

Just as she hung up, Nikki's car pulled into the driveway. Chloe quickly tossed the garbage bag into the receptacle, attempting to appear composed. "Hi! How was your day?" she greeted Nikki, attempting to divert her attention from the call she had just taken.

Nikki was in an unusually chipper mood, seemingly oblivious to Chloe's inner turmoil.

"Who were you on the phone with?"

Chloe hesitated for a moment before crafting a lie about the phone call. "It was my mom. Nothing important, just work stuff," she said, hoping Nikki wouldn't detect the unease in her voice.

As they settled in the living area, Chloe tried to focus on their conversation about work. She made notes on the management issues she was facing, but her mind kept drifting back to the encounter with Lisa. She knew she had to confront Nikki about it.

"Thanks for giving me all these pointers for work. You don't know how much this means," Chloe said.

"It's my pleasure. I don't want anything but the best for you and I'm here to guide you whenever you need me," Nikki said as she pulled Chloe into her arms.

Finally, gathering her courage, Chloe gently released herself from Nikki's embrace. "Nikki, I need to address an issue that came up tonight. Lisa came by earlier," she said carefully, studying Nikki's reaction.

Chloe was taken aback by Nikki's unexpectedly nonchalant response. Nikki laughed it off, "She is nothing more than a bitter ex," painting Lisa as a bitter ex spreading lies. Doubts lingered in Chloe's mind, refusing to disappear. Lisa seemed genuinely concerned and scared.

"I know you, but I don't know Lisa," Chloe admitted, torn between Nikki's words and Lisa's warning. "She sounded so convincing, and I don't know who to believe."

Nikki met Chloe's gaze, defending herself with conviction against Lisa's accusations. But Chloe couldn't ignore the nagging feeling that there was more to the story.

Desperate for clarity, Chloe sought reassurance from Nikki about the medication Lisa had mentioned. Nikki dismissed it as a fabrication, blaming Lisa for stealing pills from her mother. Chloe felt a weight in her chest, torn between trust and suspicion.

"I would never lie to you about something like this, and it's obvious that Lisa hasn't gotten over me," Nikki explained further, desperately pulling Chloe closer to her bosom.

Despite their embrace, Chloe found no solace. Confusion enveloped her as she grappled with the conflicting explanations from both Nikki and Lisa. She decided to push aside her doubts for the moment and enjoy the rest of the night with Nikki. But deep down, a lingering sense of unease remained, and Chloe knew she couldn't ignore it for long. As they held each other, Chloe's heart remained unsettled, uncertain of the path ahead. She envisioned a dark road with a thick and cloudy shadow as she slowly walked toward the light.

CHAPTER 43

THIS IS TOO MUCH (AARON'S CONFESSION)

Yanking his tie around his neck while pacing the floor, Aaron could not shake the uneasiness he seemed to feel. He knew too well that Chloe's leadership position on the ministry team was in danger of ending in a matter of a few short weeks. Then, her in and out of relations with Nikki was both emotionally and spiritually dangerous. These issues were too much for him to be at ease, so he determined he would have a heart-to-heart with Chloe.

"Hey, would you like to meet at my place for our final session instead of the church?" Aaron's voice was warm and unsure, a mix of anticipation hesitation as he heard Chloe's sweet voice on the other end of the phone. "I figure it would give us a different atmosphere for what we need to share tonight."

Chloe hesitated for a moment, trying to hide her unease. Especially since Nikki seemed to have some sort of power to know when she was with Aaron. "That sounds fine," she answered, her fingers nervously tapping on the phone. Aaron's offer felt a bit strange, but she didn't want to overthink it. "Please text your address, and I'll leave here in the next fifteen minutes."

"You bet. See you then."

As Aaron paced back and forth in his living room, memories and emotions collided within. The progress they had made during their sessions felt significant, but the pain of Lilly's tragedy still haunted him. He wondered if he had healed from that experience or if the old anxieties were resurfacing. Trying to steady himself, he turned to meditation and the comforting words of scripture, seeking an escape from the nagging thoughts.

The doorbell's chime broke the stillness, and Aaron rushed to welcome Chloe into his immaculate home. "Nice place," she said as she stepped inside, her eyes scanning the room. Aaron peered out the door, glancing around nervously. "Looking for somebody?"

"Just making sure you weren't followed… Anyway, make yourself comfortable," Aaron replied, trying to project an air of control despite the underlying unease.

"Followed? Wait… are you referring to Nikki?"

Aaron took a deep breath, trying to choose his words carefully. "Yes. She showed up here a couple of weeks ago, unannounced at night. Startled me."

Chloe's face displayed a mix of surprise and concern. "You never mentioned that" she said, her voice tinged with confusion.

He attempted to change the subject, offering her refreshments, but Chloe's thoughts were still on Nikki. "Can I get you a beverage, nuts, fruit?"

"No, I'm good."

"Okay, so… I want to address some of your questions about how God feels about same-sex romantic relationships. Diving right in, first off, we know that God created male and female when we study the book of Genesis, and the first marriage, performed by God, by the way… was between a male and a female. I believe we can use the Bible and discern that God's intentions for romance and marriage are between male and female."

Chloe's conviction and stern look showed she was not easily

swayed. "I understand the interpretive nature of the verse you refer to, but… why do I have a tendency toward the female gender when it comes to being comfortable in a romantic relationship? I never said I hadn't been involved in a relationship with a male, but I am comfortable with my romantic tendencies. I happen to believe it's the way He made me."

With genuine empathy, Aaron said, "Chloe, I believe you feel you were created with a tendency toward females, but I want you to carefully think about the nature of confusion when it comes to what is defined as natural and unnatural in the realm of sexuality. Just pray into this and let me know what answer you receive from the Holy Spirit. No need to be anxious. God will give you an answer of peace."

Her eyes locked with his, searching for understanding. "But what do you think?"

Taking a moment to gather his thoughts, Aaron shared something intimate. "As you know, I've always attempted to walk in the shadows of both my father and grandfather. They have groomed me for ministry since I was twelve. When I accepted God's calling on my life at the tender age of eighteen, I felt like I was ready to save the world," he spoke with both conviction and humility, pausing between sentences. "With all that being said, Lilly was assigned to me by my father. She was a complex individual who, like you, felt a tendency to be in a romantic relationship with other women. She underwent gender transition surgery but faced significant struggles afterward, including clinical depression. I became emotionally attached to her, and her tragic suicide left me devastated."

Chloe's gaze softened, understanding the weight of his past burdens. "You mentioned Lilly's depression in a conversation we had previously, but you never mentioned that she was a lesbian and all the other issues she underwent. Why tell me this now? Are you assuming my situation is like hers?"

"I'm merely explaining why I take the stand that I do when counseling. I offer a safe environment where the one being counseled can release what's in their heart and weigh it by what the text of God's word dictates. You see, sometimes we don't know what's in our hearts until we release it with words and reflection. Sometimes our way of thinking seems right, but according to God, that way is only right in our own eyes, and not His."

Chloe's voice hardened, and a touch of sarcasm seeped in. "My tendencies are not exactly like Lilly's were. I never said anything about a gender transition, and I surely do not plan on killing myself."

"Of course. I never meant to imply that you would. I want to ensure that you are free from the bondage of a possessive spirit of control that's dark and demanding. I've seen the type of spirit that operates in an individual like Nikki."

A hint of frustration colored her tone. "So now, you've assessed Nikki. Excuse me, are you a preacher or a certified therapist?"

"I have a degree in Christian counseling."

"Great. I just wish you would not have withheld information about your issues with Lilly and the degree of her problems."

"I apologize, but I honestly felt as if I conducted our sessions in the manner best for the situation. But I won't hold back how I feel about you."

With a mix of emotions, Chloe responded, "So, you feel that you're going down the same road as Lilly. Aaron, I'm sorry. I think we're done here. You and the board can decide what you want."

Aaron desperately tried to salvage the situation. "Wait, Chloe..." The loudness of the door slamming in his face felt like the earth being pulled from under his feet. What would happen next was a mystery to Aaron, as he felt his duty to make Chloe whole had just blown up in his face. The tension in the air lingered, heavy with emotions and unresolved pain.

CHAPTER 44

UNRAVELING EMBERS

Chloe's heart was heavy as she drove home after the emotionally charged session with Aaron. Tears streamed down her cheeks, blurring the city lights that passed by in a haze. Desperate for answers to resolve the turmoil within her, she clutched the leather-bound journal in her trembling hands. It held her self-discovery journey—a completed journey where she called the shots as to who she was, despite anyone else's opinions. She also pondered other accomplishments and empowerment that she'd experienced over the past four years. She had been quite proud of the clarity about her feelings, her identity, and her place in this complicated world. But tonight, she suddenly felt as if someone stole something valuable from her.

Feeling alone in her struggle, Chloe ordered her voice activation app to dial Kennedy. As the phone rang, she bit her lip nervously, wondering if it was even fair to burden Kennedy with her own uncertainties. As closely knitted as they were, they had not spent a lot of time together recently due to their hectic work schedules and personal affairs. After a few rings, Kennedy picked up the call, her voice rushed and distracted.

"Hey, Chloe, sorry, I'm in the middle of something with Greg. What's up?"

Chloe tried to suppress her sobs as she spoke, "I… I just need someone to talk to, Kennedy. I'm so lost, and I don't know what to do anymore. Thought I had a handle on things."

Kennedy's voice softened, sensing the urgency in Chloe's tone. "I wish I could talk right now, but we're kind of busy planning the wedding. Can we catch up later, maybe tomorrow?"

"It's okay, I understand," Chloe managed to reply, though disappointment weighed heavily on her heart. Hearing the soft music in the background, Chloe discerned that the two were doing more than planning their wedding.

Feeling more alone than ever, Chloe decided to visit her mom, hoping to find some comfort and understanding. But as she poured her heart out to her mother, she realized that even her own mom couldn't grasp the depth of her inner struggle. She could tell that ever since her mom and her Aunt Macy had resolved their differences, her mom tried to spend more time with her but Chloe still held feelings of resentment about the mysterious Henrietta Lawson.

"Sweetie, you'll figure it out eventually. You're just going through a phase," her mother said with a well-intentioned pat on Chloe's hand.

"But it's more than just a phase, Mom," Chloe protested, her voice cracking. "I don't fit into a neat box, and I don't know what to do with all these emotions. I need to understand who I am, and it's tearing me apart."

Her mother's eyes filled with concern, but she couldn't offer the answers Chloe sought. Starla felt helpless as she continued to stare into her daughter's face. "You'll find your way, darling. Time has a way of sorting things out," she finally concluded.

Feeling increasingly frustrated, Chloe thanked her mom and

decided to leave. She couldn't blame her mother for not understanding, but the weight of her unspoken pain persisted.

With a heart full of uncertainty, Chloe found herself driving aimlessly through the dimly lit streets. She was drawn to Nikki's place, like a moth to a flame. Maybe Nikki would understand, maybe she could offer some guidance, or maybe she would take advantage of the situation and attempt to draw her away from family and church all together.

As she parked outside Nikki's house, Chloe hesitated for a moment, her hand hovering over the door handle. She took a deep breath and finally stepped out of the car, clutching her journal close to her chest.

The walk up the lawn to the porch of the house felt like an eternity, each pace a step closer to answers or heartbreak. When she reached Nikki's door, she hesitated again, her nerves almost getting the best of her. Finally, she knocked on the door and then rang the doorbell.

Seconds passed like hours before the door swung open, and there stood Nikki, looking surprised but not unwelcoming.

"Chloe, what are you doing here?" Nikki asked, holding a wine glass, concern flickering in her eyes.

"I… I needed someone to talk to. Someone who might understand," Chloe admitted, tears welling up again.

Nikki's expression softened, and she opened the door wider, inviting Chloe in. "Come in. Let's talk."

As they sat on the couch, Chloe poured out her heart about the painful session with Aaron. She revealed her fears, doubts, and hopes, all the while clutching her journal as if it held the secrets of her soul.

Nikki listened intently, nodding at all the right moments, offering comfort when needed, and sharing her own experiences. As they spoke, Chloe felt a sense of understanding and connection, something she had longed for all along.

Nikki's words echoed in the dimly lit room, filling the space with an air of understanding and vulnerability. Chloe listened intently, captivated by Nikki's honesty about her own struggles. The flickering candlelight danced on their faces, reflecting the complexities of their emotions.

"So… Lisa was telling the truth about your mother saying that you had not taken your medication in a while," Chloe said, her curiosity piqued as she hung on Nikki's every word. "Was the rest of Lisa's story true?"

"Some of what Lisa told you was true, but not everything. Look, this is not about Lisa or me. It's about you breaking free from your family and the church board. Especially Aaron. He lied to you for crying out loud," Nikki said, her voice tinged with frustration, her wine glass swirling with emotion.

Chloe contemplated Nikki's words, her heart torn between the loyalty she felt towards Aaron and the unsettling revelations she had discovered. "I wouldn't say that it was a lie or even that he intended to deceive me, but it did hurt to find out the withheld information about Lilly."

"Hahaha… listen to you. You speak of Lilly as if she was someone you knew, or as if she's still alive. You see what this preacher man has done to you?" Nikki remarked, her laughter laced with bitterness.

"You're right. I'm too attached to the Lilly story. Listen, I do love you, but I also need space to figure out why I'm so attached to Aaron. Can you give that to me?" Chloe mustered the courage to express her truth, even though she knew it would be difficult for Nikki to accept.

Nikki's eyes softened, and she reluctantly replied, "I can. I won't lie and say I agree with it, but if that is what you desire for me to do… then I'll respect your wishes. I only ask that you stay with me tonight."

Chloe felt her heart race at Nikki's request, torn between her own needs and the powerful allure of Nikki's embrace. "I... I'm not sure if that will help the situation any."

"Are you telling me that you don't want me, Chloe?" Nikki's voice took on a hint of vulnerability, mixed with a magnetic pull that left Chloe feeling breathless. Nikki's hand grazed Chloe's thigh gently, causing her senses to spin even faster.

Stumbling to her feet, Chloe tried to regain her composure, but her head felt like a whirlwind. "I just... need some space and time to think. I forgot to eat, and I skipped lunch today as well. I'll be okay, really. Just need to eat a cracker or something... drink some water."

Concern etched across her features, Nikki picked up Chloe in her arms, effortlessly carrying her towards the bathroom. "Now I know you need to stay here tonight. You're not okay, young lady," Nikki said, her voice filled with both care and firmness. "I'll make you a bubble bath and fix you a sandwich. There are plenty of cold beverages in the fridge. Let me take care of you tonight, Chloe. Then you're welcome to continue your self-discovery journey, or whatever it is you're calling it."

Though Chloe's mind was racing, she couldn't deny the warmth of Nikki's care. Surrendering to her exhaustion and the realization that she needed to take better care of herself, Chloe decided to comply with Nikki's suggestion. It would be a long night, but perhaps in this embrace, she could find the peace in her soul that she so desperately sought. As the water ran and the scent of lavender filled the air, Chloe allowed herself to be cared for, hoping that the night would bring clarity amid the storm of uncertainty.

CHAPTER 45

IT'S ABOUT TO GET REAL (CHLOE WAKE UP)

As the week raced by, Chloe found herself caught in the crossfire of dodging Aaron's phone calls and contemplating what her life would be like without the ministry she had been a part of for years. The weight of disunity in the church burdened her, as some showed support for her, while others opposed and continued with harsh looks and gossip. The upcoming Harvest Day and quarterly board meeting added to the pressure building inside her.

"Hey, Chloe. What's up?" Kennedy's voice rang through the phone as she finally reached out, feeling guilty for the delay in getting back to her cousin.

Chloe responded, her tone snappy, "Hi, Kennedy. Just getting off. About to grab a sandwich and call it a night."

"I know I've been preoccupied lately. I'm sorry for the delay in getting back to you. So… what did you wanna discuss the other night?"

"No bother. I figured it out," Chloe answered, her voice still edged with frustration over the previous disappointment. She knew she shouldn't be this way with Kennedy, but her emotions were getting the best of her.

"Oh no you don't. Spill the tea... come on," Kennedy urged, trying to break through the tension.

"I said no bother, Kennedy. It's fine. I know you and Greg were doing your thing, and you didn't have time to listen to me whine," Chloe snapped, her frustration pouring out.

"It wasn't like that—"

"You're telling me that you and Greg were not in the middle of getting your groove on?" Chloe's words lashed out, fueled by her emotions.

"Okay, busted. But... well, you wouldn't understand," Kennedy's tone softened, trying to explain herself.

"Don't throw shade. I'm a lesbian, but it does not mean that I'm not a normal person. I do understand," Chloe retorted, her voice sharp.

"What's up with you? Look, we're not kids anymore in my bedroom telling secrets and looking out for each other. We're both adults with responsibilities. It doesn't mean that we don't care for each other."

"Save it. It's okay. I agree. Now if you will excuse me, I'm pulling up at the drive-through, and I need to order food. I'll talk to you later," Chloe said, ending the call abruptly.

Moments later, a text from Kennedy came through, expressing an apology and a willingness to listen. Chloe replied with a 'thumbs up' emoji, acknowledging the message, but still feeling the strain in their usually strong bond.

As she continued her drive home, Chloe's thoughts were consumed by the conversations she had. Her relationship with Kennedy had always been unshakeable, but now she felt a shift, a growing distance that she couldn't ignore.

When her phone rang again, she was surprised to see it was Aunt Macy calling. As they spoke, Chloe found comfort in her aunt's motherly presence, but she also learned that Macy had an unexpected encounter with Nikki at the supermarket. This revelation only added to the complexities of her emotions.

"Yea...we actually had a nice conversation. She opened up to me, Chloe. The woman is suffering from lots of past traumas."

"What? Do you mean to tell me that you happened to bump into Nikki and now you know about her past traumas?"

"Not exactly. We conversated for a moment, I invited her to have a cup of coffee around the corner. We spent a half hour together and I discerned her pain. She confided in me a little. I was able to see beyond the intelligent, career-focused individual and see the undercurrents of a woman who has masked pain for years. You need to shut down your relationship with this woman until she gets professional help, dear," Macy said with care and concern in her voice.

"Wow...this woman you're speaking of has been the only person who has been there to support my vision for my life. I don't know if I can be real with myself and pretend that I don't love her."

"Is it love, or is it curiosity, honey? Love, or infatuation? There is a huge difference, and the line is quite thin," Macy's words were drenched in concern and the touch of nurturing that mothers gave to their adult daughters. "Now, out of respect for your mother, I want to invite you to talk with her about this. I'm happy to tag along if you'd like. I think the three of us can make some headway in this serious matter."

"No thank you, Auntie. Listen, you have always been a mother to me. I appreciate all those years when my own mother was busy with her career and neglected to spend that quality time with me. I appreciate especially the family feeling that I was fortunate to experience with you, Kennedy, and Uncle Broderick. Let me handle this one on my own."

"Chloe, wake up. It's time to see that you've been placing a bandage on your own scars. Nikki is that bandage. I know she's helped you in your career, but you don't owe her anything. Your life choices should not be based around her."

"Auntie, I'm just as awake as I can ever be. I love you. We'll talk soon." Ending the call in the same manner as she did with Kennedy, Chloe felt the burden of Macy's words. So much so that she began to tense up, anxiety was taking her breath. The onset of panic and anxiety was overtaking not only her thoughts but now her body as well.

Aunt Macy's concern for Nikki's past traumas rang in Chloe's ears. She knew her connection with Nikki had been a lifeline during challenging times, but now, it seemed like a slippery slope. Her aunt's suggestion to step back from Nikki until Nikki seeks professional help resonated with her, but she couldn't ignore the pull of her feelings.

As she continued to contemplate the events of the day, a wave of panic engulfed her. Memories of her painful past resurfaced, taking her back to a dark night in Ms. Monet's cabin.

Struggling to breathe, Chloe fought the fear, shame, and pain that threatened to overwhelm her. Desperately, she cried out the name of Jesus, finding safety in faith. Slowly, her tense body relaxed, allowing her to exit the car and make her way inside.

Though she managed to find peace at that moment, Chloe knew she needed to address her anxieties and find professional help as well. The internet would be her guide, as she vowed to educate herself about anxiety attacks to prevent such incidents in the future. She found herself back on the journey to face her inner struggles and seek answers and healing along the way.

CHAPTER 46

PREACH THE WORD (AARON'S DILEMMA)

As Aaron prepared to meet his father, grandfather, and Pastor Conner for lunch, he couldn't shake the unsettling nerves in his stomach. The weight of recent events had clouded his mind, making it difficult to focus on his sermon outline for the Harvest Day celebration. Chloe's refusal to take his calls or texts added to his distraction, leaving him feeling lost in a maze of burdens and conflicting thoughts.

Staring at his traditional attire, he remembered Chloe's teasing words about his dressing habits. Deciding to reach out to her one more time, he was relieved when she finally answered his call. Her voice sounded different, less sweet, but he appreciated hearing from her, nonetheless.

"Chloe, thank you for taking my call. How are you?" Aaron began, trying to keep his anxiety at bay.

"I'm well, and yourself?" Chloe responded, her tone a mixture of politeness and distance.

"Good. I've been calling all week. Chloe… I'm sorry we ended up the way we did, is all. I wanted you to know that you were more than a congregant coming to me for counseling. We shared a lot, and I came to care about you deeply. I pray that everything works out for your good in the end," Aaron expressed sincerely.

"Thanks, that means a lot. I wanted to take your calls, but I've been doing lots of soul-searching. I accept your apology, and if it means anything… I do miss our conversations," Chloe admitted.

"Speaking of conversations… I'm meeting with all three of them in a matter of forty-five minutes. Pray for me," Aaron joked, but Chloe could sense his underlying anxiety.

"Oh boy… you mean the Pastor and your dad and granddad. Sounds like a serious affair. You've got my prayers," Chloe replied, trying to lift his spirits.

"And how are things going in your world?" Aaron inquired, genuinely interested.

"They are going. Nikki and I spent one last night together last week, and we've split up to give me time to sort some things out, with my feelings for you being included in that.

"I agree that my sudden attachment to you only added to your dilemma, but I won't apologize for my feelings."

"And you shouldn't. On another note…Nikki had a conversation with my aunt if you can believe that," Chloe shared.

"How did that go?" Aaron asked, intrigued by the unexpected twist involving Nikki and Chloe's aunt.

"It was somewhat positive. My aunt took her out for coffee and was able to discern the pain and trauma that Nikki has been carrying for years. From what I hear, Nikki has decided to talk with a therapist," Chloe revealed, surprised by the recent developments herself. "I've been trying to get her to do that for a while."

"Wow. That's great. Your aunt must be some kind of woman to get Nikki to see a therapist," Aaron said, admiring Chloe's aunt for her insight and influence.

"She's cool. So, I can hear the tension regarding your lunch meeting. All I can say is stand your ground," Chloe encouraged, hoping to offer support to Aaron.

"Right. You too, Chloe Rhodes. Talk later," Aaron replied, feeling a mix of emotions as he ended the call. The unexpected twist involving Nikki seeking therapy added a new layer of complexity to the situation, and he couldn't help but wonder what other surprises lay ahead and if Nikki was sincere in her quest to seek help.

The restaurant was unusually calm, with only a few patrons scattered across the dining area. As Aaron made his way to the back, he noticed the three men already seated, deeply engaged in conversation.

"There he is," Aaron's dad, Marshall, exclaimed, interrupting their discussion. Marshall, a middle-aged man with a distinguished salt-and-pepper beard, held a commanding presence. He was a well-educated pastor, deeply rooted in scriptural knowledge and unyielding in his legalistic and traditional preaching style. Dressed in a crisply tailored suit, he carried himself with the characteristics of a man dedicated to his faith.

The others stood up, and they all exchanged firm handshakes.

"So glad we could all meet. It's been quite some time," Aaron's grandfather, Pastor Benjamin Conner, said with a warm smile. Despite the deep wrinkles etched into his face, his voice remained resolute and strong. Pastor Benjamin was a pillar of their religious community, known for his unwavering commitment to traditional values and his encyclopedic knowledge of scripture. He, too, was dressed in a sharp suit, a reflection of the respect he held for the sanctity of their roles as spiritual leaders.

"Good to see everybody," Aaron replied, though his nerves churned within him like a tempestuous sea. He took a seat next to Pastor Conner, trying to steady himself.

"Son, Pastor Conner and I had a conversation last night. We

wanted to know how your counseling sessions went with the Rhodes lady?" Aaron's dad, Marshall, wasted no time in bringing up Chloe, cutting straight to the important aspect.

"The sessions went well. Chloe has the potential to see things through the lens of scripture, but..." Aaron began cautiously.

"But what?" Pastor Conner interjected, the intensity of his gaze causing Aaron to pause. "You know the church is on the verge of splitting over this issue," Pastor Conner added, his voice tinged with concern and stress.

"Yes, Sir. I'm aware of the disunity. Chloe needs more time. She's journaling, soul-searching, and seeking advice. She is releasing years of traumatic tension, and I believe that once she confronts those traumas, she'll find the freedom to walk in her God-given purpose," Aaron explained, hoping to bridge the gap between his convictions and the church's stance.

"Son, you're not addressing the issue head-on. It's not just about her purpose; it's about a certain lifestyle she stubbornly holds onto, believing that God approves," Grandpa Benjamin added, his words heavy with the weight of tradition.

Before Aaron could respond, Pastor Conner interjected again, steering the conversation in a different direction. "So, here's what we, your father, grandfather, and I, propose to do. The Harvest Day celebration is a significant event for our church and the community. Due to the gossip and disunity, we need a fiery sermon on the topic. While I'm not sure what you've planned, here's an outline with some verses and key points that need to be reiterated. We want the people of our church and community to understand our stand on same-sex relationships. Can you handle this?"

Staring at the page with the pre-written sermon outline, Aaron felt a mix of shock and conflict within himself. On one hand, it was tempting to accept their suggestion; it would free his mind from the burden of finding his own message. Yet, on the other hand, it didn't sit right with him, feeling like a betrayal of his beliefs.

"Well, son, do you think you can handle this, or should one of us deliver the message?" his dad asked, concern etched on his face, reminiscent of their heart-to-heart conversations from Aaron's teenage years.

"I can." Aaron replied, meeting the eyes of each of his mentors. While he struggled with the request, he was willing to comply out of respect for them, even if it felt wrong in his heart. Deep down, he knew this wasn't the message he wanted to deliver, but for now, he would do what was asked of him, hoping that someday his true convictions would be heard.

CHAPTER 47

NIKKI, MAKE PEACE WITH YOUR DEMONS

The evening unfolded with a crisp and refreshing breeze, a gentle reminder that the world was still spinning despite the weight of Nikki's thoughts. After a day filled with property evaluations, exhaustion clung to her like a second skin. With a weary sigh, she decided to embrace the comforts of solitude – a chance to order takeout, slip out of her shoes, and indulge in one of her cherished films.

Standing before the vertical mirror, her own reflection stared back, a morbid reminder of the battles she had been waging within herself. The trophies of her career accomplishments seemed dim in comparison to the emptiness that gnawed at her core. Even the recent night spent with Chloe was not compensating for the hollow place in her soul. Pouring herself a glass of wine, Nikki paced the room, her steps echoing the rhythm of her thoughts. She also grabbed a bottle of pills that she'd picked up from the drug store earlier.

"I wonder if praying and affirming will work for me," she mused, desperation weaving through her soul like a thread of vulnerability. Chloe's unwavering faith in those practices seemed like a lifeline, a path Nikki hadn't dared to tread. Her introspection was abruptly interrupted by the persistent chime of the doorbell.

"Who in the… come on, it's Friday evening and I don't wanna be bothered," she muttered, annoyance evident in her voice as she strode towards the door. The door swung open to reveal Macy, a familiar smile on her face.

"Well look who it is… Chloe's cookie-baking aunt Macy," Nikki quipped, a touch of sarcasm lacing her words as she held the door wider for Macy's entry.

Macy's response was a smirk, coupled with a gentle request, "Can I… come in?"

"Be my guest." As Macy stepped in, Nikki's invitation was laced with an undertone of curiosity.

"Hope I'm not interrupting anything," Macy said, her concern genuine.

"Actually, I was just about to order dinner and crash on the couch with a flick. Long and exhausting day," Nikki replied, the wine glass in her hand a testament to her intention. "Would you like a drink?"

"No thank you. I'm so sorry to interrupt. I should have texted first."

"Yes, you should've, but what can I do for you?"

Macy hesitated for a few seconds before revealing the purpose behind her unexpected visit. "This may sound strange, but I woke up this morning with you heavy on my mind. It was as if I carried your thoughts through the night. I'm almost certain you were in my dreams."

A teasing smile tugged at Nikki's lips. "Macy Rhodes, are you flirting with me?" Macy let out a sinister giggle.

Macy's eyes met Nikki's, unflinching. "No, Nikki. It's a gift from God. God's Spirit has revealed this to me and I'm only obeying what I feel compelled to tell you. It's supposed to give you comfort and strength. God loves you Nikki and He is waiting on you with open arms. He wants to heal you everywhere you hurt. He knows you've been looking for a home, but every place your feet tread only turns out to be an alienated land full of disappointment."

A tear welled in Nikki's eye, her emotions brimming at Macy's sincerity. "So, are you some kind of psychic?"

"No, not at all. Again, it's the power of God's love."

In a moment of vulnerability, walls began to crumble. Nikki began to unload, pouring out the burdens she had been carrying. Macy's presence was a balm to her wounds, urging her to confront the shadows that had haunted her for far too long. The shadow of a marriage, where her ex-husband physically and verbally abused her. If that was not enough, her father had done the exact same thing to her mother. Nikki revealed that her ex-husband was seconds away from strangling her to her death. Had it not been for a stranger jogging past their lawn that day, she wouldn't be alive today.

Their conversation wove its way through Nikki's defenses, breaking down her resistance. Macy's disclosure of her own journey of healing became a bridge, a connection between two souls navigating the complexities of pain and growth.

"I want to share some of my backstory. A part of my life I'm ashamed of and many haven't heard this. During my college days, I thought I was a lesbian. I experimented with same-sex encounters. I rebelled against my parents and my church family. One day, somebody special approached me, the same way I'm approaching you. The message this person shared was the message that caused my walls to crumble and at that moment in time, I realized that it wasn't about sex at all. It was about finding God's presence. Not church attendance, but truly finding God through a Savior, whose name is Jesus Christ," Macy said, her words were soothing, like a tranquilizer as her transparency spilled out like water.

"You said that I've been looking for a home in strange places.

That is so true. I've not known home in years," Nikki confessed, her voice trembling with raw emotion. "You must have some gift, Macy Rhodes. I've not made myself this vulnerable with anyone."

Macy's response was gentle and knowing. "God does exist, and He empowers us to comfort and love one another the way He loves. We need each other."

Nikki's skepticism had yielded to something deeper. "Thank you. This feels awkward, but I will try to do as you suggest. I'll contact the therapist you recommend and go from there, Nikki said as she thought her agreement would encourage Macy to leave."

As Macy's departing figure disappeared, it left behind a whirlwind of newfound freedom and a glimmer of healing for the tormented Nikki. However, beneath the surface, a dark cloud loomed over her soul, casting a sinister shadow over her fragile state of mind. Sweat trickled down her forehead, mingling with tears streaming down her cheeks, a confirmation of the inner struggle she faced.

Desperate to escape the suffocating grip of her own thoughts, Nikki sought a haven in the hypnotic allure of wine and the pills she obtained earlier. With trembling hands, she reached for the bottle, pouring the crimson liquid into a trembling glass. And just as swiftly as the alcohol touched her lips, a sense of temporary relief washed over her, calming the anxieties that gnawed at her from within.

But as the wine lulled her into a state of false tranquility, a familiar chorus of voices began to whisper in the dark recesses of her mind. They were echoes from a time she thought she had left behind, haunting reminders of a reality drowned in medication. They whispered secrets, insecurities, and despair with tormenting tongues, threatening to pull Nikki deeper into the abyss she was fighting so hard to escape.

Sobbing uncontrollably, Nikki fought back against the gross darkness, clinging desperately to her dwindling strength.

"I just want peace," Nikki murmured, her voice barely above a whisper, as she continued to drown her sorrows in the cocktail of wine and pills. The room spun around her, forming a distorted shape, and her legs gave way beneath her, sending her crashing to the floor in a heap of despair.

Gazing at her reflection on the intricately adorned glass table she held on to, she felt momentarily captivated by the unfamiliar face staring back at her. A face that seemed somehow detached from her own reality, plunging her into a state of confusion. Before she could gather her bearings, her eyes fell upon the empty pill bottle lying discarded on the table, its contents now within her. Panic traveled through her veins as the dooming predicament became clear.

In that moment, as despair threatened to consume her, a brilliant ray of light pierced through the darkness, dancing upon the glass and casting enchanting patterns upon the room. It was as though the God that Macy and Chloe had spoken about had summoned all of its powers to save her from the abyss that loomed.

With every ounce of strength she had left, she reached for her phone with trembling hands. Her fingers fumbled desperately as she dialed the three emergency digits that held the promise of salvation. 9-1-1. Her heart pounded in her chest as she awaited the connection, hoping for a lifeline to be thrown her way.

CHAPTER 48

CHLOE'S EPIPHANY

Unable to sleep, Chloe was happy to see the morning sunlight as she stumbled out of bed. A Saturday morning run sounded nice, but she felt she didn't have the energy after tossing and turning all night long. Jumping in her vehicle and heading to the park, she had the strange notion to drop by her mom's to grab some of her energy herbs. She knew her mother was an early riser, and it would give her time to hopefully become fully awake and jumpstart her day.

Parking on the side of the street, Chloe was taken aback to see another vehicle parked in the yard. "What the..." to her amazement, it looked to be the same vehicle that Henrietta was driving a few weeks ago. "This is too weird," she mumbled. Grabbing her spare key from one of the compartments of her purse, she decided to go into the house, in hope that this time, her mother would explain why Henrietta was there.

With her normal routine of entering the house and calling out for her mom, Chloe's first stop was the kitchen, then the den, and finally up the stairs to her mom's bedroom. "Mom," she continued to call out. As she entered the bedroom, voices that sounded like melancholy laughter could be heard. Confused, she quietly advanced toward the bathroom. The door was slightly cracked. Entering the adjourned master bathroom, Chloe's body tensed, as she witnessed the unthinkable.

"What is this?" she asked, her voice reversing to that of a small child, bewildered and confused, interrupting her mother and Henrietta. The two women were naked, indulged in the moment and sharing a bath together in the large, oval shaped bathtub that Chloe remembered her father surprising her mom with on one of their anniversaries. With music coming out of the Bluetooth speaker and as the room seemed to spin, Chloe walked backward until she was no longer in the room. Everything was foggy, as if she was moving in slow motion. Turning her body to depart from her childhood home, a voice could be heard in the backdrop... "Chloe, Chloe, please honey, don't leave. Let's talk about this... Chloe...I'm ready to explain everything..." but Chloe didn't stop until she was at the bottom of the stairs, desperately seeking an escape route!

Fumbling in her hip pocket to find her kiosk, she managed to enter into her car. Whipping her head to the left, there she was... her mother or whoever she now was to her was standing beside her car, tears were flowing like a river as she begged Chloe to get out of the car. Whipping her head to her right, she witnessed another figure running toward her car. It was her Aunt Macy. *Did she know all this time?* A question flashed through her mind as she sat lifeless behind the wheel, Macy on one side and her mom on the other. Looking toward the house, Henrietta, fully clothed, was entering her vehicle, preparing to flee the scene.

Minutes seemed like hours as Chloe could hear her aunt talking on her phone. As she breathed uncontrollably, she told herself that she was not going to have another panic attack and she meant it. Words from her session with Aaron, as well as the talks that she'd had with Nikki in the past swirled in her mind. Then, there it was out of nowhere, an event from her childhood Sunday school class. It was the story of Jonah, who ran from the call of God and when he finally obeyed after being swallowed by a huge fish, he was angry at God when the people that he thought should have been destroyed for their wicked and violent acts were spared by God's mercy because they were sorry for what they did. She could hear her favorite teacher ask the question..." *Why can't we give people the same grace that God gives us?"* It was in that moment that Chloe found the strength to snap out of her delusional episode. Coming back to herself, she could hear her mother sobbing and asking her to forgive her. Unlocking the door and slowly stepping out of the car, a sigh of relief swept over Starla, and she grabbed her daughter and gently led her back into the house.

"Chloe, are you okay," Macy asked as she hurried in behind them.

"No! We can handle it from here. This is my mess, I'll clean it," Starla said, her bloodshot red eyes filled with determination. Turning to leave, Macy nodded in agreement and left the scene.

"Sweetheart, thank you for giving me a chance to talk with you. You were right the other week to express that we all live like we want to and never confide in you. I'm sorry. Both your father and I have been keeping secrets from you and I wanna clear the air," she continued, as Chloe stared into the open. Gently holding her cheek and turning her face toward her, Starla continued. She explained that the marriage between her and Reginald ended several years ago. They had attempted to live together for both Chloe and the sake of their reputations in the community.

"How long have you been gay and why Henrietta?" Chloe finally asked, her voice sheepish but resolute.

"Honey, your father and Henri used to date for a bit in high school. They were planning on getting married until he and I secretly started seeing each other. We promised each other that we would discontinue the relationship, since we both loved Henri, and didn't want to hurt her."

"Well, that explains why you two never wanted me," Chloe's words were saturated in a lifetime of pain but despite the ugliness of the situation, she could feel strength coming upon her to face her mother head on.

"That's not true. We both loved you and that is the reason we did everything we could to ensure you had a good life," Starla felt strength to speak her mind, tons of weight lifted from her shoulders. "When your father left town to attend college when you were a baby, Henri started coming back around. Our friendship was restored. I always knew in my heart that your father loved Henri and tolerated me. I resented him because of it. But something strange began to unfold during the years he was away…Henri and I began to lean upon each other. She lost her father and grandfather in the same year. She was so broken. I wanted to console her…to make up for how Reginald and I had shattered her heart. I owed her something."

"This is a humble story, but it doesn't explain what I witnessed in that restaurant between dad and her and now you and her in the tub," Chloe sarcastically said, desperate to understand.

"To make a long story shorter, dear, things shifted. Henri began to be different. I was lonely because your father only visited every now and then on the weekends, since money was tight. Honey, we ended up…falling in strange love, Henri and me. I can't explain it. It all happened so fast."

"So, all this time, you could have helped me sort out my identity issues, but you were so busy deceiving me with your fake marriage. Mom this is not okay," Chloe blurted out. Within a split second, she could once again hear her Sunday school teacher's question……" *Why can't we give people the same grace that God gives us?"* Sitting up straight, she began to look at her mother directly in her eyes. During that moment, she could see pain, instead of poised business woman who was always in control of everything.

"Dear, I'm not sure why your dad and Henri met at that restaurant, he'll have to speak to that. But what I will speak to is the fact that life is complicated and if you don't get on top of your pain, it will get on top of you. I fell in love with Henri, your father seems to be in love with Henri, and Henri doesn't know which direction to take. So...your father and I agreed to fake it. It was working fine until Henri moved back here. That's enough for now. I'll let you process what you've heard."

"May I go to my room?" Chloe asked, as Starla's face held more confusion.

"Sure, honey, but why?"

"I need a nap. When I'm awake, I have something I need to tell you," Chloe said as she rose and went upstairs, leaving her mother standing in bewilderment. Starla's first thought was that Chloe was suffering from a mental breakdown, but little did she know, her daughter had experienced an epiphany moment that had been a long time coming.

CHAPTER 49

CHLOE'S EPIPHANY CONTINUES

Waking suddenly to a smell of burnt bacon and other aromas, Chloe's hour nap felt like four, as she stumbled out of her old bed and down the stairs. What she witnessed was a sight she hadn't seen in a while, her mom and dad...in the kitchen together.

"What's all this?" she asked as she stood in the entrance way of the kitchen.

"Morning!" Reginald said, walking slowly toward Chloe with arms extended. A tender embrace took place between the two; however, Chloe continued to inquire as to what was happening.

"Dear, I phoned your father and asked if he could come over and have breakfast, or something like that..." the two chuckled as Chloe continued to stare in unbelief. "Look, I wanted the three of us to share a meal and talk. I understand if you're not up for it, but I wanted to try," Starla's voice was sincere as she wiped her hand on an apron that had been in the cupboard for years.

Nodding her head hesitantly, Chloe complied. "I'd like that."

As the three sat and conversed, Chloe appreciated her parents' honesty about their past and how sorry they were that she was caught in the crossfires of their unresolved past issues. While the two continued to go on and on about making it up to Chloe by spending more family time, Chloe couldn't go another second without spilling her own truth.

"Mom...dad...I was molested when I was twelve. It happened at camp, that last time and...I lied when I was asked if I had been in her cabin those last few nights. I felt ashamed. Like it was my fault. I was traumatized and didn't know it all these years. I'm sorry I didn't confide in you," she said, gasping for air as if to drown from her tears.

"Oh my God! So, it was true? The other camp facilitator asked you, and...Chloe...so, is this what Nikki was talking about?" Starla was frantic.

"Starla, give her a moment to calm herself and settle her nerves...don't you see she is having a panic attack?" Reginald said sharply as he held Chloe's hand and began to guide her breathing. Sitting next to Chloe, Starla settled down and took Chloe's other hand.

"That's it, sweetheart. Easy does it, in and out...in and out," Reginald continued and within a moment Chloe's breathing returned to normal as she collapsed in an embrace with her dad.

"It's okay, sweetheart. We don't blame you, but we're hurt that you suffered alone," Starla calmly interjected, stroking Chloe's hair.

"Well, it's over now. You've endured this heavy load for all these years, but It's over. I want to find this person and press charges," Reginald said, pressing his lips together, the shock of it all getting the best of him.

"You've got that right! There is no telling how many children this beast of a woman has harmed," Starla added.

"No, I don't want to re-visit any of it. I want peace. I just want to heal. I've been doing research and I'm finally ready to see a therapist and if she thinks I need to face Ms. M and confront the whole thing, then I'll deal with it then. Until that time comes, please…can we put it behind us?"

"You bet, sweetheart. Give us a chance to be real parents to you. I know you're an adult with your own life, but I want to make up for lost time," Reginald said as a tear flowed from his eye.

"I'd absolutely love that," Chloe said embracing her parents and thanking God that she had been able to release what she suppressed for many years.

"So good to hear, and baby we're sorry that it came down to all of this for us to realize how important family and trusting communication is," Starla said as she held Chloe with a tight embrace.

As Chloe rested upon her parents, her life history began to play in her mind like an old flick…year by year…tear by tear…but one realization came to mind. She was ready to face the next phase of her life, no matter what fire she would pass through. Her mind seemed clear and what she heard was a voice speaking one of her favorite verses from the Bible…. *When you pass through the waters, I will be with you; and when you pass through the rivers, they will not sweep over you. When you walk through the fire, you will not be burned; the flames will not set you ablaze.*

CHAPTER 50

I AM AFFIRMED

A social media message notification flared at Chloe as she scanned her phone. After taking a couple of days off work, she felt renewed in her mind and was eager to get back into the swing of things.

"Normal does it," she whispered as she placed her files in her brief case and slipped on her shoes. Retrieving her phone, she checked the message. It was from an unfamiliar profile; thus, she contemplated whether to open it. When she did, to her amazement it was Dan Dan.

"Hi there! It's been a minute since we've connected. Can we chat a moment?"

Chloe thought it was odd to be receiving a message from Dan Dan, since they'd not spoken in years. Also, she'd heard that he was engaged to one of the nurses at the hospital he was working for.

Responding to the message, Chloe provided her phone number. "This ought to be interesting," she said as she continued to prepare herself to head out the door to work. She felt a newfound peace this morning. With her first appointment with a therapist after work, along with spending extra time reading the

Bible and praying, she already felt affirmed as someone who was loved by God and that her life would be successful no matter what. A little conversation from an old fling would not shake the strength in her emotions. Within a moments time, her phone rang.

"Good morning, Chloe Rhodes speaking," her voice sounded like music to Dan Dan as he paused before answering her cheerful greeting.

"Good morning, Chloe. Thanks for responding."

"No problem. How may I help you?"

"Chloe, I need to tell you something important. Nikki, a woman I'll never forget, was dismissed from the hospital's mental health unit yesterday," he informed, the memories of the unsettling vibes Nikki had emitted years ago flooding back. "I felt compelled to warn you, even though it's against the company's policies."

"What?" Chloe was startled, as she didn't know about Nikki's hospitalization.

"Oh, boy. So...you didn't know?"

"Know what? I've not spoken to her in a few days," Chloe, sitting on the edge of the bed with the phone in one hand and one arm in her blazer.

I don't have all the details, but there were incidents. Troubling ones," Dan Dan continued to sigh, not wanting to upset Chloe. "Look, this confidential information invades privacy laws, but...I couldn't shake the feeling that came over me. She's got some problems and was advised to get additional help, but she refused, and her mother signed her out. The reason it was so disturbing was that the woman's mother was terrified of her," Dan Dan's voice sounded sincerely concerned, as Chloe continued to listen and contemplate. "Are you there? Hello."

"I'm here. Dan Dan, thank you for your concern. I appreciate you taking this risk for me. I'll take it from here."

"So...okay. I...Chloe Rhodes, I'm getting married in a couple of months, and...well I wanted you to know that you have always been special to me, and I wish you the best. Take care of yourself and I hope that you have found yourself."

"Thank you, Dan Dan, or is it Danny or Daniel nowadays," Chloe teased, as she often did when she felt the atmosphere needed to be shifted. Chuckling on the other end of the line, Dan Dan informed her that most folks still referred to him as Dan Dan. Chloe, still feeling empowered, congratulated him on his engagement. The two casually talked for a couple of moments before ending the call. As Chloe closed her phone, a sense of normalcy settled over her as she continued preparing for her day. Little did she know, another unexpected surprise was about to rock her world as her doorbell rang a few moments later.

Opening her door, Chloe flinched, holding her chest as she beheld a strange woman in front of her. "You startled me. May I help you?" Chloe asked.

"I'm sorry for barging over, but when you didn't pick up, I thought I'd catch you before your day started...she said you were a morning person and so I took my chances coming over here. The woman had a look of suspense as she continued speaking. "Hi, I'm Margaret Witherspoon, I retrieved your address from an address book of hers."

"Mrs. Witherspoon, it's nice to meet you. What can I do for you?"

"My daughter is desperately ill, and I was hoping you could speak with her. She had a mental evaluation already but...she is refusing help and she won't take meds. I'm worried about her," Mrs. Witherspoon shared as her voice trembled. "Did you know she attempted to kill herself?"

"Oh my God! No Ma'am, I knew nothing of it. That's terrible."

"She said it was an accident. She was taking her medication because she knew she needed to get back on her meds, then she was drinking and she forgot she had taken it, or something like that. I'm terrified that her condition has worsened than from before."

"May I ask what condition you're referring to?" Chloe's curiosity was at a peak level, as she stared at the time. She knew she couldn't spend time with Nikki's mother too much longer.

"Nikki was diagnosed with post-traumatic stress disorder and other psychotic disorders like auditory hallucinations when she was a teenager. She and I both underwent traumatic experiences at the hand of her father, and then unfortunately her husband abused her. She had gotten so much better after seeking professional help, but things started turning and...I didn't know how to help her, and I know she blames me for her pain," Mrs. Witherspoon said as she wept.

"Listen, I appreciate your taking the time to inform me of Nikki's condition. I will reach out to her later today. It's going to be alright," Chloe gently said as she and the woman walked toward their vehicles to depart.

Dialing Nikki's number, Chloe panted as she recalled Mrs. Witherspoon's words earlier that day.

"Chloe girl!" Nikki blasted, answering the call on the first ring. "Dinner tonight? I know we agreed you were sorting things out, but I really need to see you," Nikki said as if her recent incident hadn't taken place.

"Nikki, I'm on my way to see a therapist, okay. I wanted to reach out to let you know that I'm texting you her information. It's time, Nikki. It's past the time for us both to heal from our past trauma."

"Who told you!"

"Nikki, calm down. I care enough about you to beg you to please, get the help you need."

"You're calling to break up with me. Yea, that's it. And to think when I saw your number flash across my screen that you were missing me."

"I won't go back and forth on this. Listen, thank you for everything, but I won't feel obligated to continue in a relationship that's not good for me or for you. I care too much, and if you care about me, you'll get help. Bye Nikki," Chloe said as sadness filled her heart. She knew she had to discontinue her relationship, but she was divided in her emotions. As she prepared to discontinue the call, she could hear Nikki's cold voice emphasizing how ungrateful she was and other threatening remarks. Chloe pushed it out of her mind and continued to walk in the affirmation that her healing was right around the bend.

CHAPTER 51

KILLING ME SOFTLY (CHLOE'S JOURNEY CONTINUES)

On the day of the annual Harvest Day Celebration, the church's sanctuary pulsed with life, filled with the vibrant congregation and eager visitors from the community. The anticipation was evident, an age-old tradition poised to unfold once again. Pastor Conner and his wife graced the scene, their attire a symphony of autumn colors, a visual testament to their leadership and unity. Despite the division that had recently clouded the church, the event commenced on a hopeful note.

Chloe found herself hiding out in the music room, the sanctuary of her solitude interrupted by Justine, a member of the liturgical dance ministry team. Justine's words carried a mix of surprise and concern, catching Chloe off guard as she meditated.

"Chloe, you're here. We weren't expecting you to—-"

Interrupting, Chloe's voice held a blend of defiance and determination. "Weren't expecting me to what? To show up as I always do, to prepare for the Harvest Day Celebration? Or perhaps you thought I wouldn't dare interpret the sermon today? Is that it?"

Justine's response was laced with humility. "I meant no disrespect. We had heard that you quit the team."

Clarifying her stance, Chloe's voice cut through the tension like a blade. "You heard wrong. I have never quit anything in my life." With purposeful strides, she walked past Justine, her daily devotional scripture a guiding beacon in her mind. A decision had crystallized within her. Chloe wouldn't be sidelined this time. She would take her place in ministry today, defying the uncertainties, and would deal with the board's decision when it was time. Amidst the chaos, she would find peace and acceptance in her chosen path, with or without her current church affiliation.

Standing on the stage, ready to interpret the first song, Chloe's hands moved in fluid motion, translating the melody into a visual language. Anxiety's grip tried to claw back into her, but Chloe summoned the strength, recollecting the essence of her ministry. She focused on the purpose that had driven her from the beginning, allowing it to guide her through the sea of faces.

With each gesture and each movement, Chloe looked to her heart's devotion. As the final notes of the song floated away, she felt an applause that vibrated like echoes of old times. Taking a breath, she stepped back, making way for Pastor Conner to ascend the podium.

As Pastor Conner's introduction led to Aaron's entrance, Chloe's gaze lingered on Aaron's face, his expression was filled with anticipation and nervousness. His tablet rested on the pulpit, ready for the words he was about to share.

Aaron's time to approach the pulpit podium arrived. His greeting resonated with warmth, his voice carrying the weight of a shared journey. Chloe, seated on the front pew, awaited the appropriate time to take her position for interpreting the sermon. She watched with pride and anxiety as Aaron's words stumbled at first, gradually finding their rhythm. As he looked towards the congregation, his tablet took a backseat to his conviction.

"Church, my brothers, and sisters in Christ… I feel as if I'm in a tug of war. You know how that feels, don't you? I mean you pull with all your might, but someone else is also pulling with all their might on the opposite end. Life can become a tug of war at times," Aaron's voice resonated with empathy, painting a vivid picture of struggle. The weight of his words hung in the air as he shared his vulnerability." Now, if you'd like, you can turn to John chapter four as we allude to Jesus's discussion with the woman at the well of Samaria." Pages began to flip in Bibles and others began to interact using their electronic devices. "Hold your places because I have a question for us? Are we, as a church body, driving people away because all we offer is a message of what God disapproves of? Do we create a safe atmosphere for people to talk openly concerning their affections and feelings, or do we make them feel like they are outside looking in? Think about it. Most of you came today expecting a fire and brimstone message to the lesbian or homosexual community. A fiery warning that God doesn't approve of their sexual preference. But I want us to think about our approach," Aaron said with passion, his eyes wandering to his left where his father and grandfather sat. Both held a stern countenance, but Aaron continued. "We need to take the approach that Jesus took when He set free the woman at the well. He didn't start out by pointing to the numerous failed marriages, nor did He inquire why she did not visit the well during the time of day the other women did. But He had a normal conversation about water and about intimacy with God! He also gave the woman the opportunity to speak her truth through admittance! *'I have no husband'* she said, although she was living with a man."

As Aaron spoke, Chloe's hands flowed like sharp blades, her face captivated many as a single tear flowed down her cheek. Several of the youth could be spotted with their eyes locked on her, rather than their usual cell phone activity. The moment was electrifying.

"Imagine being in a place where you were different and all you wanted was an understanding of intimacy and how to heal emotional wounds. All you wanted was to know your identity. You might look at me and wonder what intimacy and emotional wounds have to do with Jesus and the woman at the well in Samaria and I would answer… everything."

As Aaron delved more into the narrative of Jesus and the woman at the well, his voice became a vessel of revelation, his words drawing the congregation into a shared journey. Chloe's fingers moved to mirror his message in ASL, her fingers became a choir of dancers, her movements guided by a sense of unity.

The narrative unfolded like a hand-crafted blanket, woven from threads of vulnerability, redemption, and the pursuit of intimacy with God. Chloe's hands moved in rhythm; her own heart stirred by Aaron's words. The warmth of conviction filled the sanctuary, strong energy flowing between the congregants.

"God the Father created us with worship in mind. Before we choose a mate, a career, a church home, or anything else, He wants our hearts," Aaron's words struck a chord, resonating deeply within Chloe's spirit. "God also wants us to know, not only why He created us, but how he created us. We are spirit, soul, and body. We are human and there are cravings, lusts, and inherent weaknesses that will rise within us, even after we have given our lives to Christ. Now, there we go with that tug-of-war syndrome again," Aaron reminded as the audience chuckled.

As Aaron concluded his message, Chloe's hands stilled. Her heart felt like it had been pierced. Tears welled up in her eyes as the words of God hovered over her like a heavy blanket. She felt a tugging on her heartstrings, as if Heaven was calling to her, beckoning her closer. She let out a sob and fell to her knees, weeping at the altar as she confessed and asked for forgiveness. As she prayed, the weight upon her shoulders began to lift, and she felt a peace come over her that she had not felt in years. Her soul was released from its prison, and she felt freedom like she had never known before. Aaron's words killed her softly until she was resurrected back to life.

In the wake of the service's end, Chloe found herself compelled to address the congregation. With Pastor Conner's approval, she stood before the assembly, her parents at her side. Tears mingled with her words as she recounted her journey of self-discovery, the illumination that had dawned upon her through Aaron's sermon and her recent reconciliation with her parents.

"Now that you've heard my testimony of healing, repentance, and reconciliation, I'd like to address the board and the entire congregation. See, my sexual preference has come under scrutiny. The board is divided as to allow me the opportunity to exercise a gift that God bestowed upon me many years ago. I am not here to express whether I agree with the protocol, but I would like to echo a few of the implications from Minister Aaron's sermon by asking which one of you here is without sin? I remember from Sunday school class that Jesus asked this question to several leaders who were ready to stone a poor woman because she was caught in the act of adultery. When the leaders heard his line of questioning, none of them could cast a stone at her because Jesus commanded that whoever was without sin, should cast the first stone. Again, I'm not making excuses for sin, all wrongdoing is sin. Now, I have one more question that God pointed out to me recently, and it's this...why is it so hard for people to show the same kind of grace to others that God has shown to them? Why? Board of Trustees, regardless of what your decision will be tomorrow, I win. I win because God is pleased with me and His light shines on me continually, regardless of how you or even I feel or behave. Thank you."

As Chloe released the microphone, the congregation exploded into claps, praises, and some stood to their feet. Next, her parents stepped up to the podium and took a deep breath before they too revealed their secrets. The crowd seemed electric with emotion - some were shocked, some awe-struck, but mostly full of understanding and compassion in response to Chloe and her parents' boldness.

Their confessions inspired others to also come forward and open up about their personal struggles – things they had kept hidden for years - creating an aura of emotional healing within the church walls.

After the service, as the crowd began to disperse, and the sanctuary returned to its tranquil state, Aaron and Chloe found themselves drawn to each other amidst the hushed whispers of congregation members.

Their eyes met, and a silent understanding passed between them. The weight of their unspoken emotions hung heavy in the air as they moved towards one another, the crowd parting to make way for their meeting. Suddenly, as they clung to each other, it felt like home...finally, for both. Aaron had stood his ground and released the message within his heart despite his father and grandfather's suggested sermon, and Chloe's journey of self-discovery had taken a divine detour, one that landed her in the arms of her Heavenly Father. She felt peace regardless of how things would turn out with the board.

For Aaron, it was also a moment of realization and defiance. He had spent most of his life living in the shadows of his father and grandfather, seeking their approval and adhering to their expectations. But now, as he gazed into Chloe's eyes, his heart overwhelmed with courage, he knew that he had to break free from the chains that had held him captive for far too long.

Chloe, on the other hand, had battled with her own doubts and fears. The journey of self-discovery had been a tumultuous one, filled with moments of darkness and confusion. But as she stood before Aaron, her heart beating with fierce determination, she knew that she was ready to embrace her true identity, regardless of the consequences with Nikki, at work, church, or the community. Her epiphany resounded loudly. Her true identity as God's daughter with a destination was inviting to her soul.

Their hands reached out simultaneously, fingers interlocking as if they were two puzzle pieces coming together at last. It was an electric moment, a fusion of souls and a declaration of their shared resolve.

"I love you," Aaron whispered, his voice barely audible amongst the fading echoes of the celebration. "I have loved you since the moment I laid eyes on you, and I will continue to love you till my last breath."

Chloe's eyes shimmered with unshed tears, her voice quivering. "I have been searching for my place in this world, for a love that could fill the void within me. And now, at this moment, I realize that I have been searching for you."

Embracing once more, a clearing of the throat interrupted their fairy tale moment. It was Pastor Conner.

"Sister Chloe, the board and I have concluded that your position on the drama and praise ministry is desperately needed. It is no secret that the Lord's anointing is upon you, and we'd be delighted to have you stay on and even do some mentoring for some of the younger members."

"That sounds wonderful," Chloe responded, her voice shaking with excitement and awe, but she wondered about Aaron's father and grandfather. Would they be angry with Aaron for not using the outlined sermon they recommended? She hoped that was not the case, as Pastor Conner dismissed himself and her parents joined her.

"Dear, your mom and I are going out for lunch. We're so proud of you," Reginald said as he kissed Chloe's forehead. They were both relieved by the resolution of the board. Starla following. Looking over to her right, she witnessed Aaron with his father and grandfather. From the look of the handshakes and the pat on the shoulder, Chloe could discern the unity between the three. This added to her joy.

The Harvest Day Celebration marked not only the end of a season but the dawn of a new chapter for both Chloe and Aaron, Starla and Reginald, and the entire congregation. The news of the event would also spread throughout the entire community, as many had already begun to testify of their personal experiences during the celebration, causing many to go along their pathway thinking and evaluating their own journeys of self-discovery.

CHAPTER 52

AIN'T NOBODY MAD BUT THE DEVIL

Leaving the church, Kennedy, her fiancé, Chloe, and Aaron were conversing. The four would go out and later swing by Chloe's parents for dessert.

"So...my mom is really trying," Chloe chuckled as she and Aaron held hands walking alongside Kennedy and Greg. "Now, when we go over after we're done with lunch, pretend like her cake is the best desert you've put in your mouth, "she said chuckling once more.

"Huh? I thought Uncle Reginald was cooking the cake," Kennedy responded, laughing harder than Chloe.

"Mom wouldn't let him. I think she believes that she's turned into a Betty Crocker overnight. But I'm proud of her though."

"I know right. Well, here we are. We'll meet you guys at the restaurant," Kennedy yelled as she and Greg left the church's parking lot. Most of the other congregants had already left and only a few stragglers were left.

"See ya there," Chloe responded, reminiscing on the beginning of her journey back in college up until the present moment. *It could only go up from here, was her thought.*

As Aaron was about to open his vehicle door, Chloe gasped as she suddenly saw a mad woman charging toward them. It was as if Nikki had transformed into someone else. Her hair was not styled, eyes swollen and puffy, and no makeup…and charging in Aaron's direction as he was not alert, as he attempted to move his brief case and other items from the passenger side of his vehicle.

"Nikki, no!" Chloe screamed as she caught a glimpse of the large knife that Nikki raised as she got closer to Aaron. Letting out a horrible shriek, Nikki continued to charge toward Aaron and before he knew it, his first response was to shield his face, but Nikki was quick and sliced his arm with the knife.

"Aaron! Nikki stop!" Chloe screamed, frozen with shock.

"She's mine!" the deranged Nikki screamed.

Grabbing Nikki, Aaron began to tussle with what seemed like dead weight. Nikki's adrenaline gave her the strength of a man. Finally, Aaron was able to wrestle her down and take the knife, but unfortunately, not without taking another slice. By that time, two courageous men from the congregation intervened, their hands reaching out to assist in subduing Nikki. The scuffle left them all breathless, a stark contrast to the celebratory atmosphere that had filled the church just moments before.

As the distant wail of an ambulance pierced the silence, Chloe and the others stood motionless, their faces etched with shock and disbelief. Tears welled up, blurring their vision as the weight of the nightmare settled in. The once glorious and healing day had taken an abrupt and cryptic turn, leaving them grappling with the harsh aftermath of an unforeseen tragedy.

~

The hospital waiting area was cold and still as Chloe, Aaron's dad, grandfather, an aunt, and other congregants awaited the news from the doctor. Kennedy and Greg also joined.

"Are you alright?" Kennedy asked as she grabbed Chloe.

"I'm fine. Just a little shaken. Aaron was stabbed by Nikki with this...I wanna say knife but, it was almost like a sword from one of those Viking movies. It was terrible," Chloe answered as sobs emanated from her being. Before Kennedy could respond the doctor joined them with news of Aaron's condition. He endured two stab wounds. One on the forearm and the other on his left side. The doctor indicated that Aaron was a lucky man. The blade just missed the kidney and spleen, but his family all agreed that he was not lucky but blessed.

"Praise the Lord," Chloe said as tears gushed from her eyes. Cringing with each thought, Nikki's face and the rage in her voice resounded like a horror movie in her mind.

"I know that look. Wanna share?" Kennedy asked, gently placing her hand on her cousin's shoulder.

"I can't get pass the reality that I created this entire incident," Chloe's despondent voice revealed as she placed her head in her hands.

"Don't you dare...don't dare take responsibility for this. Nobody is to blame but the devil. Wickedness influenced Nikki to do what she did, and something tells me that this wickedness within her didn't start with you. Those demons have been with her for a while."

Embracing her, Kennedy finally convinced Chloe to visit Aaron for a few moments and then go home to get rest. Aaron would be dismissed with medical instructions in the morning. There was nothing more she could do. Arriving home, reflecting on the situation, she grabbed her journal. Looking for the words to scribe, all that flowed forth were tears.

The next few weeks were different for Chloe and Aaron, but in a positive way. The churches board had already begun implementing more robust security measures after the attack. Many also pressured Aaron with pressing charges against Nikki, which he refused.

As Aaron recovered, he insisted on one last counseling session with Chloe. They would discuss a plan going forward, not just for her ministry, but how to deal with Nikki.

As the counseling session between Chloe and Aaron ended, Chloe smiled at him from across his desk. "It's noble of you to not press charges against Nikki, and surely God will bless your decision," she said, her voice soft and full of admiration.

Aaron looked up from the notepad he was scribbling on and returned her smile. "All I can think of is an incident in my teen years when I was hanging out with some the guys in my neighborhood at a local retail store. Those guys were stealing, got caught, and the manager gave us a chance. He didn't call the police, so…I'll give Nikki the grace she needs and prayerfully she will get the help she desperately needs," Aaron explained. A quite pleasant look on his face as he peered into Chloe's face. "Let's celebrate with a cup of coffee, shall we?"

Complying with Aaron's request, the two stepped out of his office into the early evening air. He reached for her hand gently as they walked.

"I know you don't agree, but my therapist recommended that I have a virtual visit with Nikki for closure instead of seeing her in person," she said.

Aaron nodded and squeezed her hand reassuringly. "I trust you and your decision to follow what your therapist says. And look at all the progress your parents have made since they started seeing her too. Everything is going to work out just fine," Aaron answered.

Linking arms, Chloe and Aaron made their way to their

favorite cafe for coffee and an inspirational movie – time well spent calming their minds and reflecting on the path ahead of them that God had laid out. Both agreed not to rush, but to gradually allow God to make their paths straight before them.

Six months later, Chloe and Aaron found themselves embarking upon a newfound ministry, a sanctuary for those wrestling with the intricate knots of trauma and identity crises. The resilience, healing, and redemption that both had received is what they endeavored to pour out. The genesis of the ministry was organic, but slowly began to sprout, breaking through hardened soil. The ministry seemed to bloom silently, rooted in the shared scars of its foundation.

Within six additional months, the ministry burst forth overnight. It was not by social media nor marketing techniques, but word of mouth and evident fruit flowing from the lives of the individuals who had been touched by what Chloe and Aaron had to offer.

On a quiet Saturday evening during one of their Identity Crisis conferences, amidst the dimmed conference hall lights, Chloe and Aaron scanned the diverse faces in the crowd, spotting a figure that once harbored chaos but now radiated tranquility—Nikki Witherspoon. It was not the face of a madwoman but a testament to the untold capacities for change nestled within every soul.

Joy surged within them, not just for their own journey but for Nikki's metamorphosis. God's grace, like a masterful Artisan, had turned Nikki's tumultuous tale into a harmonious melody, aligning her footsteps with the divine rhythm of her destiny.

"And so, everyone's journey is filled with twists and turns, but choosing the path aligned with divine purpose leads to a place of peace and fulfillment," Chloe proclaimed in her closing remarks as Aaron stood beside her adding a call to action to their audience.

"We invite each of you to reflect on your own detours and the divine exits that have guided you back to the main road. If you're lost, let us pray for you," Aaron added as a flood of people of all ethnicities, races, and geographies flooded the front of the venue in order to receive prayer. Nikki Witherspoon was in that flood of souls, who were desperately looking for the main road.

Life, as they had learned, was a journey full of detours, a mountain of choices that could either lead astray or guide back to the main road. And there, upon the stage, Chloe, whispered a truth learned through winding paths that she would later journal, "Sometimes it takes numerous detours to eventually arrive at the conclusion that just as we don't understand the the way of the wind, or how the bones grow in the womb of a pregnant woman, we surely don't always understand why God allows some of our twists and turns. Trusting the plan of God is the key." The words hung in the air, a timeless truth echoing in the hearts of those who had navigated the winding path and found peace and safety in the sacred dance of their God-given destiny and purpose.

EPILOGUE

FOR WITH GOD, NOTHING IS IMPOSSIBLE...

The passage of time brought with it a tapestry woven from healing, growth, and the courage to face life's trials head-on. In the wake of Chloe's journey through therapy with her family, her heart emerged stronger and more resilient than ever before. The wounds that had once festered in silence were now open to the soothing balm of time and understanding. Chloe found herself walking a path illuminated by purpose, a purpose that reached far beyond romantic inclinations.

It was during a crisp autumn day, as golden leaves danced on the breeze, that Aaron took Chloe's hand in his own and gazed deeply into her eyes. It was as if the surroundings spoke not only to the changing of seasons, but to the beauty and renewal of what relationships should be. With the weight of vulnerability, he never took his eyes off her. Their shared journey had been one of mutual healing and growth, and at that moment, as the sunlight painted their world with warmth, he dropped to one knee. With a heart brimming with emotion, Aaron asked the question that had been echoing within him: "Chloe, will you marry me?"

Time seemed to stand still. It wasn't just a proposal; it was a declaration of commitment forged in the fires of their past challenges. Her eyes, reflecting the emotions within her, met his with a depth that surpassed mere acknowledgment. It was an affirmation of the sanctuary they had become for each other amidst the chaos., The culmination of their experiences, the trials and triumphs, the pain and joy, it all converged into a resounding "yes." Their engagement was more than a union of hearts; it was a celebration of two souls who had weathered life's storms and found solace in one another's presence. "After all I've learned on my journey, I can't help but accept this proposal. I've truly come to know myself and I'm not complete apart from you."

Meanwhile, on the other side of the journey, Nikki had also taken the brave step towards healing. Engaging in therapy, she confronted the shadows that had once fueled her possessiveness and control. The wounds that had driven her to use her success as a shield began to mend, layer by layer. Therapy was not a simple remedy; it was a complex excavation process, delving into the depths of Nikki's past to unveil the roots of her struggles. With each session, Nikki peeled back the layers of her past, revealing vulnerabilities that had long been hidden.

And then, slowly but surely, a transformation unfolded. Nikki's strength evolved from a facade of power to an inner resilience rooted in self-awareness and compassion. As the walls around her heart crumbled, she found herself embracing the possibility of genuine connection, not fueled by manipulation or need, but by the authenticity of her own growth.

In the quiet moments of reflection, Nikki found the courage to confront her past, paving the way for a future unburdened by the shackles of unresolved trauma. She eventually found that main road leading her back to a career in finance and real estate. But more importantly, a newfound relationship with her mother.

In the end, the lives of these three individuals intersected through pain, healing, and transformation. Chloe's journey of self-discovery not only brought her to a place of purpose but also paved the way for others to find their own paths to healing. With hearts mended, souls illuminated, and a shared bond that transcended the past, Chloe, Aaron, and even Nikki, found themselves on a path of resolution that was as heartfelt as it was inspiring. The echoes of their stories, whispered through the winds of time, filled with the melody of triumph over adversity. The tapestry bore witness to the profound truth that healing is not just a destination; it is a sacred journey—a symphony of redemption and the unwavering resilience of the human soul.

"You make known to me the path of life; you will fill me with joy in your presence, with eternal pleasures at your right hand." Psalm 16:11 (NIV)

ABOUT THE AUTHOR

In addition to writing Christian fiction and non-fiction, she is a licensed minister of the gospel of Jesus Christ, a playwright, and a liturgical dance educator. Denise is an award-winning, best-selling author who desires to take her expertise as both the wife of a Pastor and a gospel teacher and weave principles into a narrative. Her stories are both based on personal experiences as well as the experiences held by those she has served.

Denise is married to Pastor DeForest Godfrey, she is the mother of two and is a loving grandmother. She has served the Banking Industry for over 30 years and enjoys aerobic exercise, reading, and spending time with her family.

ALSO BY DENISE COOK-GODFREY

When Willows Weep

Haunted by the abandonment of her mother and father, Willow embarks on a relentless quest for answers, driven by an unfillable void within her soul. But as she confronts buried secrets that threaten to unravel her world, she must overcome relentless opposition that could destroy everything she holds dear.

Willow, like a resilient flower breaking through life's concrete constraints, carries a name bestowed by her estranged mother—an aspiration for her to mirror the strong willow tree, flourishing against all odds. Battling childhood bullying fueled by her devotion to church traditions, Willow's journey intertwines with Titus, a young man from a different ecclesiastical world.

Their rare and blossoming love faces a relentless challenge from denominational customs and suffocating legalism. The rigid mindsets within Willow's respective church erected an insurmountable barrier between them. Post high school, Titus and Willow take separate paths, attempting to forge ahead and leave their shared history behind. Yet, within Willow's journey, there's Paxton, her husband of three years, and an unyielding pursuit of her long-lost mother, unearthing a concealed secret behind her disappearance.

As suspense thickens, love, drama, and redemption converge in this gripping story. Will the courage to embrace their present season without being entangled in the past allow Titus and Willow to find solace? Their journey unravels a riveting narrative, brimming with emotions that will captivate readers until the final revelation. Get ready for a rollercoaster ride of emotions as the threads of love and destiny weave through a story that will keep you on the edge of your seat.

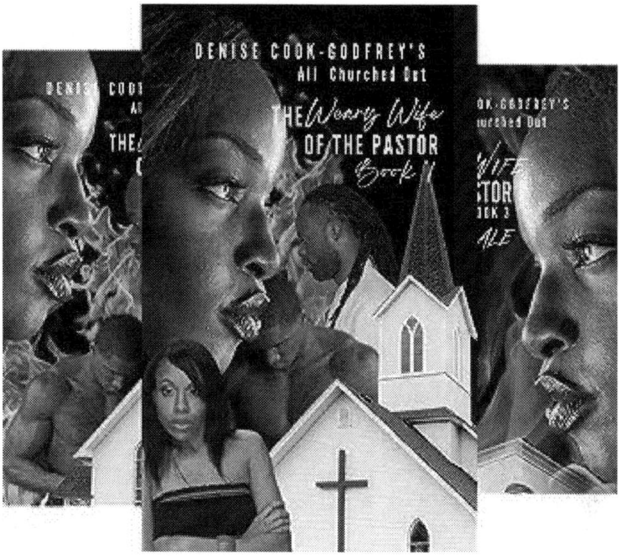

All Churched Out

Leah Westchester-Jackson is a woman torn between two worlds. One of those worlds revolves around God's unique gifts and passions from within her but the other revolves around chaos, betrayal, legalism, and hypocrisy.

Walking in the shadows of her late mother as the First Lady of Shady Hill Missionary Baptist Church, Leah loses a sense of restraint when her heart becomes shattered into millions of pieces. At that point in her life, she plummeted onto a journey where she searches for completion outside of the walls of the traditional church.

This is the gripping story of a woman scorned while attempting to define true worship, spirituality, and love. "Leah", whose name means "weary", portrays the kind of character who takes the term "level up" to a new level.

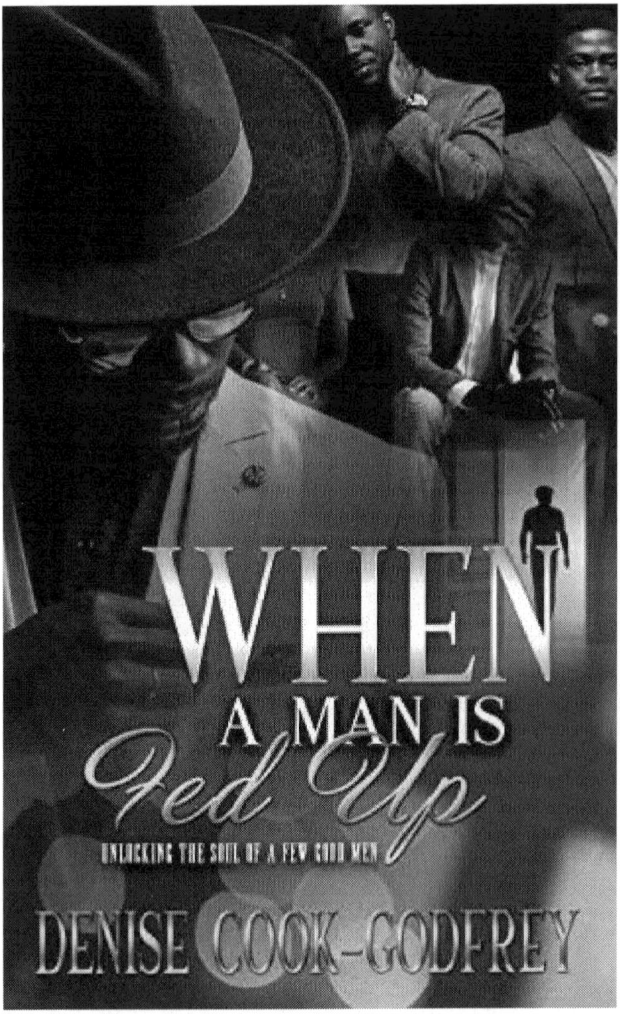

When a Man is Fed Up

Staggering through the shadows of rejection and abandonment, Xavier Taylor eagerly embraces the transition into adulthood; but he must face the demons from his childhood closet! Hiding his heart within the security of childhood friendships, writing rap lyrics, and leaning upon the faith of his grandmother, will Xavier discover his real purpose and destiny?

Sometimes what appears to be anger within a man is not anger at all...but the manifestations of trauma! This is the gripping story of rescuing the little boy to save the man while wading through pitch-black nights anticipating the brightest of mornings.

UNEQUALLY
Yoked
THE PLEASURES OF SIN LASTS FOR A SEASON- BOOK 1
DENISE COOK-GODFREY

Unequally Yoked

Christine is in desperate attempts to find her purpose amidst the horrible bullying and other dysfunctions from her past. Her naivety and the inclination to soothe her wounds through toxic relationships may prove fatal to her destiny when buried secrets resurrect in her pathway.

Christine Wells is a young woman stripped of esteem and identity by poverty, bullying, and family dysfunctions who is determined to reach her destination of identity and purpose. These dysfunctions cause her to choose to engage in sexual relationships at a tender age. When we open ourselves up to sexual sin at an early age, do we also open a Pandora's Box filled with pain and emotional baggage that could affect our adult life?

This Novella is a compelling story of influence, choices, consequences, and the offer of redemption that some receive, and others reject. There is a quote provided by best-selling and award-winning Author Michelle Stimpson. Download your copy now!

Unequally Yoked: Reaping the Harvest

This book is the compelling sequel to the continuing saga of events evolving from book # 1: "Unequally Yoked- the Pleasures of Sin Lasts for a Season."

After coming face to face with the grief, anguish, and heartbreak from her past, Christine Wells forges ahead in contemplation of picking up the broken pieces only to discover lessons in reaping and sowing. Will Christine be able to endure the night seasons of wrestling, pushing, and pulling to see the dawning of her day of destiny? Download your copy today!

Feel free to follow me on Amazon to receive alerts when new novels are released at *https://www.amazon.com/stores/Denise-Cook-Godfrey/author/B00B8KDHH4*

Made in the USA
Columbia, SC
26 March 2024

33641033R00187

GAGA,

HAPPY BIRTHDAY OLD MAN!

Rich

LIFE & GOLF ARE SUPPOSED TO BE FUN!

GO WITH THE FLOW ~

RAND